# Barking at the Moon

# Barking at the Moon

## Nene Adams

P.D. Publishing, Inc.
Clayton, North Carolina

ISBN-13: 978-1-933720-53-1
ISBN-10: 1-933720-53-0

9 8 7 6 5 4 3 2 1

Cover design by Nene Adams
Edited by: Day Petersen / Lara Zielinsky

Published by:

P.D. Publishing, Inc.
P.O. Box 70
Clayton, NC 27528

http://www.pdpublishing.com

To Carmela, who wanted to know what happened next, which inspired this story. Thanks!

## Chapter ONE

Sheriff Annalee Crow walked towards the knot of flannel-clad men huddled together on the sagging porch attached to the front of Gunn's Pro Shop. "Good morning, gentlemen," she said, pausing at the foot of the warped wooden stairs. She used the word in the loosest sense; there was absolutely nothing gentle about these men.

The oldest man in the group spat a wad of tobacco juice in her direction, just missing her shoes. The others remained watchful and silent. Every face turned towards her was eerily similar — dark, suspicious eyes gazing at her from beneath lowered brows, acne-pitted skin stretched tight over prominent bones, a smattering of freckles and irregular moles, greasy black hair worn too long in the back. Like many of the other families living in and around the Deep who had scratched out a subsistence for the last two hundred-plus years, the Gunns' genealogy was as tangled and knotted as a discarded fishing net.

*Borderline, and in some cases not so borderline, incest leaves its mark generation after generation,* Annalee thought.

"Morning, Titus," she said to the tobacco spitter, being sure to turn slightly so a beam of sunlight lanced dazzling bright off the sheriff's badge pinned to the front of her brown uniform shirt. The display was a little reminder of her authority, not that she really expected them to respect her. The Gunns respected nothing and no one except their own insular clan. She rested a hand on the thick leather belt slung on her hips, her fingertips close to the grip of her service weapon, a .38 caliber Smith & Wesson that had belonged to her late father, Jefferson Crow, the former sheriff of Daredevil County.

"I heard tell some of your boys got into a scuffle over to Hallelujah Ridge last night." Annalee kept her tone pleasant despite the stony silence. "Something I ought to know about that? Your boys want to tell me their side of the story?"

Titus regarded her a long moment before answering in his high reedy voice, "Ain't nothing we can't handle." He paused, then added grudgingly, "Sheriff."

Annalee did not allow him to intimidate her. She hardened her expression, letting the façade of friendliness slip away. "No matter what you believe to the contrary, old man, this county isn't your private domain. God damn it, the law is the same for everybody, including you. I'm not going to tolerate any more violence between your family and the Skinners. Am I making myself rightly understood? Make no mistake, Titus — the next time your boys go looking for trouble, I'll be giving them all they can handle and then some."

A teenager with a wandering eye sneered at her, baring teeth already nicotine stained. "You? Give us trouble? That's pretty damned funny. Ain't no bitch alive gonna collar us big dogs. Ain't no way, no how."

Murmurs of assent from the others made her stiffen. They were like a pack of wild animals, feral and primed to attack any perceived weakness. In her experience, there was only one way to deal with their kind of antagonism: show no fear. She walked up the steps and stood on the porch facing them. Chips of "haint blue" paint from the flaking underside of the roof crunched underfoot. Her back already ached from her belt's weight, but she would not have traded her weapon, her back-up .22, speed-loaders, and radio for anything short of a Remington 870 shotgun, which she had left in the trunk of her patrol car.

"You want to try some shit with me, boy?" she asked, pitching her voice low and threatening. First rule of dealing with testosterone-poisoned idiots: never be shrill. Men tuned out a female who sounded like a dentist's drill. "You got the balls, or ain't they dropped yet?"

He flushed and threw her an ugly look. Annalee tensed, anticipating a move, but one of his brothers — she thought it was Dewey — let out a bray of laughter and hit the teenager on the shoulder, almost knocking him sprawling. The other men chuckled while Titus cackled with unrestrained glee.

"Sweet Jesus weepin' on the Cross! Never mind my grandson; you got some balls on *you*, Miz Crow. Big shiny brass ones, if I ain't mistaken," Titus finally croaked, settling the feed store cap more firmly on his balding head.

Annalee made no reply. She kept her attention split, half on Titus, the other on the rest of his boys. If anybody wanted to take the situation to the next level, she was ready.

The smile suddenly vanished from Titus' face. He looked like an Old Testament prophet, filled with a wrathful, dead certain righteousness no power on Earth could shake. "Now I'll tell you something for free, Missy: stay out of the Gunns' business. Them Skinners ain't nothing but heathen peckerwoods and white trash, not worthy of your time."

He started to stump around her on his bowed legs but stopped and peered into her face. His breath was foul. A thin line of tobacco juice glistened on the side of his bristly chin. "They do say it was curiosity killed the cat," Titus told her, his voice filled with a malevolence that crawled electric on her skin. He continued with a smirk, "Well, I don't know about that, but I'm pretty sure it was curiosity that killed the crow."

Annalee froze. She knew Titus was referring to her father. Jefferson Crow had been murdered six months ago, his body found dumped on a deer trail in the four-thousand square miles of old growth forest called Malingering Deep. The case remained open, the killer unknown; the investigation had gone cold due to a lack of evidence and an absence of leads. The only thing Annalee knew for certain was that her father had been investigating something in the Deep, some secret he had kept from her. Now Titus seemed to be hinting that the Gunns had been involved in the murder. A white-hot explosion of fury drew her lips back from her teeth in a snarl, but she retained enough presence of mind to not draw her weapon.

"If I find out you or any of yours killed my kin," Annalee said, forcing the words to come out controlled through her rage, "they'll pay, by God. They'll pay in full." At that moment, she was less a representative of law enforcement than a hill woman with blood-feud bred in her bones, taken in with her mother's milk, learned on her daddy's knee.

"Would that payment be by God's law or man's?" Not waiting for her reply, Titus touched a gnarled finger to the brim of his cap. "Good day, Sheriff. When you're next in Lingerville, do drop by the house and make your polites."

He swaggered his bowlegged way off the porch, followed by the rest of his boys. They piled into a pair of Superman blue pickup trucks and tore off down the gravel road, kicking up a thick veil of orange, iron-tinged dust that hung in the air, scarcely stirred by the breeze whispering through the cottonwoods.

Annalee watched them go and blew out a breath, shaking her head. The swell of anger she felt was tinged with grief and the sadness that never completely went away. She missed her father every day and often found herself turning to ask him a question or make an observation, only to remember he was buried in the Holy Mount of Jesus Cemetery next to her mother.

As the engine noises lessened in the distance, she heard the hum of the Coca-Cola vending machine behind her, and a mockingbird perched on top of an electricity pole beside the shop, warbling an ever-shifting pattern of stolen songs. Annalee closed her eyes against a stab of loss, thinking about her father, the strongest and best man she had ever known. *So many memories...* She had always been close to him, especially after her mama died.

The sudden, unexpected male voice that boomed behind her made Annalee nearly jump out of her skin.

"You get far with them assholes?" the man asked.

Annalee turned around to see her chief deputy smiling down at her from his superior height. Noah Whitlock was related to the Skinners on his mother's side; he had his maternal family's almond-shaped brown eyes, thick blond hair, and wide toothy smile.

Annalee uncurled her fingers from the gun butt, her heartbeat slowly returning to normal. "Do I need to put a bell on you?" she asked. "Jesus, Noah, learn to make some noise when you walk and quit that pussyfooting around. You scared the ever lovin' crap out of me."

"Sorry." Noah did not sound the least repentant. "So how'd it go with Titus?"

"Well, not quite as bad as a poke in the eye with a sharp stick, but it was a near thing," Annalee said. "You?"

"I had the talk with Uncle Ezra this morning. He's a lot more reasonable once he's had a few cups of coffee and some of Aunt Rachael's sawmill gravy."

"What'd he have to say?" Annalee knew Ezra Skinner's three oldest sons had gotten into a tussle with some of the Gunns at Hallelujah Ridge near Ogee. She had heard about the altercation from Junior Tishamingo, who lived near the site. Last night, he had called the office to complain about the noise, and a late-shift deputy was dispatched to deal with the nuisance. There were no serious injuries so no arrests had been made, but an official report had been filed. Annalee had come out to the Pro Shop that morning to issue a caution to the Gunns, while Noah had done the same for the Skinners.

"Luke, Matthew, and Mark are fine, just some bruises and a fat lip," Noah said. "It was the Gunns that started it, you know, but Uncle Ezra don't want to press no charges."

"Of course he doesn't," Annalee said in disgust. There was no question in her mind that the Gunns had started that fight. The whole family loved nothing better than stirring up trouble and strife, but it was damned difficult to do anything about it if nobody pressed charges against them. "How the hell am I supposed to keep the peace around here when them stubborn sons-of-bitches won't let me?"

"No idea. Don't ask me, Sheriff...I'm just the hired help around here."

She reached around and slapped his arm lightly in reproof. "You're more than that and you know it. What was the fight about, anyway?"

A corner of Noah's mouth quirked in a not-quite smile. "The usual crap teenage boys fight about when they're plumb full up with puberty and contrariness — somebody talks trash, somebody else takes offense, somebody stirs the pot, tempers run high, and blam! Next thing you know, there's fists flying, bloody noses, and bruises. If I was Junior Tishamingo last night, I'd've turned the hose on every one of them idjits." He hitched at his utility belt and changed the subject. "You want to help me eat some breakfast at Old Lady Magee's diner?"

"You didn't have sawmill gravy with Ezra?"

"He was feeling none too sociable," Noah replied mournfully.

"Yeah, sure, why not?" Annalee shrugged. "Old Lady Magee makes the best buttermilk biscuits in the county, bar none, and her nephew just made a fresh batch of sausages. Maybe she's got some of her special hashbrown casserole, too." Her mouth was beginning to water in anticipation of the kind of meal that would make her doctor purse his lips and deliver a lecture on cholesterol and saturated fat, had he known.

Noah grinned. "I live in hope, my hand to God."

The dry breeze freshened and caught a long strand of Annalee's mouse-brown hair, whipping it against her eyes, making them sting. Cursing under her breath, she re-pinned the wayward lock and wondered, not for the first time, if she ought to just get the whole mess cut off, but her father had often complimented her long hair, saying it made her resemble her mother. She had not had the length more than trimmed since she was seventeen, sitting in the kitchen before Mama's funeral, a towel tied around her neck and Great-Aunt Myrtle snipping at her hair while she tried not to cry. Another gust of wind drew her mind back to the present.

Sniffing the air, Annalee detected the faintest hint of ozone she reckoned was distant lightning. "Smells like rain's headed our way from over the hill," she commented.

"Also smells a lot like blood," Noah added under his breath. When Annalee glared at him, he shrugged in his turn. "The Skinners protect their own, Sheriff. You know that. They're not going to let you do it for them. You're not family."

"I know it all too well," Annalee said, "but the last thing we need is an all-out war."

There had been a Skinner in her class at the J.D. Knowles High School in Brightbrook, a shy girl whose thick mop of blond hair had hidden most of her face except her eyes, almond-shaped and brown as dying leaves in autumn. *What was her name?* Annalee asked herself, sliding behind the steering wheel of the patrol car. The Skinner girl had gotten teased by some of the meaner natured kids until a mysterious incident in the showers after gym class. Annalee couldn't recall the details — she had been taken ill that day and stayed at home — but whatever happened, no one bothered the Skinner girl again.

*Come to think of it,* she thought as Noah settled into the passenger side seat, *that girl was always hovering around the fringes. Never speaking, just watching, staying close. Always had her eyes on me. Didn't bother me much, though. Least she was quiet. Lou Ella. That's her name! No, no, not quite right. Close, but no cigar. Damn it, can't remember shit no more.*

She was about to ask Noah for the girl's name when she was interrupted by a squawk from the radio.

"Sheriff, we have a report of a D.B. at Yellow Jacket Pond." The call was slightly fuzzed by static, but Annalee recognized the husky, cigarette-laced voice of Minnie Lee Hawkins, the day-shift dispatcher. A mental image of its owner supplied the voice with cat's-eye glasses, floral smocks, and hennaed hair teased as high as gravity and industrial-strength hairspray allowed.

"Acknowledged, Dispatch," Noah replied into the handset. "This is Charlie One-Oh-One, we are underway. Has the M.E.'s office been notified?"

"Copy, Charlie One-Oh-One. M.E. and CSU are en route to scene."

"Copy, Dispatch. Out."

"So much for breakfast and probably lunch, too." Annalee sighed. Ignoring her stomach's growl, she started the engine and gave the car some gas, fighting the steering wheel's tendency to pull to the left. She had tried to requisition more four-wheel drives from the State, which would have been far more practical on the dirt trails that were masquerading as roads, but Daredevil County was barely a blip on the budgetary radar. The morons who monitored the bottom line had decided that one SUV was enough for her office — one SUV to be shared amongst herself and all her deputies in a backwoods county where paved roads were the exception rather than the rule. She snorted. It was far more important for the governor to have a fully tricked-out helicopter so he could ferry his hunting and fishing friends around in the season. *That asshole won't be getting my vote again,* she decided. Annalee viciously wrenched at the wheel, her wrists feeling the strain as the patrol car bumped through a pothole that left her wincing in sympathy for the chassis. The Motor Pool boys were going to skin her alive, since they had recently realigned the damned thing.

Yellow Jacket Pond was about a half-mile from Hallelujah Ridge, which was in turn ten miles from Lingerville and Gunn's Pro Shop. The last three miles, Annalee was able to turn off the switchback gravel road onto the smooth blacktop of Route 82. She could have sworn the car sighed in relief. Beside her, Noah let go of the "oh-shit" strap and relaxed.

They were the first people at the scene apart from a red-faced teenager, Buddy Nowland, whose expression screamed guilt. It was not long before Annalee found a half-stick of short-fuse dynamite in a Ziploc bag under the thwart of an old rowboat, a fixture at the pond, abandoned years ago and available for anyone's use. The explosive, as well as the fish floating belly-up on the water's surface, told her what the idiot child had been doing.

In her opinion, it was unnecessary to call in the Bomb Squad. The dynamite was stable and the date stamped on the side indicated it had been manufactured in 2002. She would make sure the explosive was disposed of properly after she finished her business here.

"Don't you know what kind of trouble you can get into with that stuff?" Annalee asked, noting the cell phone sticking out of Buddy's shirt pocket — she supposed it was the source of the 911 call.

Turning her head briefly, she watched Noah wade out into the pond to get a look at the naked body floating facedown among the dead fish and water weeds. The corpse's pallid skin had a definite greenish tinge to it. Annalee hoped Noah had the sense not to disturb the floater if it was too ripe. She did not want to have to drag the pond for internal organs if the body burst, and besides, a dismembered corpse would tick off the county medical examiner no end.

"Damn it, Buddy, you could get classified as a terrorist suspect!" Annalee went on.

"It was just a little fun, Sheriff," Buddy said, cringing.

She resisted the impulse to slap the boy upside that thick-as-a-brick head and raise a knot a calf could suck on. He was seventeen years old and thought he was immortal. Cause and effect were foreign concepts to a hormone-addled mind. Annalee shuddered to think what could have happened. *The velocity of detonation is greater than a thousand yards per second*, she thought, *and he'd have been right on top of the explosion, right at Ground Zero. Christ! We'd have been taking two dead bodies out of that pond, one in pieces you could fit in a matchbox. Closed casket funeral for sure, damn it.*

"Dynamiting fish is illegal, Buddy," she said, summoning her most authoritative tone. "Possessing dynamite without a license is *very* illegal. I could call the Feds and they'd throw your sorry ass in prison. Do you want your poor mama to have to visit you in Edgewater Correctional? Maybe them Federal boys or Homeland Security decide you're a terrorist and you get sent to Guantanamo Bay, which ain't no vacation spot, believe me. You ain't gonna be fishing out there in Cuba, son. That there's stone-cold hard time. You want to squat in a cell with terrorists for five years or better, no contact with family? No? Then tell me, where'd the explosives come from? Who gave the dynamite to you? Where did you buy it?"

He still looked sullen. Annalee prodded him with a finger. "Go on, son. Tell the truth and shame the devil. That's the only thing you can do. The water in Shit Creek's rising and you're about over your head."

Buddy said nothing. He crossed his arms over his chest and shuffled his feet.

She tried again. "Somebody sell the stuff to you? One of them illegal fireworks vendors, maybe? Give me a name, a location. I give you my word the D.A. will grant you immunity from prosecution in exchange for your testimony." She waited for an answer. It was after July Fourth but there were fireworks sellers who slipped over the state line almost every weekend in summer, hawking their cheap, volatile, overseas-manufactured merchandise at flea markets, gun shows, and other places. Sometimes they had dynamite, too, obtainable if one knew the right questions to ask and had the money to pay for it.

"Not from a fireworks guy. Got the stuff from Papaw," Buddy finally mumbled.

Annalee hid her surprise. Obadiah Nowland was a stubborn old coot and a hell of a character, a dirt farming survivalist who probably had enough weapons cached in his private concrete bunker to subdue a small Latin American dictatorship. However, he was also a die-hard advocate of gun responsibility. Obadiah would have never given dynamite to an inexperienced youngster, especially his only grandson, on whom he doted.

"You mean you took it without your Grandpa Nowland's permission," Annalee stated flatly. It was the only explanation that made sense.

Buddy's flush deepened. "Don't tell on me," he whined. "Daddy'll have a cow."

"And Grandpa Nowland will probably have triplets, one after the other." Annalee turned when she heard a sloshing sound. Noah was wading back to shore without the body in tow. His expression was grim. She called out to him, "Hey, what's the news, Deputy? Got an I.D. on the D.B.?"

Noah did not answer at once but kept walking toward her. He had taken off his utility belt, shoes, and socks prior to wading into the pond; his tan uniform trousers were wet to mid-thigh and sticking to his legs. He brushed past a clump of sweet flags growing in a fringe near the pond's edge, his bare feet squelching through the wet clay mud. The sun picked out reddish highlights in his blond hair but also cast his eyes into shadow. An oddity of the light hollowed his cheeks in deepest shade as well, lending his face a disquieting skull-like aspect.

Premonition made the skin on the back of her neck prickle. *Something wicked this way comes.* Annalee listened to her instincts. She said to Buddy, "Go sit in the patrol car, son." The boy opened his mouth, and she added quickly, "Don't make me tell you twice."

Once Buddy was safely in the backseat of the patrol car, out of possible harm's way, Annalee shut the door and switched her attention to Noah. "Well? Who is it?" Her gut clenched in anticipation of bad news.

"It's Reverend Lassiter."

"Oh, God save us." Annalee pushed her bangs back from her sweaty forehead and wished she had not gotten out of bed that morning. The fallout from this was going to be nasty; she could feel it in her bones. "That's all we need. You know, I really hoped he'd run off to Tijuana with the offering money and the church secretary. Please tell me he got drunk, accidentally fell in the pond, and drowned."

"No such luck." Noah's frown deepened. "He was shot in the throat."

Annalee leaned a hip against the side of the car, ignoring Buddy's tentative rap on the window while she considered the murdered man, Reverend John Delano Lassiter. He was an evangelical preacher, leader of the Church of the Honey in the Rock with a congregation of about two dozen of the wealthiest citizens in Daredevil County. Lassiter had disappeared about a week earlier, but now she would be looking into a homicide rather than a missing person's case. She went through the current investigation in her mind, gathering details, making mental notes. She had put together a list of possible suspects by the time a dusty white van bumped off the blacktop and rolled to a halt on a patch of reasonably dry ground. Annalee smiled when a silver-haired, dark-skinned woman hopped out of the van.

"Hey, Doc," Annalee said, waving a greeting. "Looks like murder."

Dr. Betty Vernon shaded her eyes with a hand, peering at the pond and the floating corpse tangled in water weeds. "I thought that was my call to make, Sheriff."

Annalee thought Doc Vernon was good people, even if the woman was a transplant from Up North. "Be my guest. The scene's kind of wet, though."

"I'm not made out of sugar, Sheriff," was Betty's tart reply. "I won't melt." Annalee noticed that the medical examiner nevertheless took a pair of dark green neoprene, boot-foot chest waders out of the van, stepping into them before entering the pond.

Retrieving the body from the water was tricky, but Betty managed it with her assistant's help. In the meantime, Annalee contacted Minnie Hawkins at the sheriff's office and told her to get Obadiah Nowland or Obadiah Junior down to Yellow Jacket Pond, and to also request the Georgia State Police dispatch a diver to search the pond for evidence. She avoided stating the victim's name, well aware there were some people in the area with scanners who had nothing better to do all day than monitor radio traffic. This category included journalists. She wanted to keep the press out of the investigation as much as possible, especially in the early days when they could ill afford media interference.

Lassiter's disappearance had already become a statewide news item thanks to a public campaign engineered by the reverend's devoted follower, Abner Cutshall, who owned the *Daredevil Trumpet* and the *Huntswell Star*. In addition, Abner was a big noise in the county seat, a very wealthy man who was not opposed to passing out "greenback handshakes" to political and religious causes that jibed with his personal philosophy. The man had serious connections and plenty of juice at the highest levels of local government. Annalee knew the minute Abner found out about Lassiter's death, he would be pestering the governor, the mayor of Huntswell, the county commissioner, the Chief of Public Safety, and anybody else he could influence to put pressure on the investigation.

*It ain't what you know, it's who you know,* Annalee thought, hating politics as usual. It seemed half her time was wasted on placating and reassuring politicians who appeared determined to drive her around the bend. Some days, she forgot why she had wanted to be elected sheriff, then she remembered her father. By the time Jefferson's body had been found in the forest, insects had eaten his eyes. She would never forget the shock of that discovery, a slam to the gut that still reverberated six months later. Her father's eyeless face returned to her dreams with haunting regularity.

Betty came over, snapping off her disturbingly purple nitrile gloves. The sharp sound brought Annalee out of her musing.

"GSW to the throat," Betty reported. "The extent of the damage is consistent with a close contact shotgun shooting. I'll need to open him for the official COD, but let's say initially that death was caused by hemorrhagic shock due to injury of the external carotid artery. He bled out. Whether he was still alive when he went into the water, I can't say yet. Wait for the autopsy, which I'll schedule for tomorrow."

"I'd like to take a peek at the victim," Annalee said.

"Be my guest." Betty waved a hand at the medical examiner's van. "By the way, if you find a suspect shotgun, I can test for tissue and blood in the barrel."

"You think there might be blowback?"

"Absolutely. I'd say from the dermal inclusion of gunpowder around the wound margin that the killer held the shotgun less than a foot away from the victim."

"Thanks, Doc."

Stooped over inside the van, Annalee zipped open the body bag and took her time examining the victim. In life, she recalled, John Lassiter had been a well-fleshed fellow, tall and paunchy, with big callused hands and big square teeth that had reminded her of tombstones crowded together in his jaw. Stripped of his clothing as well as his dignity, his naked flesh bloated with putrefaction, he did not resemble the dynamic, charismatic, loud-spoken preacher who had entranced some folks and antagonized others.

*Like the Skinners*, she thought. Lassiter had a definite grudge against the Skinners. For some unknown reason, the man had regularly denounced the family from his pulpit, calling them irredeemable sinners and worse, or so she had heard from a private source. The church's membership was highly exclusive; no one whose net worth was under seven figures need apply. She had never attended a meeting herself, but rumors and hearsay were rife.

Had the Skinners decided to wipe out Lassiter's offenses with blood? At this point, Annalee could not say for certain. It was a possibility. In the hills, men might shrug off an insult, though the grudge would never be forgotten, or they might lash out in violence that would lead to more violence. *Unto the seventh generation, as the Good Book says.*

She checked the throat wound that looked like a second mouth, the ragged lips bleached pale by prolonged immersion in the water, although the gunpowder tattoo stood out. The wound was not centered but off to one side and at an angle, piercing the carotid artery as Betty had said. Pond dirt peppered the skin, which had a greasy sheen. A gleam of jellied white shone from beneath the victim's lowered eyelids. She had the uncomfortable sensation that the dead man was watching her, and she was being judged and found wanting.

Annalee turned to the medical examiner, who was standing just outside the van, and asked a silent question with a raised brow: *through and through?* When Betty nodded, Annalee carefully raised the victim's head and checked the massive exit wound that left the top of the spine exposed, the vertebrae alabaster against the darker muscle area.

"Are you sure this is the crime scene and not a body dump?" Betty asked.

"No idea yet. CSU's on the way." Annalee did not see any other injuries on Lassiter's body except for a few bloodless nicks on his shins and calves. She indicated the wounds. "Any idea what caused these?"

"Snapping turtle?" Betty suggested, shrugging. "Fish? Outboard motor? It'll be in the autopsy report. You about done?"

"Time of death?"

"The skin of the hands and the fingernails has only started to separate, so I'd estimate time of death at about a week, but I won't know for sure—"

"Until the autopsy. Yep, you're coming in loud and clear." Annalee clambered out of the van, allowing the assistant — she could never remember the young man's name so she called him "Igor" in the privacy of her mind — to enter in her wake and shut the doors.

Betty walked down to the pond's edge to take water temperature readings, balancing carefully in the slick mud.

Noah beckoned to Annalee. He was standing beside a couple of young ash trees, frowning down at the grass. She joined him, following his line of sight to the ground. The grass was scuffed, and in one spot had been torn apart to reveal bare earth the color of rusty iron. Someone had excavated a hole approximately twelve inches in diameter and about six inches deep. Annalee believed there was dried blood mixed with the lumps of clay.

"Okay, this looks like the principle crime scene," she said. "Let's cordon it off and wait for CSU to get here."

Annalee registered movement in the corner of her eye. She turned and caught a ghostly shape lurking about a hundred yards away, beneath a stand of pines. To her surprise, the image resolved into a wolf, one of the rare blond-furred breed that could only be found in Malingering Deep. She had no idea what the animal was doing so far from its usual habitat.

The wolf's pale fur stood out in sharp contrast to the pine trees' rough red-brown bark. It seemed to her as if the wolf was not trying to hide, but deliberately putting itself on view. It pointed its sharp muzzle in her direction. She knew she was being watched, and shivered as the hair on the back of her neck tried to bristle. Before she could call Noah's attention to the oddity, the wolf turned tail and vanished, leaving her with a strangely bereft feeling.

Another vehicle arrived at the scene, parking near the medical examiner's van. Annalee dismissed the wolf as unimportant, and squinted in the vehicle's direction, determining it was not the Crime Scene Unit or the state police diver, but Obadiah Nowland, Jr., Buddy's father. He was a big man, bull-necked and broad-shouldered from twenty years of working at the slaughterhouse in Ogee, jointing carcasses and hauling sides of beef. Nowland caught sight of Buddy sitting in the back of the patrol car, and his face screwed into a scowl made even more hideous by the vascular birthmark that stained his right temple and eyelid like a splash of spilled wine.

Annalee nodded at Noah, trusting him to set up the perimeter while she hastened to speak to Nowland before he lost his temper and started shouting. She had neither the time nor the inclination to put up with a grown man's hissy fit.

"Your son was dynamiting fish," she said, preempting whatever accusation or demand he had been about to make. Nowland's mouth snapped closed and he glared at her. The man had little respect for law enforcement in general, and even less for her personally. He had been loud in his objections to a female sheriff. Fortunately for her election campaign, he had not possessed any influence beyond a few like-minded friends.

Relishing the opportunity to lecture a vocal opponent and all-around asshole, Annalee went on, "We both know possession of dynamite without a proper license could get you, your father, and Buddy into serious trouble with the Feds."

"Now, Sheriff, Buddy's just a boy, he don't know no better," Nowland said. He sounded confident, but beads of perspiration glittered in his thinning hairline.

"That may be, but the law's the law." Annalee had him firmly by the short hairs and they both knew it. She let him sweat a long moment before she tilted her head and gave him a small, tight smile. "Look, Junior, I don't want to have to arrest you or Buddy or Grandpa Nowland. That's too much paperwork. I surely don't want to involve the Feds, who ain't a damned bit of good for man or beast. So here's what we're going to do — I am going to let y'all off with a strong warning. I am going to put you down for a five hundred dollar contribution to the Police Benevolent Society. I am going to assume that Grandpa Nowland moves his stash of dynamite where Buddy can't get at it, because if I catch the boy again, he *is* going to jail. And since you don't want me to execute a search warrant on your property, don't let me hear tell of any more dynamite explosions anywhere in Daredevil County."

He swallowed hard, gave her a fish-eyed look like he couldn't believe she was showing him mercy, and finally put on an "aw, shucks" grin that did not fool her one minute. Underneath, she knew he had to be seething. "Why, thank you," Nowland said. "That's mighty good of you, Sheriff; I do appreciate your kindness to my family. I'm much obliged."

"Don't forget that donation," she said dryly. "I'll send you a reminder in the mail. You can take your boy home now, and if I was you, I'd give him a good dose of what-for."

Nowland cut a glance toward his son, whose dismayed face was pressed against the window of the patrol car. "Boy's so dumb, if brains was gas, he wouldn't have enough to drive a piss-ant's go-cart around a Cheerio. Believe me, when I'm done with that child of mine, he's going to have trouble sitting down for a spell. I guarantee he ain't going to forget the difference between dynamite and a fishing pole any time soon, Sheriff."

Annalee stood aside and allowed the man to fetch his son.

The CSU van finally made an appearance, and technicians began processing the crime scene in earnest. At the area of disturbed earth, a tech took samples from the hole, spading through the iron-oxide clay with as much delicate care as an archaeologist at a dig site. Annalee happened to be present when the tech discovered what he believed might be human tissue — specifically, brain matter and fragments of bone.

The picture of the crime was becoming clearer in her mind. Annalee decided that unless further evidence proved her wrong, her working hypothesis would be that Lassiter had been lying on the ground, the killer standing over him, pressing the shotgun to his throat. Afterward, the killer had dragged Lassiter's body to the pond, then returned to remove the shotgun pellets that had penetrated the earth. Collaring another tech, she directed the woman to search a stand of nearby trees at ground level, checking for high-velocity blood splatter, stray pellets, and gunpowder residue. The entire scene within a thousand yard radius would need to be searched for discarded cartridges or stray wadding.

It was not until after noon that the state police diver arrived. By then, Annalee's stomach was gurgling loudly in protest at having missed breakfast. Fortunately, the diver came bearing a bag of jelly donuts, which he shared with fairly good grace.

Noah directed the search of the pond from the rowboat while Annalee assisted the crime scene technicians, taking scores of pictures and measurements so dear to a forensic analyst's heart. Betty and her assistant departed, taking the body to the county morgue in Huntswell. Ten minutes after the M.E.'s departure, a Jeep painted in black-and-white stripes skidded off the road and into the grass, the wheels chewing up turf and throwing gobbets of mud against the patrol car's door.

"Shit!" Noah exclaimed, his voice carrying across the pond. He stood up, keeping his balance despite the boat's inclination to rock back and forth, and shook a fist at the zebra-striped vehicle. "I just had that car detailed, you crazy fool!"

Deuteronomy "Ron" Cutshall, Abner's youngest son, flew out of the Jeep almost the second it came to a halt. "Is it true?" he panted, his blue eyes widened by excitement. "Is it Reverend John? Did you find him?"

Annalee ignored his question. Ron was a reporter for the *Huntswell Star*, and she was not prepared to give official statements to the media yet, especially when both the reporter and the newspaper represented Cutshall, who was, in her opinion, a person of interest in a murder case. "How the hell did you hear about that?" she asked.

He huffed and shook his head as if chiding her for ignorance. "Chatter on the scanner from the state police boys," he said.

"They've got more discretion than that," Annalee declared, keeping her uncertainty to herself. The explanation was credible as well as troubling; some LEOs were not as close-mouthed as she might wish. There would have to be another memo sent out from her office regarding confidentiality when it came to ongoing investigations.

"Then maybe I've got a source which I'm *not* going to identify," he said impatiently. "Heard of the First Amendment?"

When it seemed as if Ron would simply jog around her, Annalee blocked him. Ron was taller but he was skinny as a beanpole, and Annalee possessed a solid, heavy-boned physique. She pushed him backwards, not giving an inch and not caring when his expensive Italian shoes sank into the mud.

"You contaminate my crime scene, and all your daddy's money won't save you from a record breaking ass-whuppin'," she said, glaring at him and setting her jaw.

"Did you find Reverend John?" Ron repeated, apparently unfazed by her intimidation and unconcerned about the ruination of his leather loafers.

"Just what's your connection to the reverend, apart from your father's joining the Honey in the Rock's congregation?" Annalee asked, still determined not to answer him. "I thought you had nothing to do with Lassiter's brand of religion."

Ron sighed and scratched his fingers through the chaos of red hair that blazed like fire on top of his head. "Sheriff, it's a scoop."

"Yep, sure is, and for your daddy's paper, too. How 'bout that?"

"In case you haven't noticed, my father's an obsessed man, really obsessed, to the point that he truly believes Reverend John is an agent of the Lord. Hell, he worships the man like he can walk on water or turn it into wine."

"You're not answering my question." Annalee was deliberately curt.

"And you're not answering mine!" Ron flared. He subsided when she frowned at him, and he went on earnestly, "Since the man's disappearance, my father's promised a reward for anyone who brings him real information on Reverend John."

"A reward, huh? How much?"

"Fifty thousand dollars."

Annalee whistled, impressed. That was more than her annual salary. On the other hand, fifty grand was probably loose change to the great Abner Cutshall, multi-millionaire extraordinaire. He owned a good chunk of the county and had inherited a sizable fortune from his daddy and granddaddy as well, not to mention having married an heiress who had the good taste to die after giving him several sons to continue the Cutshall family line. The Great Man was sitting in the catbird seat, no mistake about that.

"I'm surprised most of the county isn't out there beating the bushes for Lassiter," she commented.

"He didn't make the offer public for that very reason."

"Who knew about it?"

"Only the church members and whoever they told, which I presume was family members and close friends. C'mon, Sheriff, help me out here."

"Why shouldn't I make you wait until the official press conference?" Annalee asked after glancing back at the crime scene, hoping he would take the hint and leave.

Ron assumed a knowing expression. "I'll split the reward with you," he offered.

She almost laughed but managed to strangle the impulse at the last second. Hurting his pride would do no good. Her expression schooled to seriousness, she said, "Trying to bribe a police officer is a felony offense."

His face fell. "Please," he said at last. "I need the money, Sheriff. I need it real bad."

"Don't your father pay your bills?" she asked, surprised.

"It's my wife, Doreen. She's been gambling again, after she swore to me she'd quit. You know how Daddy feels about that. He said to me last time she got caught, 'Wealth gotten by vanity shall be diminished: but he that gathereth by labor shall increase.' Daddy won't pay, not one thin dime, and you know what happens to people who welsh on their debts." Ron's voice lowered. "Doreen's a good woman but she's sick with gambling fever. Sick in her head. I'm going to send her to a Baptist retreat, but first I gotta make sure she'll be safe. I sure don't want her to end up in the hospital, beat to hell on account of those bloodsuckers."

Annalee swore under her breath. "The Ricketts still running that operation out on Route 82?" When Ron hesitated, she took hold of his bicep and squeezed it, willing him to cooperate. "You want me to shut them down to save your wife's skin, you've got to tell me the truth. Help me and I'll help you."

It was his turn to frown. "You shut them down one week, they're at it again the next."

She had to admit he had a point. The Ricketts ran an illegal mini-casino — poker, craps and blackjack — that moved from place to place. Their drivers used prearranged stops on Route 82 where gamblers could be picked up and transported to the week's secret location. Her father had made several related arrests in the last couple of years, but that was not enough to prevent the Ricketts from continuing their illicit activities.

*The Ricketts are like cockroaches*, she thought. *Crush one under your heel, ten others come scurrying out of the walls to take its place.* It was too bad the U.S. Attorney wasn't interested in bringing a racketeering indictment against the Ricketts' organization. The matter was far too picayune for the federal government to take notice.

"How much does Doreen owe?" she asked.

"Twenty-five grand," he said, taking a deep breath. It was clear how much he hated the situation his wife's addiction had put him in. Annalee did not blame him. Cleophus Rickett and his brothers, Manassas and Gideon, were savage, vicious enforcers for their family's gambling racket, collecting unpaid debts by any means necessary. She had files in her office containing photographs taken in the Emergency Room of men who failed to pay the Ricketts what was owed. She recalled one victim who lost the use of an eye; another had six of his teeth pulled out with pliers. None of them pressed charges.

She let the moments pass in silence, waiting for him to make his decision.

Ron finally told her in a dead voice, "They're over at Doodlebug McKenzie's this week."

Annalee nodded. "Okay, there'll be a raid later today, so keep Doreen at home, and for God's sake, don't tell her or let her near a phone. If she finds out and tips them off, I *will* bust her for obstruction." It was time to show Ron the stick. "I guarantee I'll find a judge who isn't one of your daddy's fishing buddies, and when she's found guilty, the D.A. will ask for the maximum at sentencing. You sure as hell don't want to have to schedule conjugal visits with Doreen at Lakeside Women's Correctional for the next seven to ten years."

Just to mess with him a bit, she started to move away, saw him twitch, then halted and added over her shoulder, "Reverend

Lassiter's been dead about a week. Doc's got his body at the county morgue." That was the carrot, his reward for obedience.

Ron stammered his thanks, leaped into the Jeep and sent it tearing back onto the blacktop, headed east toward Huntswell and his father's mansion. Noah brought the boat in against the bank, muttering curses at the mud splashed on his newly detailed patrol car, but he quit complaining fast when Annalee brought him up to speed on her plan to go over to Doodlebug's house that afternoon and execute a raid on the Ricketts' gambling operation.

"Sounds good to me," Noah said, adding, "No joy on the shotgun. Diver turned up nothing except some beer cans, an old outboard motor, and this thing near the bank." He held out a thick silver chain.

Annalee took the chain, turning it this way and that while she examined the broken clasp. "Looks like it was torn off, maybe snagged on something." There was a minute tuft of hair caught between two of the links. She quickly bagged the evidence, presuming the chain had belonged to the victim. They could check with the reverend's wife later.

Returning to the office, Annalee blessed Minnie, who had made a fresh pot of coffee and ordered a late lunch delivered from the Smog Hut barbecue restaurant. After inhaling a plate of chopped pork, coleslaw, Brunswick stew, baked beans, and roasted corn on the cob, Annalee typed up her initial report and helped log the evidence found at the scene. She also organized the planned raid. At around four o'clock, she and Noah, accompanied by two other deputies, drove to Doodlebug McKenzie's residence about a mile from the Lingerville exit off Route 82. The house was set far back from the access road on a slight rise, surrounded by the thick growth of pine, oak, and hickory trees that comprised Malingering Deep.

Annalee got out of the patrol car, shutting the door behind her with a minimum of force. Noise out here carried surprisingly far. They were on the edge of the forest; the air was filled with the loamy green scent of earth and growing things, as well as the taint of decay. The odor was familiar, since her own home was also on the edge of the Deep.

Beside her, Noah stiffened. Annalee caught a glimpse of a pale blur flitting at ground level through the trees before it disappeared behind the house. It did not seem human shaped. "What was that?" she whispered.

Noah shrugged. The other two deputies, Jeeter Murphy and Cynthia Starbuck, came up behind them, silently waiting for orders.

Another movement in her peripheral vision made Annalee draw her .38, the weight comfortable and familiar, right down to the slight burr in the trigger guard that itched where her forefinger rubbed against it. She scanned the area but found nothing out of the ordinary. Holstering her weapon, she decided somewhat sheepishly that the movement had been made by an animal of some kind, not a threat.

"Jeeter, you and Cynthia put on your gear and go around to the back of the house," Annalee said as she strapped a tactical vest over her uniform shirt. At thirty pounds, it was an uncomfortable but necessary safety precaution. "When you hear me and Noah go in the front, that's your cue to bust in from the rear. Y'all ready?"

The deputies nodded, putting on their tactical vests and protective helmets. Annalee was not expecting armed resistance, but she thought donning full gear was good practice for more serious future operations. At her gesture, Cynthia and Jeeter ghosted to the side, keeping just behind the tree line to avoid being seen as they maneuvered their way to the rear of the house. Annalee gave them a few moments to get into place, then nodded at Noah.

"Let's go," she said, striding boldly to the front porch. She doubted the Ricketts had lookouts posted to give warning, and if anybody managed to get away, the state police had promised to have prowl cars roaming east and west along Route 82 to pick up escapees.

The pillars that held up the porch roof were slender tree trunks, well weathered and bug-drilled but still solid. As usual in these parts, the underside of the roof was painted haint blue, the traditional bright hue that was supposed to ward off evil spirits and ghosts. A whippoorwill's call burst out of the woods, startling her. She grimaced at the tightness in her chest, trying to breathe through it. When she was six years old, her mother had told her that a whippoorwill singing near the house was a sign that someone was going to die. Annalee did not believe in such superstitions now that she was an adult, but information absorbed in childhood had a tendency to linger when it was no longer desirable.

Noah made a faint sound that she interpreted as nervousness. She glanced at him and mouthed, "Ready?"

He nodded.

Annalee had used Ron Cutshall's testimony to gain a search warrant from a friendly judge, so anything they found would be admissible in court. Any gambling equipment could be confiscated and destroyed, hopefully before the Ricketts hired a lawyer. In her opinion — and her late father's, it had to be admitted — the only way to stop their illegal operation was to make it too expensive for them to continue, just keep hitting them in the wallet until they took up some other scheme or moved out of the state, preferably both. Putting some of the Ricketts into Edgewater Correctional Facility for a ten to fifteen year stretch would be a good start.

She glanced at her deputy. Noah was toting a twelve gauge shotgun loaded with frangible, semi-solid breaching rounds packed with fifty grams of zinc powder and wax. The rounds were designed to blow off door locks, deadlocks, and hinges, and immediately disperse without the possibility of ricochet or endangering anyone on the other side of the door. He put the shotgun stock to his shoulder, taking close aim at his target. Annalee turned aside, the strap of her helmet digging into the soft flesh beneath her chin. She closed her eyes. He fired once, the explosion painfully loud, leaving her ears ringing. She opened her eyes. The round had destroyed the brass lock, left a splintered hole, and damaged the wooden frame. Noah drove his boot heel into the door, crashing it open.

"Police!" Annalee shouted at once, stepping inside. "Nobody move! You are all under arrest. Stay put, keep your hands in plain sight, and don't be stupid."

The room was clear of furniture except small tables and chairs, and a long pine bar topped with bottles of cheap bourbon and whiskey. Annalee looked around, trying to see everywhere at once and identify potential threats. There were two dozen people around the playing tables, eight dealers, and a pretty girl in Daisy Duke cut-offs and a halter top, carrying drinks. Her mouth was an "O" of astonishment, as comically round as her blue eyes framed in false eyelashes that resembled spider legs. The condensation-beaded glasses slipped out of her hands and smashed on the wooden floor, sending shards of glass scattering. The sharp scent of alcohol bloomed in the air, joining the nose-itching fug of cheap cigar smoke.

Noah was shouting as well, and from the rear of the house came Cynthia's treble voice raised, backed by Jeeter's rumbling bass. Annalee was about to holster her weapon — everyone was staring at her in paralyzed consternation, no one seemed inclined to resist, this was going to be a cakewalk — when Barabbas Rickett barreled into the room, swinging up the muzzle of an FN P-90 compact submachine gun. The bore was like a dead black eye staring Annalee full in the face. She let out an inarticulate yell, her .38 aimed at the center of the man's chest, knowing it was too late to squeeze off a shot that would count. Even if she hit him, Barabbas would not die instantly. At such close range, his return fire — fifteen 28mm rounds per second, her memory supplied, if the P-90 was fully automatic — would in all likelihood kill her stone dead despite her tactical vest's ballistic panels.

The sound of her breathing as loud in her ears as a hurricane's roar, Annalee took in the split-second scene: Noah holding plastic flexicuffs, about to restrain a middle-aged male prisoner; Barabbas' mouth dropping open, spittle flying as he screamed; the gun clutched in her hand heaving into her sight as she raised it a little higher, her finger curled around the trigger. She heard Cynthia's shout, then a pale blur streaked across her vision, resolving into...a dog? *Big damned wolf* suddenly registered, making her instinctively scramble backwards. It was moving too fast for her to catch more than a handful of details, but the wolf seemed to be composed mostly of masses of thick, white-blond fur and a black-lipped muzzle bristling with teeth. The wolf leaped snarling at Barabbas, straight for his unprotected throat. Shaking, Annalee raised her gun again, only to have it knocked aside by Noah.

"Don't," he gasped, his gaze locked on the scene. "Don't hurt her."

Barabbas went down hard, flat on his back, the wolf planted solidly on top of him. His shriek trailed off into a wet gurgle as that sharp-toothed muzzle darted forward and closed over his sunburned neck. The wolf's ferocious growl made Annalee's chest lurch, a weird fluttering sensation that took away her breath. Barabbas' P-90 discharged a chatter of bullets as his finger convulsed. Annalee crouched, half expecting to feel the burn of injury, but the rounds chewed their way up the wall and across the ceiling, sending plaster and plaster dust raining down on her head. By the time she blinked her vision clear, the wolf was gone and Barabbas Rickett was dead, his open eyes glazing over, his throat a mangled mess of blood and torn flesh. Crimson arterial spray was fanned over the nearby wall, and a pool of blood was spreading over the floor and mingling with the spilled alcohol.

The waitress sucked in a breath, letting it out in a scream that drilled straight through Annalee's skull, where an ache of mammoth proportions had started gnawing behind her eyes.

Furious, Annalee barked at Noah, "Shut her up, Deputy, and secure the rest of the goddamned prisoners." She had stood by and let a man be killed by a wolf. A wolf! Jesus Christ on roller skates! The county would be lucky if the Ricketts didn't sue them back to the Stone Age. "Murphy! Starbuck!" she shouted. "Where the hell are you, damn it? Playing mumblety-peg? You were supposed to secure the rear."

Cynthia stumbled into the room, Jeeter hot on her heels. "Sorry, Sheriff," the woman panted, her face pasty with shock. "We were securing prisoners."

"You let a wild animal loose in here," Annalee said, reining in the impulse to scream at them until the rest of the ceiling came crashing down on her aching head.

"We couldn't do anything," Jeeter insisted. He was looking a little wild around the eyes himself. "It just ran in through the door, quick as never-you-mind."

Noah put a hand on her shoulder in what was an obvious attempt to calm her frazzled temper. "Barabbas was going to kill you," he said.

Annalee very carefully did not shrug his hand away and punch him in the face for stating the obvious, which was her first inclination. Instead, she forced herself to a semblance of calm. Venting on subordinates might be satisfying for the moment, but it damaged morale and did more harm in the long run. Besides, no matter how the pooch got screwed or who did the screwing, it was ultimately the sheriff's responsibility for what happened at a crime scene.

"Secure the rest of the prisoners," she said. "I'll radio Dispatch to send the M.E. along to pick up the body." She lowered her voice and added to Noah alone, "When I get a free minute, you and me are going to talk about that stunt you pulled. Got it?"

Noah inclined his head, but the stubborn set of his mouth told Annalee he had no regrets about stopping her from shooting the wolf. *Maybe he has a point,* she thought. *One bullet might've just pissed the critter off.* Wolf bites were dangerous in more ways than just the obvious. She did not relish the thought of a round of rabies shots and the danger of blood poisoning, not to mention the potential crisis if one of her arteries was nicked.

It was not until the last prisoner was safely in the transportation bus guarded by state troopers that she allowed herself to tremble in reaction to the near-death experience. Annalee tried to believe it was the adrenaline kick wearing off, crashing her down from a fight-or-flight high, but that self-deception was not very convincing. She knew her nightmares would be starring Barabbas Rickett and his shotgun for a while.

"Here." Noah nudged her and held out a can of off-brand cola.

Annalee popped the can open and took a swallow. The sugary liquid was so cold, it made her stomach muscles cramp, but it soothed her throat and the caffeine helped ease the post-crisis jitters. "Thanks," she said, wiping her mouth with the back of her hand.

Noah nodded. "Found some drug paraphernalia, cocaine, ether...looks like Barabbas was freebasing and went nuts when we busted in. We also turned up a box of marijuana cigarettes, some mixed baggies of pills — probably Special K, methamphetamines, Ecstasy — and what I think is amyl poppers, but the lab'll know for sure."

"That would explain why the crazy sumbitch attacked us." Freebasing cocaine caused acute paranoia over time, and Barabbas had a record of aggressive, violent behavior anyway. "So much for a cakewalk," Annalee muttered bitterly, finishing the cola in a few gulps that made her headache more acute, a spike of pain that had crimson light bleeding into the edges of her vision. That reminded her of the bloody mess left of Barabbas' throat.

"Tell me, Deputy Whitlock, why'd you feel it necessary to prevent me from saving Barabbas' life?" she asked.

His sidelong glance was cautious. "You mean the wolf? My family's full of conservationists, you know, and the Deep wolves are an endangered species. I just reacted automatically, without thinking about the consequences."

Annalee crushed the empty cola can in her fist. "You want to explain to me why that wolf decided to run inside the house at exactly the right moment to rip Barabbas a new one before he could blow my head off? Or how the hell you knew it was a female? 'Don't hurt her,' that's what you said."

"Told you, my family's trying to save the wolves in Malingering Deep."

It was an answer, but not to any of the questions she had asked. Annalee watched Betty Vernon and young "Igor" wheel the gurney with the body bag out of the house, carefully bumping it down the porch steps with the help of a pair of husky state troopers. Acid scorched her stomach and a sour taste flooded the back of her throat at the visual reminder of her failure. "Conservationists, huh?" she grunted.

"Yes, ma'am." The dying sunlight caught Noah's eyes, making them glint amber.

Annalee turned away, unsure if she was asking the right questions, and equally unsure if she really wanted to know the answers anyway. Her father had loved the wolves. They were not often seen, but anyone who lived around Malingering Deep had heard their howling. On many nights, huddled under a pile of quilts in winter or sweating under a sheet in summer, Annalee had listened to the high, wavering wolf-song serenade from the safety of her bed.

She muttered, "You're taking the witness statements and writing the report. If it's believable, I'll sign off on it. But don't do it again, Deputy. Don't ever let me hear you say that you didn't stop to think about what might happen before you jumped into a dangerous situation with fangs out and hair on fire, hear me?"

Noah repeated, "Yes, ma'am." His tone was soft and respectful. Annalee glanced at him to make sure she was not being mocked, but he seemed sincere.

Later that evening, when the arrests were processed and the paperwork done, she felt a soul-deep gladness on returning home. Twilight turned the world a soft lavender-gray, blurring the trees that reared tall behind her house, built by her great-grandfather's great-grandfather and improved by successive generations. Annalee had been born here; she had been raised in the house and lived in it all her life. While memories of her grandparents, her mother, and father haunted every nook and cranny, she still loved it with all her heart.

She stopped her truck at the end of the driveway to check the mailbox, finding a couple of bills, a postcard from her cousin Hannah in Tennessee, and coupons for the new pizza place in Brightbrook, then continued the short drive to the house. As always, she parked under a crabapple tree planted by her great-great-great grandfather in the same year that a mortar round was fired at Fort Sumter, beginning the War Between the States.

Her cat Mongo waited for her by the front door. He was a Maine Coon crossed with God-knew-what, a rescue from the Humane Society. Annalee liked to believe he had some jaguar in his ancestry. He was much bigger than the average cat and quite the hunter; he liked to bring her rabbits, their necks neatly broken. Mongo usually left these love offerings on the back porch step. She leaned over and scooped up the cat, burying her nose in the thick silvery fur of his ruff. As usual, he smelled of feline musk and the outdoors. His purr rumbled through her body like the vibration of a passing express train on a rail.

Mongo hung limp against her, a soft bulky weight that made her shoulder muscles protest. Annalee managed to juggle him, the mail, her key ring, and the plastic bag containing her dinner without dropping anything as she struggled to get the door open.

Inside, the house was faintly scented with beeswax and coffee, as well as a floral trace from a lilac bush that grew around the side. She let Mongo slip from her arms. His heavy body landed on the floor, rattling the teacups in the china cabinet, her grandmother's prized Andromeda pattern Spode. Mongo stalked off grumbling while Annalee moved to the kitchen where she tossed the bills and pizza coupons on the counter. The bag was emptied on a kitchen table, the wooden top bearing the scars of hard use.

Annalee had stopped at the grocery store on the way home and picked up a rotisserie chicken and potato salad. Combined with some sliced tomatoes and corn relish, it would make a good meal. Taking out the pins and running a hand through her unbound hair, she wondered once again if she ought to schedule an appointment with Arlene at the Curl Up n' Dye salon for a buzz cut. *Not today*, she decided. She went to the back door, opened it, and stepped through to the porch.

The trees formed a densely packed line beginning at the furthest edge of her backyard, which was nothing more than clipped grass, and what used to be a small vegetable patch until she let it go to seed and weed, having no time to care for it. Apart from a few birds, rabbits — less every spring when Mongo was on the prowl — and the occasional deer coming to browse on the lilac bush, Annalee did not see many animals, which suited her fine. She inhaled and smiled, her emotions settling for the first time all day. Her smile faltered when she spied a pale form moving low near the tree line.

It was a wolf.

Whether it was the same wolf she had seen that morning by Yellow Jacket Pond, or the one that had killed Barabbas Rickett, she could not tell. The animal picked its way delicately over the grass, apparently headed for the porch. Annalee's heart thumped so hard, she thought it would smash through her ribcage. She stood frozen to the spot, unsure if she should risk trying to get back into the house before the wolf could spring on her. The door was near, but sudden movements attracted predators. It was an age-old dilemma — fight for her life if attacked or take a chance, turn her back, and try to outrun the threat.

The wolf moved closer, its tongue lolling out of its muzzle in what looked like a good-natured grin but might well have been a smile of anticipation for a tasty meal. Wolves did not attack humans, according to the experts, but they also did not run into the midst of a police raid in order to kill a random stranger. The wolf's anomalous behavior at Doodlebug McKenzie's place was disturbing, and it meant she could not predict with any degree of accuracy what *this* wolf might do. It was a wild animal, and she was defenseless. Those were the only two facts that could be relied upon.

Annalee regretted leaving her service weapon in the locker at the office. There were hunting rifles in the living room above the fireplace, but they were out of her immediate reach. In a way, she was glad. It would be a crying shame to kill such a magnificent creature.

A furry brush against her ankles made Annalee glance down. Mongo was winding himself around her legs, purring loudly. She tensed. Although she had never heard of a wolf attacking a house-cat, she had read that in the western United States, coyotes were known to kill cats and eat them. Coyotes and wolves were both canines. Were their eating habits similar? She prayed that supreme dumb-ass Mongo would show some sense and go back into the house, but he only tipped his head back, looked at her, and let out a piercing meow. Annalee quickly switched her attention to the wolf, afraid it might show an interest in her cat, but it merely tilted its muzzle and gazed at her inscrutably.

After about thirty seconds, Mongo lost interest and wandered away. She could hear the scrape of his claws as he pawed the screen door open just enough to slip back inside the house. Relief swept through her. That was one potential disaster averted, but what if the wolf actually had a hankering for human? Should she try to run? Wait the wolf out until it got bored and left? A chill trickled down her spine like ice water. Her options were limited.

While she was attempting to make a decision, the wolf paused about ten feet away and raised a forepaw. In the hazy gray light, it looked as insubstantial as mist. The wolf regarded her steadily, without a hint of wariness. Annalee stayed still, her fear slowly turning to a sense of wonder and delight. The blond-coated animal was beautiful in a way that made the breath catch in her throat. She watched, entranced, her pulse slowly returning to normal.

Annalee could have sworn she felt a sensation like tickling fingers ghosting over her ribs, her shoulders, between her breasts. Her skin tightened at the phantom touches. Staring into the wolf's luminous golden eyes, she thought she heard someone calling her name from a great distance, and she started when a soft voice spoke in her ear: *Mine.*

Suddenly, the wolf whirled around and loped back to the trees where it disappeared from sight, leaving her alone.

Released from the spell, Annalee blew out a sigh, wondering if her imagination had been in overdrive. She waited a few moments, but the wolf did not reappear. The chill of loneliness that ran through her went deep, beyond the bone; it raised a feeling inside her akin to bereavement, as if she had lost something precious. She inhaled sharply, forcing down the pang of loss, and went back inside the house.

Annalee cut up the chicken, sliced some tomatoes, and took a half-empty jar of corn relish out of the refrigerator. When Mongo padded into the kitchen, meowing for his share of the chicken, she dropped a few tidbits on the floor. She was going to eat standing at the counter, but decided it was too quiet in the kitchen and took her plate to the living room. The canned laughter of a sitcom was not that much better than the silence that usually filled the house, but at least it was noise.

That night, when Annalee went to bed, she dreamed of running through Malingering Deep in the company of wolves...

Then the dream changed.

The hands that slid over her body were callused but not rough, a woman's touch. Annalee bit her lip and arched her back in a silent plea for more. God, this was good! Better than good. It had been too long since a lover had stroked her body this way, reverent yet beautifully assured, trailing almost unbearable sensations in the wake of bold caresses.

When she opened her eyes, her lover's face and figure were shadowed, too vague to make out in any sort of detail, yet this did not alarm her in the slightest. Annalee accepted it, just as she accepted the sudden wet heat of a mouth on her nipple. Each tug of her lover's lips made her feel as if she had been flayed wide open, every nerve ending exposed. The other nipple crinkled tight, aching for attention. Her lover found it, circling and scratching the sensitive point with the edge of a thumbnail until lightning flashed inside Annalee's head, pleasure with a sharp shining curve of pain.

A groan vibrated out of her throat as her lover's mouth worked against her skin, painting secrets in white-hot flame with the tip of an agile velvety tongue. Annalee reached out helplessly but her hands remained empty, grasping nothingness. Her elusive lover slipped over her, and now she could feel the press of another woman's breasts, another woman's weight straddling her, preventing her from flying away. The smell of sweat and arousal filled the air, a seashell musk that increased her desire to a fever pitch.

Feather-light touches skimmed the places where she burned fiercest. Her lover kissed the tautly stretched tendon in her neck and, without warning, bit the pulse point at the base of her throat — gently at first, then harder, licking and sucking with bruising force. Annalee was sure her lover had drawn blood but she was past caring. She writhed and panted, shaken by jolts of delight that threatened to overwhelm her utterly.

Her lover's weight lifted, then breath came in puffs of heavenly coolness on the backs of her knees, her belly, and the inside of her thighs. Annalee twisted, offering herself without shame to the sensual drag of fingertips over her overheated flesh. A hand slid between her legs, cupping her slippery center. She splayed her thighs further apart and ground down, rocking her hips. Annalee felt utterly wanton, abandoned to a passion that was stoked higher when the hand was replaced by lips and tongue. Her lover lapped at her, long languorous strokes which left her whimpering. It was too much and not nearly enough. Fingers finally pushed inside her, and she clenched around them, shuddering.

Annalee's breath came in urgent, agonized gasps. Her lover's tongue was thick and greedy and far too clever, but the fingers thrusting into her body set a more leisurely pace, the counterpoint driving her out of her mind. She fisted the sheet beneath her, hanging on while the blood roared through her veins. Sounds were ripped out of her throat, animal cries she could not contain. Her entire body felt swollen, stretched from horizon to horizon.

Teeth nipped her clitoris, ruthlessly demanding her surrender. Lighting flashed again, this time coursing over her skin, sizzling and incandescent. Annalee let go of the sheet, desperate for a living anchor, and her flailing hand found coarse hair to grasp. She seized a handful in a convulsive grip, holding her lover's head locked in place.

She howled and tensed for a long impossible moment when her climax rolled over her, a juggernaut of excruciating pleasure that caused the world to vanish in an explosion of white light. When she came back to herself, limp and languid and sore, she glanced into her lover's face, and to her profound shock found a pair of golden eyes staring back at her.

Golden eyes in a pale-furred wolf's face.

Mine.

Annalee bolted awake, sweat pouring off her. She was sitting bolt upright in bed, the perspiration-damp sheet tangled around her body. The room was dark, the window showed no trace of dawn in the sky, only the glimmer of stars and a haze of moonlight. Glancing at the clock on the nightstand, she realized it was four o'clock in the morning.

"Jesus Christ," she murmured, rubbing her neck. "I seriously need to get out more."

It was not the first time she had dreamed such an amazingly vivid sexual scenario, she thought. The dreams had started in high school, clearly explicit visions in which a shadowy female lover worshipped her body, at first slightly awkwardly, as if the lover had as little experience as Annalee herself, then more confidently as they went on. She had known she was attracted to girls since puberty, so that aspect was no surprise, but at the time she had even found herself drifting into pleasantly lustful fantasies during class.

*Haven't had one of those since after graduation*, Annalee thought. Her life had become busy with community college and an accelerated program at the police academy, then working with her father as a deputy. She had forgotten about the dreams. Remembering when she had cherished the shiny new secret of her imaginary lover made her feel kind of bereft. None of her real life sexual encounters had been as satisfying. None of her one-night stands had given her half as much pleasure as she had found inside her own mind.

She straightened the sheet, chased Mongo off the spare pillow, got a drink of water to soothe her dry mouth, and lay back down, staring at the bedroom ceiling for a while. She could not forget the incredible sensations generated by her dream. Her body tingled as if she was experiencing the aftermath of a powerful orgasm, and there was an uncomfortable clamminess between her legs. The whole encounter had seemed so real. She reached up and tentatively brushed the base of her throat, half-expecting the ache of a bruise.

There was nothing.

Annalee's disappointment brought tears to her eyes. Turning over, she buried her face in the pillow and tried to go back to sleep, but sleep was a long time coming.

## Chapter TWO

The next morning brought an unexpected development, not wholly disagreeable — the state police commissioner had decided to take over the investigation into the Ricketts' gambling operation.

"They want the credit, that means they can also take the blame for Barabbas Rickett's death," she told her deputies, who had descended en masse to tell her the news as soon as she arrived at the sheriff's office. "I'm not going to fight them over this. You've got to pick your battles, and I'd rather save myself for the budgeting wrangle next month. Starbuck, you send 'em the witness statements, copies of the evidence logs, and all the reports before they call and ask for them. That'll take some wind out of their sails and make us look competent. Hey, no sulking, boys and girls. We have Reverend Lassiter's murder to occupy our time, not to mention one or two other things, such as Deputy Murphy. I do believe, Deputy, it's your turn to man the speed trap out on the Taliaferro Freeway loop."

Casting her thundercloud looks, Cynthia and Jeeter went to their tasks. Noah handed her a mug of coffee, strong and black, the way Annalee liked it.

"Doc Vernon called to ask if you want to attend Lassiter's post mortem today," he said. "By-the-by, her office has been getting calls from Abner Cutshall and the rest of the church's congregation, wanting Lassiter's body released to them for immediate burial. Cutshall is threatening to get an injunction to stop the autopsy."

"Not gonna happen, no matter what kind of fit he pitches," Annalee said wryly, taking the mug into her office. Noah followed her inside, shutting the door. She went on, "Abner Cutshall has no grounds for an injunction. Lassiter's death is clearly murder, unless he shot himself in the throat and managed to conceal his weapon before expiring, so unless you think maybe the state police diver missed a thirty-six inch long shotgun on the bottom of Yellow Jacket Pond, there's nothing Abner can do. The law's on our side. The sheriff's office has an obligation to investigate homicides in Daredevil County, and the medical examiner is legally required to perform autopsies on suspicious deaths. Period. End of statement. Stick it in a box marked 'Done'."

"Somebody ought to tell Mr. Cutshall that."

"I aim to, if he tries that moonshine on me. He may be the Great Man of Daredevil County, but I'll be damned if I'm going to let the tail wag the dog. This is a homicide investigation, not subject to Cutshall's influence. Not while I'm still the sheriff, anyhow. Anybody don't like that, they can stick it where the sun don't shine." Annalee tried a sip of coffee, careful not to scald her tongue, and wrinkled her nose at the taste. Somebody had added chicory to the pot. "Anything else I ought to know about?" she asked.

Noah rubbed the back of his neck, his expression suddenly doubtful. "Um, look, Sheriff...about yesterday, at the raid..."

"That ship's sailed, son," Annalee said, moving around her desk and sitting down. Her IN box was full, as usual, and she noticed that Minnie Hawkins had changed the screensaver on her computer. Instead of a sheriff's badge bouncing from corner to corner, she now had an illustrated Tarzan swinging on a vine. Each arc blew up his leopard-spotted loincloth, revealing a different cartoon phallic symbol between his thighs — a stick of celery, a power drill, a rocket. It was unsubtle, crude, and hilarious, like Minnie herself.

Annalee made a mental note to shut off her computer before any meetings with the county's bigwigs — in her experience, career politicians had no sense of humor — and continued, "If you'd shot Barabbas Rickett, we wouldn't be having this conversation, right? Dead's dead. We'll let the state boys take the fallout for that one. They want the credit, they can take the blame, like I said. However, if there's a next time when you have to choose between saving a human life and shooting a wolf, even an endangered wolf, I expect you're going to make a better choice. Is that clear, Deputy? Am I getting through to you?"

"Clear as crystal, Sheriff."

"Good." Annalee leaned back in her chair, drinking her coffee. The biting bitterness suited the darkness of her mood. She felt restless and unsettled. Part of her wanted to strip naked and run through the trees, run headlong into the heart of Malingering Deep while wolves surged around her like a pale-furred tide, just the way it was in her dream. She took a breath and put the coffee mug on her desk. It was not the first time she had been forced to strangle the impulse to chuck civilization out of the window. That urge was something she had known all her life — the beckoning, near-irresistible call of the wild, wild wood.

"Come with me to the post mortem," she said at last. "Afterwards, we'll go have a talk with the reverend's widow and your Uncle Ezra."

"You think Ezra's involved in Lassiter's death?" Noah frowned.

"If this is going to be a conflict of interest..."

"No, no, don't think so; that's not worrying me one bit," Noah said, throwing up a hand as if to ward off Annalee's query. "If a Skinner was responsible, if they broke the law, they have to pay. That's a no-brainer."

"I'm so glad you approve." Annalee winced at how dry she sounded. "You have any idea why Lassiter preached against the Skinners? I heard he could be pretty scathing."

Noah shook his head. "Who told you that?"

"Common knowledge." Actually, Annalee had gotten the story of Lassiter's vituperative denunciations of the "generation of vipers" from her hairdresser, who had heard about it from her cousin's wife, Jane Darnell, the church's hired cleaning lady, who was apparently an incurable eavesdropper. She was not going to tell Noah that.

"Lassiter had something against my uncle," Noah admitted, "but I don't know the details." He scrubbed a palm over his hair. "Really, Sheriff, I'm just a Whitlock to them. There's family things they don't share with anybody who ain't a Skinner, and that's a fact."

"I reckon Ezra will have more information." Annalee swallowed another mouthful of coffee, grabbed the fried egg sandwich Minnie had left wrapped in a paper napkin next to her OUT box, and stood up. She would deal with the never-ending paperwork later. "Let's head over to the morgue. Doc prefers to do her cutting early."

The county morgue was not Annalee's favorite place. The puke-green walls, black-and-white linoleum floors, missing or stained ceiling tiles, maze of corroded pipes, fluorescent lights, the pervading scents of disinfectant and death — these things never failed to make a cold, sick feeling blossom in the pit of her stomach. She went in through the front door and showed her I.D. at the security desk, where she was waved through by a uniformed guard. The man paid scant attention to her or to Noah; he was busy knitting a red, white, and blue scarf and watching a football game on a portable DVD player.

The walk down the corridor always gave Annalee the heebie-jeebies. It was too cold, the atmosphere too clammy for comfort, and far too quiet. The clicking of her shoe heels echoed hollowly with each step. Walking through the swinging doors and entering the autopsy room, she automatically reached for the industrial-sized jar of Vicks mentholated Vaporub on a nearby shelf. The sharp, eye-watering eucalyptus fragrance scoured the back of her throat, but it helped cut the sickening smell of decomposition. Floaters were notoriously nauseating. Noah smeared a fingerful of the glistening salve beneath his nose, as well.

Dr. Betty Vernon stood beside a gleaming steel autopsy table. The fluorescent lights overhead and the green scrubs she wore deepened the dark color of her skin to a hue approaching ebony, relieved by the hot pink slash of her lipsticked mouth. "We discovered something interesting when we washed the victim's body down," she said without preamble.

Annalee moved closer to the table and looked at the body of Reverend John Lassiter, bloated and monstrous in the harsh light. Betty had already made the Y incision that went from shoulder to shoulder meeting at the breastbone, then angled into a straight slash arrowing to the pubic bone. The soft tissue had been peeled back and the ribcage cut away to expose the internal organs. An overpowering stench drifted from the open cavity, strong enough to linger on the back of her tongue. This was not her first post mortem examination, but Annalee was already regretting eating a greasy fried egg sandwich for breakfast.

Betty indicated the victim's flaccid arm, the bicep marred by an age-blurred United States Marine Corps tattoo. "Note the unusual coloration of the skin," she said.

"To be honest, I don't see anything special, what with all the decomp." Annalee accepted the magnifying glass Betty offered her and examined Lassiter's arm, wrist, and hand. After a moment, she was forced to shrug. "Sorry. You want to clue me in here?"

"It turns out Reverend Lassiter was using some kind of cosmetic base, probably theatrical." At Annalee's blank look, Betty went on, "Greasepaint, Sheriff. Insoluble in water. When we cleaned the body, we found it on his face, neck, and hands. He was covering up his skin. I'll send a sample of the cosmetics to the state lab for analysis but I have a feeling it's going to be a common theatrical variety, impossible to trace."

Annalee looked at the corpse again, somewhat bewildered by Betty's statement. "Was he...oh, hell, you know what I mean, was he trying to pass?"

"You mean was he a black man trying to pass for white?" Betty smiled, seemingly amused by Annalee's attempt at delicacy. "No, he's definitely Caucasian. The victim wasn't a drag queen, either, in case that's your next question. At first I thought the discoloration was due to cyanosis, but then I remembered a case study I'd read recently and did a punch biopsy on his skin. Lassiter was attempting to conceal a medical condition."

"What condition?"

"Argyria. It's a non-reversible, rare cutaneous discoloration. The skin turns a bluish-gray color due to the ingestion of silver salts over a period of time," Betty explained. "Silver particles have collected in high concentrations in the victim's perifollicular sheaths, capillary walls, elastic fibers, macrophages and fibroblasts, and in the basal lamina of the epidermis and blood vessels. There was also about a gram of unabsorbed silver in the small intestine. X-ray microanalysis confirmed it."

"Silver does all that?" Annalee frowned. She felt Noah leaning closer to her, his body heat a blast of warmth against her side.

"The culprit's probably colloidal silver," Betty said. "I'll send the stomach contents and blood samples to the lab for toxicology but judging from the argyria's severity, our victim's been taking a silver-laced solution for quite some time, possibly years. I even found granular silver in his eyes, a condition called ocular argyrosis. Unless he worked in a silver mine, which I doubt, I'm opting for the most likely source, which is colloidal silver. It used to be employed as a water purifier, but these days it's mainly sold as a homeopathic medicine meant to improve health, cure diseases, and allergies." She snorted. "That's pure snake oil. The only thing you can get from ingesting silver is permanently blue-gray skin."

"Okay, I'll bear that in mind. Did you find water in the lungs?" Annalee asked.

"No. The victim wasn't breathing when he went into the water. The cause of death was hemorrhagic shock, as I stated at the scene. Traumatic injury of the external carotid artery resulted in exsanguination. Death occurred approximately six to seven days ago." Betty pushed back the flap of skin and tissue that had obscured Lassiter's face, revealing the man's slack features. "The throat wound has abundant gunpowder residue, so the shooting occurred at very close range and at an angle suggesting the killer stood over the victim, who was lying flat on his back on the ground with his head turned slightly to one side."

"That much I already figured," Annalee said.

Betty gave her a half-smile of approval before continuing. "I recovered pellets from the wound as well as fragments of wadding. The killer used a 20-gauge shotgun. During the autopsy, I also discovered basilar skull fractures, but those injuries occurred perimortem."

"Fracturing the base of the skull takes considerable force."

"Yes, it does. In this case, when the killer shot the victim at close range, the projectiles permitted the entry of gases sufficient to shatter the skull."

Annalee nodded. "Anything else?" she asked.

"Another oddity. See here?" Betty pointed at the ragged upper edge of the throat wound. "The perimeter here is too irregular, like it's been...well, chewed up is the best description I can use. Not something I'd expect to see in a GSW."

Annalee used the magnifying glass to look at the area. "If I didn't know better, I'd swear this was an exit wound," she said at last.

"It's not, believe me. The victim was definitely facing his killer."

"What about those little wounds on his shins and calves?"

Betty was stripping off her purple gloves. She paused. "Dog bites would be my best guess. Well, nips, actually. The bruising is fresh and there's no sign of healing, so they must have occurred perimortem or just prior to death." The gloves were tossed into a disposal bin.

"You're kidding me," Annalee blurted, surprised. "Dog bites?"

"I've seen it before. Some dogs are aggressive; they nip to keep the owner in line."

"Didn't know you were an animal behaviorist," Noah said, his brows tightening in a frown.

"My ex-husband owned a Chihuahua with a serious attitude problem. Little ankle-biter thought he was a pit bull." Betty turned her attention to Annalee. "I sent a sample of the hair caught on the silver chain to the lab. From a simple microscopic examination, I can tell you it's not human. The rest will have to wait until the results come back, but my bet's on canine."

"Okay, that's good enough for a start. CSU's got a picture of the chain; I'll get a copy and see if the victim's family can identify it. Thanks, Doc."

Betty waved at them in clear dismissal, her attention already switching to "Igor", who had entered the morgue carrying a folded paper bag with an ominous stain on the side.

Annalee hurried outside, grateful to get away from the morgue. It felt as if she had been in there for hours. She stood in the parking lot, wiping the Vicks off her upper lip with a paper napkin and gratefully breathing fresh air for several moments. Noah stood beside her, rigid as a statue. He seemed offended, but by what, she could not tell. Annalee decided to ignore him for the time being. There was no point stirring up trouble. If Noah had a problem with Doc Vernon, she would hear about it eventually.

"Get that picture from CSU," she told him after settling her hat on her head. "I'll wait for you out here. After that, we'll go have a talk with Lassiter's wife."

Noah went back inside the squat building, a seventies monstrosity composed of thrusting angles, embellished concrete block, and smoked glass. Annalee looked away from the offensive sight — the polyester-and-love beads wearing architect had probably been smoking "wacky tobacky" when he designed the morgue way back when — and instead gazed at a straggling fringe of pines that separated the parking lot from the busy street on the other side. It was early but already hot enough for her to imagine the gasping heat that would be beating down before lunchtime. Annalee half turned when motion registered in the corner of her eye and her fingers drifted to her belt, just above the butt of her gun.

A woman in her mid-twenties was walking across the white-lined asphalt, headed in Annalee's direction. The newcomer was of average height and she was sturdily built, with short stocky legs, a long torso, and the barest indentation of a waist. She wore faded jeans and a flannel shirt open at the throat. Her hair was thick and wheaten blonde, cut to just below shoulder length. As she drew closer, Annalee saw her eyes were brown. There was a family resemblance to Noah Whitlock, so she guessed the woman was probably a Skinner.

Annalee thought the stranger also seemed very familiar, although she remained blank as to when and where she might have seen her before. Movement on her other side divided her attention. She relaxed slightly when she recognized Noah exiting the building, holding a manila envelope. He spotted the young woman and stopped, smiling hesitantly.

"Cousin Lunella, what are you doing here?" he asked.

*Lunella! That was the name of the Skinner girl from high school*, Annalee now recalled. She studied Lunella, comparing her to memory. The gawky, awkward girl had grown into a pretty, good-looking woman. *Actually, a damn fine woman*, she thought. The heavy bones that had been too blunt for a teenager's face now lent an agreeably sculpted aspect to the adult countenance. While Lunella was husky and broad shouldered, with very few feminine curves to speak of, she was nevertheless attractive, exactly the kind of woman who attracted Annalee. She tried hard not to stare and told herself not to drool.

"Hey, cuz. I was looking for the sheriff," Lunella replied, her generous mouth curving in a cool answering smile.

"You found her," Annalee said, fascinated by the faint blush that crept up Lunella's neck to stain her cheeks pink. "What can I do for you, Miz Skinner?"

"Oh!" Lunella blushed brighter. "Yeah, well, I heard y'all found Reverend Lassiter over to Yellow Jacket Pond yesterday."

Annalee tilted her head, waiting for Lunella to continue. She had learned early in her career that if you were quiet, if you kept your mouth shut, and pulled an air of expectation around you, most people felt almost compelled to fill up the silence with words. Noah stirred beside her. She stilled him with what she hoped was a subtle gesture.

When Lunella spoke, the words came out in a staccato rush, as if they had been memorized from a script. "Anyhow, Uncle Ezra sent me to say that he'll be home today after two o'clock, on account of he's gone up to Mercy Ridge to check his traps. And you ain't s'posed to question Matthew, Mark, or Luke unless he's there or Aunt Rebecca is there 'cause the boys are underage, and he says if you go over to the house and do anythin' without his permission, he'll hire the slickest lawyer in Huntswell to sue your ass."

"Uh-huh." Annalee bit back a smile. "You can tell your uncle that if it makes him feel better, he can have a lawyer present when I question him and his boys. That's his right."

"Sure, I can tell him that."

Noah cleared his throat. "That's good, Lune. If Ezra wants help..."

Lunella's eyes flashed gold. "We don't need your help, Deputy," she snapped, suddenly not shy at all. She pronounced his title like it was a dirty word.

*Seems like a bit of a family feud going on there*, Annalee thought. She knew better than to get involved. Interference in domestic matters usually ended in tears, if not outright bloodshed, when the combatants invariably closed ranks against an interloper. Such disputes were better left alone if possible, and she had no intention of intervening. "We'd best be on our way, Deputy. Miz Skinner, it was a pleasure meeting you," she said.

"Yeah, sure, Sheriff, likewise," Lunella replied, giving her sidelong glances that Annalee found simultaneously amusing and kind of endearing. In fact, her face ached from the effort not to grin like a goof at Lunella's sheer cuteness.

She stopped that thought in its tracks. There was no misery like a hopeless attraction to a straight girl, unless it was compounded by the fact that the girl was her deputy's cousin. Hell, yes, Annalee was attracted. She wasn't made of stone, and Lunella was her type. Very much her type, in fact, but she would not act on that attraction, especially since a little lesbian liaison would probably spell the end of her law enforcement career if it ever became public knowledge. The county Bible-thumpers would be all over *that* like flies on crap.

It was not just because she loved her job; she needed to remain in the sheriff's office until she solved her father's murder and brought whoever was responsible to justice. After that accomplishment, the county commissioners could kiss her ass if they were so inclined. Annalee was used to being alone. When she desired intimate company, there was always a weekend trip to Atlanta to ease her itch, a visit to the clubs and bars where she was just another stranger meeting other anonymous bodies.

*Or I could just have another dream like the one last night*, she thought. Weird though it had become at the end, the dream had also been incredibly arousing, and about the best sex she had ever experienced. Just remembering it made damp heat bloom between her thighs. She resolutely turned her mind away from the shadowy fantasy lover of her imagination, only to find her thoughts drifting back to the subject of Lunella Skinner.

Despite her resolution not to show interest, she remained curious. *Wouldn't hurt to find out a little more*, she told herself, recalling the golden glint in the woman's eyes. Lunella's instantaneous switch from shy to snappish was intriguing; she had always preferred women who struck sparks. There was also the nagging sense she knew Lunella better than their brief acquaintance suggested. In high school, they had barely spoken, and had not seen each other since graduation day. Annalee would swear to that.

In the patrol car on the way to Lassiter's house on the other side of Huntswell, Annalee tried for a casual tone and asked Noah, "So, what did happen to your cousin Lunella after our high school graduation? I don't remember seeing her around."

"She went up to Canada for a spell," Noah answered.

Annalee was not aware the Skinners had connections outside Daredevil County, let alone the country. "To Canada? You sure?"

"Some family thing," Noah said, fiddling with the brim of his hat. "I can't really tell you about it. I mean, I don't know the whole story."

"Fair enough." She decided to ask Minnie Hawkins about it later. The dispatcher was a veritable font of gossip who could dish the dirt on damn near anybody.

The drive continued in silence.

Reverend Lassiter had lived in the wealthy neighborhood known as Nob Hill, although when she was a kid, Annalee and her friends had called it "Snob Hill". Each of the houses was a different architectural style, some whimsical — like the A-frame glass pyramid owned by the CEO of a string of grocery stores — and others classical, like the Tudor-style home given to Lassiter by a devoted congregant of the Honey in the Rock church. The reverend's widow opened the door after Annalee rang the bell.

Ruth Lassiter was a very well-preserved brunette, her hair backcombed, sculpted, teased, and sprayed into a puffy bouffant 'do that resembled a helmet. She was dressed in a lavender knee-length skirt and matching cashmere sweater. The string of pearls around her neck was discreet and tasteful, and no doubt real. She smelled like Chanel No. 5, but when she opened her mouth, Annalee was nearly overwhelmed by the sharp odor of mint and menthol underlaid with alcohol. It seemed Ruth was a closet drinker and, from the fumes, Annalee thought bourbon was the woman's poison of choice.

"Can I help you, Sheriff?" Ruth asked, her voice slightly slurred. Sunlight was not kind to her, revealing patchy places where foundation, powder, and rouge had been too hastily applied. There were blots of mascara around her eyes. Her dark blue eyeliner was crooked as well, and there was a smear of coral lipstick on her front teeth. While some rather obvious cosmetic surgery had helped erase many of the signs of encroaching age, at that moment Ruth looked like a barfly on the wrong side of fifty, the morning after a monumental debauch.

"I'd like to speak to you about your husband, Mrs. Lassiter," Annalee said, taking off her hat and tucking it under her arm. "May we come in?"

"Of course." Ruth stood aside, allowing Annalee and Noah to pass in to the foyer.

It was much cooler inside the house. The atmosphere was hushed, the curtains drawn at all the windows, the interior dim. As Annalee followed Ruth into the living room, she noticed a hall mirror had been covered with a cloth, the sort of thing people did after a death in the family. It surprised her, seeing this evidence of superstitious belief in such a deeply — at least publicly — Christian household. The significance of the covered mirror struck her and she frowned. There had been no official police notification of Lassiter's murder to his surviving family, but somehow Ruth already knew. Annalee blamed Abner Cutshall. *He must have called the widow after his son Ron showed up with the news that we'd found the body.* Nevertheless, Annalee would follow protocol and do the notification properly.

Ruth settled on one of the impractical white leather sofas, her hands folded in her lap, her lavender leather pumps precisely aligned on the shag carpet, her posture rigid. She and her deputy sat opposite Ruth on another white sofa. The cushions were far too soft, giving under their weight until Annalee and Noah slid together to a mutual slumping halt in the middle, their knees and shoulders rubbing together. It was a damned awkward position that made Annalee's back ache, but each time she shifted, the leather creaked with a sound like a dry fart, so she made an effort to remain still.

"I'm very sorry to tell you, Mrs. Lassiter, that we found your husband's body in Yellow Jacket Pond," Annalee said softly, watching the woman's reaction. Ruth did not seem shocked. Her carefully plucked eyebrows raised a trifle, but that was all. *Well, that don't mean much,* Annalee thought. *Grief takes people differently, and besides, this can't be news to her. On the other hand, looks like the surgeon screwed her face so tight if she tried to pull an expression, her nose might pop off.*

Annalee continued, "He was shot and we are investigating his death as a homicide."

"I see," came the calm reply. "Thank you, Sheriff."

Annalee waited a moment, but Ruth's mouth compressed into a thin line. It did not seem as if the widow had anything further to add, and was certainly volunteering no additional information. Annalee saw no point in beating around the bush. She took the envelope from Noah, opened the flap, and slid out the photograph of the silver chain that had been found in the pond. "Did this piece of jewelry belong to your husband?" she asked.

Ruth's gaze flickered to the photograph, then back to Annalee. She hesitated, licking her lips, and finally answered in a reedy voice, "Yes."

"Do you have any idea how the clasp was broken?"

"No."

Annalee held the photograph loosely between her fingers, tilting it back and forth. "Your husband took colloidal silver pretty regularly, didn't he?" she asked.

Again, Ruth hesitated. "He had an allergy," she said at last.

"To what?" Annalee's interest was piqued by Ruth's odd behavior.

Ruth's gaze cut to Noah and she sat up a little more rigidly, the toes of her pumps denting the carpet. The pearls she wore had a subtle gleam, like beads of ectoplasm wrapped around her stringy neck. "John was allergic to dogs," she enunciated clearly.

"And was he under a doctor's care?" Annalee asked.

Ruth ignored Annalee. She went on speaking to Noah, grating words out between her lipstick-smudged teeth. Her eyes were cold, her features tightened to a mask of hatred. "Filthy, disgusting animals with filthy, disgusting habits," she pronounced, her hands clenching into white-knuckled fists. "'*Give not that which is holy unto dogs.*' They are worthless scavengers, shit-eaters that lick Jezebel's blood from the street and returneth to their vomit! '*And whatsoever goeth upon his paws, among all manner of beasts that go on all four, those are unclean unto you.*' Unclean! Do you hear me? Unclean!" She was shaking with fury, spittle flying, her face mottled crimson.

Annalee feared the woman might blow an aneurysm or give herself a heart attack.

Noah shot to his feet, leaving Annalee toppled and struggling to extract herself from the sofa's clutches just as a man entered the room. Ruth stopped speaking, her mouth closing with an audible snap while Annalee managed to get up without further humiliation. She clamped a hand around Noah's forearm as a precaution. He was clearly fuming, and although she was confident he would behave in a professional manner, she wanted to remind him their business here was official. Personal indignation could wait.

She assessed the newcomer with a practiced glance. His salt-and-pepper hair was slicked back, emphasizing a broad, unlined forehead. He had an expensive-looking tan and manicured fingernails, and was wearing what could only be an Armani suit that fit his toned body beautifully. Annalee had an inkling that, like Ruth, the man's unnaturally smooth facial features were the result of Botox and cosmetic medical procedures. *What is wrong with aging gracefully*? she wondered. It seemed to her the more money someone had, the more desperately they sought to retain the appearance of youth. It was a ridiculous endeavor and ultimately doomed to fail, but she supposed plastic surgeons had to make a living.

"Ruth, my dear, I understand we have callers," the man said, flashing a smile that had probably cost him more than Annalee's monthly salary. His air of bonhomie was fake, but the Patek watch strapped to his wrist was real. "Will you make the introductions?"

Annalee decided to make no pretense of social niceties. Unless the man was blind, he could see they were in uniform, and unless he was stupid, he knew about Lassiter's death. "Sheriff Crow," Annalee said. She did not offer her hand. "And you are, sir?"

His smile did not falter one whit. "I'm Aiden Thompson, senior partner at Thompson, Thompson, Camp, and McElwee. Our firm is based in Atlanta. Mrs. Lassiter is not only a client, but a personal friend of mine. I flew down to see her last night."

His statement confirmed Annalee's suspicion Ruth had already been informed of her husband's murder, although if they wanted to play it cool, she could do that.

Ruth got up from the sofa and walked over to Aiden, moving with the exaggerated grace of a secret drunkard. The man shook a cigarette from a crumpled pack taken from his jacket pocket and lit it with a Zippo lighter. Ruth pressed herself against his side, an arm around his waist. The glance she gave Noah was scathing. Annalee did not understand the animosity; as far as she was aware, Noah had never met Reverend Lassiter or his wife.

"The sheriff has been telling me that John was murdered," Ruth said.

"Really?" One of Aiden's eyebrows jerked higher. He gave Ruth a sympathetic glance that Annalee felt was the one thing not feigned about this situation. "Oh, honey, that's terrible news." He put an arm around her shoulders. The cigarette smoldered between the first and second fingers of his free hand, thin tendrils of smoke curling towards the ceiling.

"Do you need anything?" Aiden asked Ruth, his attention focused solely on her. "A sedative, perhaps? Should I call a doctor?"

"No, I'm fine." She patted his arm. "John was called home; it was the will of God," Ruth said. "I'm so glad you're here to help me carry this burden."

"I'll be here as long as you need me," he said, smiling fondly down at her.

"Mrs. Lassiter, I need to know if your husband owned a shotgun, or if you have a shotgun in the house," Annalee said, breaking up the mutual love fest before she started gagging. Was Mrs. Lassiter having an extramarital affair with Aiden Thompson? If so, had her husband known? Did the obvious bond between them have anything to do with the murder? Most victims knew their killers, which was why close family members were always the priority suspects in a homicide.

Aiden pulled Ruth closer against his side. A weight of ash crumbled off the end of his cigarette, soiling the carpet near his brightly polished wingtips. "Sheriff, Mrs. Lassiter has just learned she is a widow. Have you no compassion? Can't your questions wait?"

"I'm very sorry for your loss, ma'am, but I wouldn't be doing my job if I didn't pursue every avenue of investigation." Annalee was not going to be intimidated by some high-falutin' legal eagle from Hotlanta. "Did your husband share your feelings about dogs?" she asked the woman, ignoring Aiden's questions.

"He hated them," Ruth muttered.

Annalee made a mental note to check Lassiter's record and find out if he had ever been accused of, cautioned against, or arrested for animal cruelty. "Since your husband was allergic, do you have any idea how dog hair could have gotten caught on Reverend Lassiter's silver chain?"

"No."

"Did your husband own a shotgun?" Annalee repeated.

"Yes, he did. They're in his den. You can have them," Ruth said, her expression disdainful and her tone clipped. Aiden bent his head to murmur in her ear. She shrugged and continued to Annalee, "I have nothing to hide, Sheriff. Take the shotguns, much good may they do you."

Annalee nodded. "Do you mind telling me where you were last Wednesday evening?"

"Sheriff!" Aiden exclaimed. "Such a question at such a time!"

"I remind you again that I'm doing my job, counselor." Annalee tried hard to keep any hint of hostility out of her voice. It would not be productive to rile the man to anything beyond professional indignation on his client's behalf.

Annalee turned to the widow. "Mrs. Lassiter, I know you want to see this killer brought to justice," she said. "We have to eliminate people who had nothing to do with the case so we can focus our efforts on finding on the one who actually took your husband's life. Will you please tell me where you were last Wednesday evening?"

Ruth did not answer. Her lips remained stubbornly pressed together.

"Really, Sheriff, I must go on record as protesting this most unreasonable and insensitive interrogation—" Aiden began, but Annalee interrupted him.

"Your client can answer my very reasonable questions here, in the comfort of her own home, or she can do so at the sheriff's office," she said. "It don't make no never mind to me."

Aiden grimaced, but he held a whispered conference with Ruth that lasted about sixty seconds. When it ended, he glanced at her and said, "You may question my client, Sheriff, but I warn you, if I don't like what I hear, I will end the interview."

"On your head be it." Annalee wondered if the widow had something to hide, or if the lawyer was just being obnoxious because he could. "Okay, Mrs. Lassiter, for the third time, where were you last Wednesday night?"

"At Abner Cutshall's house in Huntswell," Ruth answered, glancing at Aiden, who nodded. She went on, "We were having dinner with some of the congregants, and afterwards there was a prayer session."

"I'll need a list of the other dinner guests," Annalee said.

"You'll get it, solely for the purposes of establishing my client's alibi. I trust you'll be discreet, Sheriff," Aiden replied.

"I'll try. Next question: did Reverend Lassiter have any enemies?" Annalee asked.

Aiden squeezed Ruth's arm in apparent warning, flicked ash from his cigarette and answered the question himself. "John Lassiter was a soldier of God engaged in a war against evil," he said. "The reverend fought sin and corruption wherever he found it. The enemies of the Lord were his enemies, too, Sheriff Crow."

Annalee pursed her lips. "I had in mind something a little more secular, Mr. Thompson. For example, did the reverend owe anyone money? Was he a gambler? Had he done anything that might open him up to blackmail? Please don't be offended, ma'am. Believe me, if there's anything to be found, if we don't uncover it, a defense attorney will, should we make an arrest. There ain't no secrets that won't come to light eventually."

Ruth's mouth worked as if she might spit. "My husband was a good, kind man whom I loved dearly," she said at last, "and I repeat, I have nothing to hide."

"That's it, Sheriff," Aiden said, frowning. "I really must insist you go now."

"After we collect those shotguns, if you don't mind." Annalee did not think the guns had been used to kill Lassiter, but she would have them tested anyway to cover all the bases. "Once they've been examined by Ballistics, they'll be returned to you, provided we don't need 'em for evidence." Annalee returned the photograph to the envelope, taking her time just to needle him. Aiden looked mulish, but he waited her out without protest.

She asked for directions to the study and made a point of having the lawyer present while she and Noah bagged three 20 gauge shotguns from an unlocked, glass-fronted case. The room was very masculine, decorated in dark woods and subdued colors, with hunting prints hung on the walls and shelves full of leather-bound books that looked as if they had never been cracked open. There was an oversize, elaborately bound Bible on a gilded stand. A glance showed the book was open to Leviticus. The overly sweet scent of vanilla pipe smoke lingered in the air, threatening to give her an instant migraine.

"If we have further questions, I trust you'll be available?" Annalee asked on the way out of the house.

Ruth nodded. Aiden scowled but waved a hand in acknowledgment.

"We'll keep you apprised of the case's progress as much as possible," Annalee said. "Should you recall any information you believe might help us, please don't hesitate to call."

Ruth made no reply. Annalee thought it quite likely the Devil and his minions would be ice-fishing in Hell before she heard another voluntary word from the widow. Certainly her pet lawyer seemed poised to create obstacles at every turn.

After giving the hovering Aiden her business card, she led Noah outside, keenly aware of Ruth's gaze burned a hole between her shoulder blades. Once in the patrol car, she turned to Noah and asked, "What the hell was that back there?"

He stiffened. "Don't know what you mean."

"The widow ranting about dogs. Seemed to me she was directing that speech at you."

"Remember those nips on Lassiter's shins?" Noah asked, giving her a look that was probably supposed to be innocent but seemed more like deer-in-the-headlights desperation. "Could she have been referring to them?"

"I doubt it, Deputy. How could she have known about Lassiter's dog bites unless she witnessed the murder? And I'm willing to bet her alibi checks out." It was interesting, the way he tried to change the subject. There was something he was trying to hide and she was determined to find out what it was. Annalee shoved the key into the ignition and started the engine. "Anyhow, is there some bad blood between you and Lassiter?" she asked.

"Apart from the way he regularly abused the Skinners in his sermons? I heard about that. Pretty sure everybody's heard about that. Lassiter didn't exactly make it a secret." Despite being restrained by the seatbelt's chest strap, Noah contorted around in the passenger seat so that he could face her more directly. "Look, it's true Reverend Lassiter hated the Skinners. They're my cousins and stuff, so yeah, I didn't like the guy. Don't know why he acted like he did, but I thought he was a Grade A asshole. That don't mean I can't do my job."

"Did you and Lassiter ever have words on account of his sermons? Maybe more than words? Y'all took a trip to fist city, you'd best tell me before it turns up in the investigation. I get sandbagged with some shit, I can't help you if them bastards at I.A.D. gets involved." Annalee did not look at Noah as she backed the patrol car out of the driveway. Every interrogator knew it was often easier to obtain a confession if the other person did not feel they were being watched and judged. The crunch of gravel under the tires was not loud enough to drown out Noah's soft-voiced response.

"Nope. Never spoke to the man," he said. "I seen him around, of course."

"Of course."

"But I swear to you, I never touched him. Never talked to him. Never. Anybody says different, they're a goddamned liar."

"Okay, okay," Annalee said, hearing the ring of truth in Noah's voice. "Don't blow your O-ring, son. I believe you."

In the rear view mirror, Annalee caught a glimpse of pale fur against a green hedge, and on an inexplicable impulse stood on the brakes, flinging out a hand across Noah's chest as the patrol car lurched to a halt. Continuing to gaze into the mirror, Annalee watched a wolf walk across the gravel drive twenty feet behind their car. Noah pried his clutching fingers off the dashboard, muttering something under his breath that she did not quite catch.

"I thought they didn't leave the Deep," Annalee said, her voice hushed. The wolf had paused and was pointing its muzzle in their direction.

"They don't." Noah leaned over so he could also peer into the mirror. "Damn it."

"Problem?"

Noah unfastened the seat belt and twisted further in his seat, craning his neck to see out of the rear window. "There are some folks who take pot shots at the wolves, ignorant peckerwoods that ought to know better but don't, which is the main reason why they're all supposed to stay in the woods. The wolves, I mean."

His choice of words seemed a trifle odd to Annalee but she replied, "Well, I don't think anybody's going to be shooting at that wolf while we're sitting right here."

"Maybe."

The wolf abruptly took off, belly low to the ground, its tail streaming out behind it like a flag as it raced out of sight. Noah rolled down the window and checked outside. Annalee did the same, and saw Aiden Thompson standing on the house's threshold. The lawyer had a rifle in his hands. Annalee wondered where the hell the weapon had come from; she had not seen a rifle in the case in the study. Was it his own? If so, why had the lawyer brought a rifle with him on a bereavement call? The passenger door opened, interrupting her thoughts and grabbing her attention. It seemed Noah was about to get out of the car.

"Hey, where do you think you're going?" Annalee asked, snagging his sleeve.

"To find out if Thompson has a license for that rifle," Noah replied grimly.

She retained her grip, preventing him from leaving. "Don't you dare piss in that guy's cornflakes," Annalee warned. "He's not a suspect, and you don't harass a lawyer without a damned good reason. Even then, you'd better be prepared for a shit storm to end all shit storms. Guy like Thompson makes a stink, you'll end up in the unemployment line."

Noah narrowed his eyes. "Thompson was going to shoot at her."

"Who? Mrs. Lassiter? If you mean the wolf..." Annalee shook her head. "You jackass. Get your butt back in the car before I smack you hard enough to make you cough up bones."

Noah slid his legs back inside the patrol car and closed the door. The solid clunk made Annalee's ears pop. When her hearing returned, he was saying, "...don't trust Thompson as far as I can throw him. My gut tells me he's a sleaze."

"Do you have something on him? Anything at all he can be charged with? Prima facie evidence of wrongdoing of any kind?" At Noah's reluctant negative reply, Annalee sighed. "Look, let's concentrate on figuring out who killed Reverend Lassiter and why, okay? Unless you actually witness Thompson shooting at an animal on the endangered species list and gather evidence to prove same in a court of law, leave the man alone. The last thing we need is a harassment suit that'll bring the governor's wrath down on your pointy little head."

Noah shrugged, but he looked mutinous.

"I'm going to drop you off at the office," Annalee decided aloud, putting the patrol car in gear. She was in no mood to deal with her deputy's attitude. "You can go over the reports and make me a summary so I don't go blind trying to read Starbuck's bad handwriting. Girl writes like a blind monkey on crack."

He did not smile at her comment. "Where are you going to be?"

"I'm taking the SUV and driving out to the Skinner place."

"Sheriff, you'd better take me with you. The house is pretty far back from the road."

On reaching the intersection of Sycamore and Bland, Annalee brought the vehicle to a stop and checked both ways to set a good example before driving on. "Hush your mouth, Deputy. I grew up around the Deep, same as you," she said. "It ain't likely I'll get lost. All I have to do is follow that track off the Lauder extension road."

"Yes, but—"

"But me no buts, Deputy Whitlock. You're going to update the paperwork before I start fielding angry calls from the D.A.'s office. I'm going to question some persons of interest in the Lassiter case as is my duty to the good taxpayers of Daredevil County, who expect to see justice done competently by their legally elected sheriff, namely me. Get it?"

"Got it." A muscle twitched in Noah's jaw.

"Good." Annalee pulled into the parking lot of the sheriff's office. "Now go away and do your job, and let me do mine in peace."

Noah got out of the patrol car and almost — but not quite — slammed the door shut behind him. Annalee rolled her eyes at the man's pique, then ducked inside the office long enough to collect a set of keys from Minnie Hawkins and sign out the Toyota Land Cruiser from the Motor Pool. It had been confiscated from a drug dealer in Huntswell and was their only off-road vehicle. Their budget was tight, and since the Cruiser ate gas like a Baptist preacher scarfing down fried chicken at a church social, she routinely ordered the SUV to stay garaged unless there was official business to be done.

The interior of the Cruiser still smelled factory fresh, but the "new car" scent was tainted by a chemical whiff which Annalee identified as the enzyme-based cleanser used to lift the dealer's blood out of the upholstery by the crime scene clean-up crew who had the county's contract. The pine scented air freshener dangling from the rear view mirror did not disguise the odor. She rolled down the window, tuned the radio to a country and western station, and enjoyed the ride out to the Lauder extension road curved snake-like between Malingering Deep on one side and the Ateeska River opposite.

Just past mile marker fifty-seven, a worn dirt track meandered across a short grassy field and into the trees. A battered, oversize mailbox was planted on a pole near the side of the road. Annalee turned off the blacktop and followed the track, the SUV's tires bumping over the rutted surface. Sunlight filtered through the trees, casting dappled light on the windshield. She turned down the radio's volume until Waylon Jennings and Dwight Yoakum were the barest murmur of sound and twanging rhythm. It seemed sacrilege to spoil the forest's majesty with loud music.

After about twenty minutes of careful, slow driving, she came to a large metal gate blocking further vehicle access. It looked new and there was no way around it; the trees on both sides grew too closely together to admit anything wider than a roller skate, much less an SUV. She parked the Cruiser, got out and inspected the thick chain and padlock holding the gate shut. She did not see any solution except to climb over it and continue on foot. She was about to do just that when Lunella Skinner popped into sight from behind an oak tree. Lunella's smile was shy but seemed welcoming.

"Miz Skinner, I need to ask your aunt and uncle a few questions," Annalee said. "You mind unlocking the gate and letting me in?"

"I ain't got the key, but if you jump over, the house isn't too far along," Lunella replied. "I'd be happy to take you up there. You got no fear of dogs?"

"Never met a hound I couldn't handle," Annalee answered truthfully. She loved Mongo, but she owned a cat mainly because she wasn't at home very much, and knew a dog required more attention than she could give it at this point in her life.

Lunella's smile widened into a positive grin. Her teeth were very white, the canines a bit too pronounced, but Annalee found the expression charming. "Then I don't think you'll have any trouble in these parts, Sheriff," Lunella said.

Annalee climbed over the gate. When she hopped down to the ground, the other woman steadied her landing with a hand. Annalee was surprised by the strength of Lunella's grip. She not only looked strong, but clearly had muscle to spare. The thrilling realization made Annalee wish she had met Lunella in a big city club, where they could smile at each other, eye fuck a little, and try to make conversation over the pounding music before slipping away to privacy. The pit of her stomach dropped out and her mouth went dry.

"Thanks," Annalee said after clearing her throat. She followed Lunella, admiring the smooth curve of her buttocks encased in dark blue, form-fitting jeans. Damn, she was a tempting sight! If Lunella had not been Noah Whitlock's cousin...if they did not live in such a small town with the usual small town prejudices... *If wishes were horses*, Annalee thought, her chest tight with a mixture of desire and frustration. She did not like hiding an essential part of herself from everyone, but it was the only way to keep her job.

*And I'm going nowhere till I figure out who killed Daddy*, Annalee thought, brushing past a clump of wild ferns and scattering a few tiny jumping spiders.

Lunella halted and turned around to face her. "Are you all right?" she asked, pausing as if choosing her words carefully before continuing, "You seem...well, kind of tense."

Annalee put on her best poker face. "I'm fine, Miz Skinner."

After a moment, Lunella nodded, although she was still frowning. "You need to relax more often, Sheriff. It'd be better for your blood pressure." That did not sound like a suggestion but a command, and Annalee did not know what to say. Lunella did not wait for her to reply; she turned around and began walking again, her hips swaying as she moved.

Lunella was barefoot. Her feet made virtually no sound as she walked down the dirt path that had been cleared of dead pine needles and last year's fallen leaves. Her wheaten blond hair — an unusual color that Annalee was sure was not due to a peroxide bottle — was pulled back into a ponytail that twitched from side to side between her shoulder blades. There was a proud tilt to the woman's head which belied the appealingly shy demeanor. The seeming contradiction made Annalee want to learn more.

"So, I hear you went to Canada after our high school graduation," Annalee said, keeping her tone light so as not to give the impression of an interrogation.

Annalee could almost hear the smile in Lunella's voice when she replied, "Just visitin' kin, Sheriff. I'm home now, hopefully to stay."

"Visiting for...what, a good five years?"

"We have a lot of relations up there in the north."

"Huh." Annalee avoided a tree root that humped out of the ground at the right height to trip the unwary "Whereabouts in Canada?"

"I'm sure you ain't never heard of it — itty bitty place in the Northwest Territories, they call it. Very nice, lots of trees, snow..." Lunella waved a hand. "It's different than here."

Annalee tried to imagine being away from Daredevil County for half a decade. She knew she would miss the familiar places and familiar faces, miss them like crazy. "Homesick much?" she asked.

"Yeah." Lunella glanced at Annalee over her shoulder. "Pretty much cried the first three weeks I was there." She let out a rueful chuckle. "I got over it, though. It was kind of hard to leave when...well, when I came back home. Here, home to the Deep."

"I've lived around the Deep all my life—" Annalee stopped speaking when an agonized animal howl sliced through the air. The awful cry wavered for several seconds, hurting her eardrums, before it cut off with a series of loud, shrill yelps.

Lunella's head snapped up, her almond-shaped eyes flashing gold. Her expression was so murderous, Annalee took an instinctive step backwards.

"Stay here," Lunella said through gritted teeth, "and don't leave the trail." She took off at a loping run towards the source of the howl, but Annalee had no intention of standing there with her metaphorical thumb up her metaphorical ass while God-knew-what was going on.

She followed Lunella as closely as she could, sticking to the woman's heels as they crashed through the undergrowth. Lunella seemed to know exactly where she was going, or at least she was moving with a confidence that appeared unshakable. At a certain point she paused, threw her head back and sniffed the air, drawing in several huge breaths, her breasts rising and falling under her flannel shirt. Annalee waited, trying not to pant too harshly. She had thought she was physically fit but she was barely keeping up. Lunella turned in a different direction and went on, ducking under a tree limb. Annalee stifled a groan and stumbled along in the woman's wake. She had the feeling Lunella was deliberately holding her speed back a little so she would not fall far behind.

At last, they reached a place where a large animal — *another big damned wolf* went through Annalee's mind, one somewhat bigger than the one she had seen at Doodlebug McKenzie's place during the ill-fated raid — was lying in a heap near the base of a hickory tree that seemed very old to her, as though it might have been a sapling when rebel American guerillas sniped at British redcoats more than two hundred years ago. The wolf's thick coat of fur was white-blond, identifying it positively as a member of the breed indigenous to the Deep. Annalee came to a stumbling, panting halt, fighting to stay on her feet rather than collapse face down in the bracken and never move again.

Lunella did not hesitate but started straight toward the injured animal. Shocked, Annalee hissed at the woman to stop, afraid to yell lest the wolf panic and start attacking them. It was in obvious pain...damn it. She had her cell phone but that would do no good out here where there was no signal, therefore no way to call for help. She drew her service piece, thanking God she was at the right distance and the right angle to make a one shot kill a fair certainty, provided the wolf did not move or Lunella get in the way.

"Get back over here," Annalee ordered, taking aim.

"Don't you *dare!*" Lunella spat, giving her a furious glare. The injured wolf whimpered, drawing Lunella's attention. She went closer, kneeling down next to it while Annalee held her breath and tried to sidle around to acquire a better firing angle in case she had to shoot it. The second glance the woman gave her was so filled with disdain, Annalee's heart contracted and she swallowed hard. Lunella laid a hand on the wolf's head. The wolf's eyelids cracked open a slit, revealing irises shimmering like flake gold.

"It's a trap," Lunella said, a world's worth of scorn in her voice. "Put your stupid little pea shooter away, Sheriff, and help me." When Annalee did not respond, standing frozen by a combination of apprehension and astonishment, Lunella made an impatient sound. "I said, *help me,*" she repeated in a growl that made the hairs on the back of Annalee's neck stir.

Annalee holstered her weapon and wiped her sweaty palms down her pant's legs. Her mouth was dry but she got out, "What do you want me to do?"

Lunella sighed in apparent relief. "He's caught in a leghold trap. The jaws are smooth, not toothed, so the skin isn't broken but the bone may be. At the least, he's hurtin' pretty bad. We're gonna let him loose. You release that spring lever there," she said, indicating a piece of metal on one side of the trap, "and I'll do t'other. Don't worry, I won't let him bite."

The wolf gave another soft whimper. Lunella stroked its ears, murmuring under her breath. After a moment, she shifted and gestured to Annalee with her free hand. "Come on over here," she said. "When I tell you, release the lever."

Annalee had never been so close to a live wolf. A musky scent came from its fur. Curious, she held out a hand and after glancing at Lunella for permission, gently touched the wolf's ruff. It was much softer than it looked, like silk against her palm.

"Uh-huh, that's nice," Lunella said with a small approving smile. "That's real nice. Now let's get him out of this trap. Ready?"

"Okay, okay, yeah." Annalee knelt down and positioned herself, her hands on the lever. At Lunella's nod, she depressed the lever, sensing the other woman doing the same underneath the wolf's body. The trap sprang apart and the wolf stood, limping a few steps away on three legs, its injured left foreleg held curled against its chest. The plumed tail hung low, as did the massive head. Annalee got to her feet and the wolf sidled further away, its muzzle wrinkling into a snarl that displayed big, sharp teeth.

"Quit that!" Lunella thumped the wolf on its shoulder. Bending over at the waist, she manipulated its injured leg while Annalee cringed, waiting for the inevitable snap of those wicked jaws. The wolf tolerated the touches with astonishing patience, whimpering occasionally but showing no inclination to bite.

"The bone's not broke that I can tell. Can you get home by yourself?" Lunella asked, as if the animal could understand her. "If you can, just go on. I'll take care of stuff here."

The wolf eyed her in what Annalee could have sworn was a sour manner, but it turned and limped off quickly, disappearing into the forest. Lunella straightened, tucking locks of her hair behind her ears. She kicked the trap, scowling. "Damned poachers," she spat. "Ought to be put in jail, you ask me."

"That type of leghold isn't illegal in this state," Annalee pointed out, not yet prepared to address the Twilight Zone weirdness of a wolf apparently obeying the young woman's commands. Perhaps it was a tame animal, a pet? If so, it was mighty damned intelligent.

"That shit's illegal on Skinner land." Lunella gazed angrily at the trap and the steel chain wrapped around the base of the hickory tree, holding it secure.

"Then it's poaching and you have a legitimate complaint, which I'm happy to make official by filing a report, starting an investigation, and arresting the people responsible." Annalee remained calm, slipping into her law enforcement role with practiced ease. She would deal with the oddities later, once she had a chance to assimilate what she had seen and experienced. "Are there any identifying marks on the trap?"

"Belongs to them no 'count Gunns," Lunella answered. "There's a sort of cartoon rifle scratched onto the jaw, near the spring lever on the right."

Annalee squatted down to check and found the mark right where Lunella said it would be. "Okay, I'll have to bring this in for evidence. You got a bolt cutter?"

Lunella nodded. "Over to the house."

"I can take some pictures with my cell phone, but I have to tell you that the worst the Gunns will face is a fine if they're found guilty. There's not a judge in Daredevil County that'll give out jail time for poaching."

"Then what good is man's laws? What in the hell has that ever done for us?" Lunella's shrug, the hard set of her mouth and the flicker of resignation in her expression told Annalee this was not the first time the woman had felt screwed over by the law. "Come on, let's go," Lunella went on. "Just leave it be. We'll deal with the problem in our own way."

"I don't want you or your uncle doing anything foolish, anything that can't be taken back," Annalee said firmly as the two women trudged back to the trail at a more reasonable pace. "I don't want to see y'all end up in court or in jail over this, okay?"

Lunella did not answer. Her silence became grating after a while. Annalee felt as if she had been judged and found wanting. She said, "Look, if an animal trap belonging to the Gunns injures a person, then I can charge them with reckless endangerment and whatnot, maybe get some jail time depending on the offender's record. You catch anybody on your property without an invite, you call me and I'll arrest 'em for trespassing."

"Man's laws," Lunella scoffed.

Annalee took Lunella by the shoulder, feeling the shift of solid muscle and bone beneath the soft flannel shirt. A momentary flashback struck her — the touch of another woman's body straddling her in that damned erotic dream she couldn't seem to shake. She pushed the unwelcome memory away and said, "I'm serious about not doing anything rash."

"Then we let them do what they want, when they want, where they want?" Lunella snarled, her eyes turning gold again. She pushed forward, right into Annalee's space. They were almost the same height but Lunella seemed to loom over her. "The Gunns have no right to be on our land, Sheriff. Our land! They have no right to hunt us, trap us, hurt us..."

Annalee's heart thudded faster. Jesus Christ, the woman was sexy! Lunella's shyness was appealing, sure, but when her temper flared and she got a bit more aggressive, showed the steel beneath the softness, it made Annalee want to howl. She forced down the disconcerting flare of desire and became aware that Lunella's expression had changed, somehow narrowing and becoming more feral, her face more angular and pointed.

Suddenly, Lunella sniffed the air, much as she had done before. Her posture — head slightly back, nose tilted up, nostrils flaring — reminded Annalee of a hunting dog questing for scent. A brief thrill of anxiety replaced desire's pangs. She had showered that morning but undergone some strenuous activity since, and was sweating like a whore in church, as her papaw would have put it. Had her deodorant given up the ghost? She would have tried for a surreptitious sniff of her own but Lunella was too close and too observant.

After a moment, Lunella's mouth curved into a wide grin that showed an awful lot of teeth. "Let's go on up to the house," she said calmly, having apparently forgotten or put aside her fury at the Gunns' poaching and the law's ineffectiveness.

"Uh, okay, sure," Annalee stammered. She was uneasy about the way Lunella gazed at her, in an odd combination of surprise and what seemed to be a kind of amused affection, like she was seeing something in Annalee, something unexpected but not unwelcome.

They began walking again, except this time Annalee noticed that Lunella had become more solicitous toward her, holding aside tree branches until she passed, taking her wrist to guide her around obstacles. Annalee found the attention disquieting but a part of her welcomed it. In Lunella's presence, she felt stripped of artifice, her inner core exposed without making her vulnerable. Undeniable electricity crackled between them. Every casual brush of Lunella's hand or body against hers was both a torment and a delight.

Reminding herself she was the sheriff and had a job to do, Annalee tried to maintain some professional distance from Lunella, refusing to allow her insane attraction any leeway. She had almost convinced herself it was working when at last they broke through the tree line into a clearing, and she got her first view of the Skinners' house.

*More like a compound*, she thought. There was a single main building, a large two-story structure built from logs that were weathered and mossy between the chinks. The wood shake roof supported a tall antenna. A covered porch stretched across the entire front of the house, made colorful by hanging baskets full of impatiens. Smaller buildings were scattered around the cleared space, including a henhouse inside a fence. There was no grass to be seen — far too many trees on the perimeter for the necessary sunlight to filter through the canopy — but the ground was covered in a mulch of age-browned pine needles and chipped pine bark. A couple of dinged-up Ford trucks were parked to one side.

A pale blur streaked across her vision. The image resolved into a wolf, smaller than any of the ones Annalee had already seen, running up the porch and through the main house's open front door. The impression she got from her fleeting view was that the wolf was a half-grown adolescent with gangly, too-long legs and an awkwardness that would disappear with age. *Another pet, perhaps? A rescue animal?* She turned to ask Lunella, but the question was forestalled by the fond look on the woman's face.

"That's Daisy," Lunella said. "Come on. I'm pretty sure Uncle Ezra's to home."

Going into the house, Annalee was immediately struck by the smell, a strong musk laced with more than a hint of what she could only describe as "wet dog". The living area was huge, taking up the bulk of the ground floor. No carpeting, Annalee noted, just wooden floorboards that were scuffed and scratched and bleached from years of scrubbing. The walls were whitewashed, undecorated except for a couple of woven Pendleton blankets in bright colors and geometric patterns, one of which she recognized as an Iroquois turtle design. Three leather sofas had seen better days; the arm of one of them had been torn open, fluffy white stuffing leaking from the hole. No television was in evidence, only a ham radio set-up, which explained the antenna on the roof.

Ezra Skinner heaved himself off the damaged sofa when she and Lunella walked into the room. He was a big-bellied man, tall and heavy boned, his hair the same wheaten blond color as Lunella's. His eyes were sherry brown, good humored but somewhat guarded. "Sheriff Crow," he boomed, thrusting out a hand. "Good to see you."

Annalee took the offered hand, wincing when his grip ground her bones together. "Mr. Skinner. How are you today, sir?"

"Never been better," he replied. "Snared some beautiful rabbits. Going to take the boys huntin' white-tail this weekend. Maybe get some boar, too."

It was not hunting season, but the man was free to hunt and trap on his own land, so Annalee did not make a fuss. "I need to ask you about—"

"Lassiter," Ezra interrupted. "Sit down, Sheriff. Can I get you a drink? Beer? Sweet tea? A cold co-cola?"

"No, thank you."

Lunella asked, "Aunt Rachael in the kitchen?"

"Sure, honey, sure." Without shifting his gaze from Annalee, Ezra flapped a hand at Lunella as if she was a pesky fly.

Annalee was about to start asking questions when Lunella broke in. "I found a leghold trap just off the trail," she said in a low growling tone that Annalee found unbearably sexy. "One of the Gunns' traps. Bear was caught in it."

That got Ezra's attention. His eyes narrowed and he tensed. "Is Bear alright?"

"I'm pretty sure his leg ain't broke, just bruised. Told him to go home."

"Well, go on and tell your aunt, girl. The sheriff and me are goin' to talk business." Ezra waited until Lunella left the room, then said, "If I catch them Gunns on my land—"

"I hope you'll call me so I can come and arrest 'em rather than take the law into your own hands," Annalee said, trying her damnedest to show him her sincerity. "Mr. Skinner, I do appreciate your concern, but I can't condone starting an armed conflict. You shoot any Gunns on your property, unless they're in your house and threatening your family, I've got to arrest you for manslaughter at least. The exact charges'll be up to the district attorney. I don't want that, sir, and I'm sure you don't want that, either. Maybe a jury would acquit, but even if they did, the shadow would haunt you for the rest of your days."

Ezra nodded slowly. "I respect your honesty, Sheriff. That's a rare thing these days." It seemed as if he might add something else, but he asked instead, "So, what-all do you want to know about that no-good sumbitch Lassiter?"

Annalee took off her hat, tucking it under her arm. Her hair was damp with sweat, and there was more sweat gathered between her breasts, clammy and unpleasant. Recalling the way Lunella had sniffed the air around her, she fought not to blush. The thought that Lunella had been *smelling* her...well, that was kind of embarrassing, and a lot more of a turn-on than she might have believed before it happened, almost as intimate as a kiss.

Wrestling her mind back to the case, she asked, "Mr. Skinner, what can you tell me about Reverend Lassiter?"

He moved over to a sofa and sat down, the cushion sinking under his weight. "Lassiter...one of them Bible-thumpin', holy rolling, hellfire-and-damnation preachers."

"I hear he had a grudge against you," Annalee said, keeping her tone and her expression neutral. She found a seat on the sofa opposite him. The scarred leather cushions were covered in a fine dusting of dog hair, which she ignored even though her every movement sent a small cloud of dust and dander rising into her face and up her nose.

Ezra snorted. "Grudge ain't a strong enough word, you ask me."

"Why don't you tell me about it?"

"It's family business."

Annalee scratched her nose, stifling a sneeze. "Mr. Skinner, this is a homicide investigation. You can answer my questions here, or we can take a trip to the sheriff's office, but I promise you, sir, I will get answers one way or the other."

At first, she was not sure how Ezra would react, then he grinned, showing teeth as prominent, profuse, and sharp as Lunella's. "I like you," he said. "You've got what they used to call moxie, so I'm findin' myself inclined to tell you a little story."

She gingerly settled back against the sofa cushions. "I'm listening."

"John Delano Lassiter weren't always a preacher," Ezra said. A shaft of sunlight illuminated his face, throwing the wrinkles at the corners of his eyes into prominence, like slashes of ink on his skin. Beard stubble gleamed silver on his cheeks and chin. "Don't quite know when he got religion, but before he took the Good Book so much to heart, his name was Shadrach Rafferty. His momma was a Skinner — my second cousin, Jerusha."

Annalee made a mental note to look up Shadrach Rafferty in the system to see if he had any prior criminal record. If so, he would not be the first man to camouflage his sins behind a Bible. "Would he be related to the Raffertys that live over to the cemetery?"

"Yes, that'd be the ones, though Jerusha left her husband when Shadrach was six years old, and as far as I know, Alonzo Rafferty drank himself to death shortly thereafter. His liver was shot. Them Raffertys ain't a damn bit of good, as you ought to know. Nothin' but a bunch of chicken-rustling sneak thieves, too fond of gettin' liquored-up."

"What about Lassiter...I mean, Shadrach?" Annalee prompted.

"Shadrach — maybe I ought to call him Lassiter anyhow, be less confusin' for the both of us — was brought up here mostly by my own momma and daddy." Struck by the syrupy yellow light streaming through the window, Ezra's irises seemed to turn the color of gold. "Look, Sheriff...Lassiter almost died when he was a young man. There was this sort of accident, see, and that created some bad blood between him and us."

"What happened?"

For a moment, Ezra's gaze went distant, as if he was recalling the past, then his focus returned to her. "I ain't at liberty to say," he said.

Annalee frowned. He had been cooperative thus far, why the reticence now? "Mr. Skinner—"

"No, don't ask me 'cause there's some things I'm not gonna tell you."

She studied the man's stubborn expression and decided not to press him on the issue. "Okay, fair enough. Did you have any contact with Lassiter?"

"Not so much. I knew he was in town, but we ain't exactly cozy."

"Why did he preach against you?"

Ezra shrugged his meaty shoulders. "Who knows why a man's heart prompts him to act in one way or another?"

Annalee thought he was being evasive. "It had nothing to do with the 'bad blood' you say was between you and Lassiter?"

"I can't tell you what was going on in the man's head," Ezra answered, a sour twist to his mouth. "Maybe he had a grudge, maybe not. We ain't spoke in many years."

"But surely you were angry about his preaching."

"Don't know exactly what Lassiter had to say or how he chose to say it. Not like me and mine was invited to his church, Sheriff."

Annalee decided to abandon the unproductive line of questioning. There was no point wasting time on Ezra's reasonable denials. She could return and press him harder on the topic if or when it became necessary in the course of the investigation. At the moment, she needed more answers and was unwilling to alienate him without cause.

She asked, "Last Wednesday evening...can you account for your whereabouts?"

He squinted at her, a slight smile returning to his face. "I was here at home with my wife, my three sons, my two daughters, my niece Lunella, her brothers, my grandfather...quite a few people was here all damned night."

Which was no kind of alibi as far as Annalee was concerned, but she would let it slide unless the evidence led her to believe otherwise. "Is there anything else you can tell me about Lassiter? Did he have any enemies?" *Besides you* went unspoken.

"He was never a good boy," Ezra said. "Oh, he tried and we tried, but he never really fit in around here. And then...well, he grew hard, Sheriff. Hard in his heart. He went away and he came back a hardened man, a man on a mission."

"What mission was that?"

She thought for a moment he was going to answer, but a teenage boy walked into the room. He was blond, of course, and brown-eyed. The boy's complexion was clear except for a nasty red rash around his mouth. Not acne, she believed, but an allergic reaction. The painful-looking welts were already scabbed over, so she supposed it had happened earlier in the week.

"Hey, Daddy," the boy mumbled.

"Johnny, shouldn't you be in bed?" Ezra seemed half-amused, half-concerned.

Annalee did not catch Johnny's reply.

"Bear got caught in a trap," Ezra said as if answering a question.

"He okay?" Johnny's bottom lip cracked when he spoke. He wiped away the trickle of blood on his chin with the back of his hand, smearing crimson along his jaw.

"Lunella says so. Why don't you go out there and check on him? And take somethin' to your little brother while you're at it, an ice cream, maybe."

Johnny walked out of the room, slouching as if his backbone was made of spaghetti. *Typical teenager*, Annalee thought. *Wait twenty years, kid...you'll be wishing you'd paid better attention to your posture when you're saving money for that orthopedic mattress.*

Now that the distraction was over, Annalee tried to bring Ezra back to the business at hand. "I believe you were about to tell me about Lassiter's mission," she said.

"Was I?" He shook his head. "I don't think so, Sheriff."

*Perhaps a little baiting might be in order*, she thought. *Shake the tree, see what falls out.* "A man named Aiden Thompson, a lawyer out of Atlanta, told me that Lassiter was a soldier of God fighting evil, corruption, and sin."

Ezra's expression turned furious. "That is the biggest pile of bullshit I've ever heard!" he cried, his balled-up fist striking his knee. "Lassiter was a goddamn parasite who didn't care who he hurt to get his way! And he was working with that crazy sumbitch Alex Dempsey—"

A woman's quiet voice cut into his diatribe. "Ezra, that's enough."

He swung his head around, clearly startled by the interruption. Annalee followed the line of his gaze and saw a tall, thin woman whose hair was quite dark blond, much more so than the other Skinners. She was standing in the doorway, frowning at both of them.

Ezra stiffened, then the bulky lines of his body softened. "My wife, Rachael," he said.

"Pleased to meet you, ma'am," Annalee said, putting on her friendliest smile.

Rachael came into the room. Not a very physically imposing woman, she wore a pair of dirty jeans that looked ready to fall apart and a ratty Lynyrd Skynyrd T-shirt, but her self-confidence and aura of command was dazzling. She ignored Annalee's overture and focused on her husband, saying, "Ezra, honey, you'll excuse us, I'm sure."

He popped off the sofa in a surprisingly graceful move and shuffled out of the room without an argument. It was perfectly clear to Annalee who really ruled the Skinner clan, and it was not Ezra. "I came to talk about Reverend Lassiter," she said.

Rachael nodded. Her manner was reserved, even cold, and her expression gave nothing away. "I think you've been given enough information today."

Annalee was going to protest, as she had not yet questioned the three boys, but a thought struck her. She still had the picture of Lassiter's silver chain, and recalling that the coroner had believed the pale hairs caught in the links were canine... She pulled out the photograph and showed it to Rachael. Perhaps despite his allergy, there was a connection between Lassiter and the wolves of the Deep.

"Have you ever seen this necklace, Mrs. Skinner?" she asked.

Rachael's reaction was instantaneous and shocking. She did not appear to move, but suddenly she was right there, hovering over Annalee, pressing her into the sofa cushions with the weight of her anger. "This isn't a game," Rachael snarled, showing far too many teeth for Annalee's comfort. "This is about survival, Sheriff. Our survival."

Annalee tried to force her heart to stop trying to batter its way out of her chest. There was real menace in Rachael's tone of voice, in the way she gripped Annalee's upper arms, in the fierce golden burn of her eyes and the musky, bittersweet animal scent that rose around her in a dizzying cloud. Atavistic fear insisted that Annalee flee, but horrified fascination kept her where she was, staring into the sharply honed gaze of a predator.

Rachael backed away, but not quite enough to reduce Annalee's apprehension. The woman's body was tense in a way that was even more suggestive of a carnivore ready to pounce. "Take your picture and your questions and go," she said. "Don't come back."

"I can't..." Annalee did not know what she was trying to say. Her mind was frozen, stuck in a rut carved by fear. The photograph was crumpled in her hand and she had no idea how it had happened. She swallowed around the knot in her throat, gathering her scattered thoughts and trying to compose herself.

Lunella was abruptly there, pushing Rachael aside and kneeling on the floor next to the couch. "Are you okay?" she asked Annalee.

"I'm...I'm fine." Annalee became aware that she was sweating heavily, even more than when she had been running in the forest. She blinked, her eyes stinging.

Lunella turned her head to address Rachael over her shoulder. "Don't do that again."

"Don't you tell me, girl..." Rachael's eyes were gleaming golden slits.

Snarling a word that sounded like, "Mine!" Lunella shoved into Rachael's space so quickly, Annalee was not able to register the movement between kneeling and standing. She sucked in a startled breath. Lunella was more physically imposing than her aunt, husky and muscular to the other woman's more petite body structure, but Rachael seemed to grow larger, swelling with cold fury, her hair bristling coarsely around her angular face. She and Lunella stared at each other for a long moment. Tension ratcheted higher until Annalee felt as if the room was filled with static electricity, invisible sparks snapping against her raw nerves. The two women did not make any threatening moves; they simply gazed at one another, each twitching slightly, communicating some silent message she did not understand. A violent clash seemed imminent. Annalee sensed the wrong word or movement at the wrong time would swing that potential her way.

Pressure built to a near agonizing height. Annalee's skin crawled. Sunlight spilled white into her vision, creating a halo around the two women, blurring their outlines. Annalee's mouth was dry, her chest spasmed painfully; she could feel the banging of her pulse inside her head, a muttering *boom-boom-boom* that did not exactly hurt but did not feel good either.

Finally Rachael shattered the spell. "Are you challenging me, girl?" she asked in a whisper.

Lunella seemed startled. She replied uncertainly, "No?"

Rachael's hand shot out and cracked cross Lunella's face with enough force to knock her off balance.

Annalee sprang to her feet in instant response, watching them carefully, ready to intervene in the domestic dispute if she deemed it necessary. Before she could say anything, Lunella straightened, touching her cheek. A handprint was blazed there, red against her otherwise shocked pallor. The color of her eyes seemed to fade from amber to brown as her shoulders slumped.

"Sorry," Lunella muttered, not looking directly at her aunt.

"You can take the sheriff back to her car," Rachael said. She did not sound smug or triumphant, just matter-of-fact in a way that chilled Annalee's blood.

*How often does that little scene play out?* Annalee wondered. An ache in her hand registered. She glanced down and realized she had a stranglehold on the butt of her gun. Blind instinct put it there, she thought, the impulse to protect Lunella from a threat. Her attraction to Lunella was no excuse; pulling a firearm in such a situation would have been like chucking gasoline on a fire, reckless and very stupid. She eased her fingers off the butt, troubled by how quickly her law enforcement training had been suborned.

Annalee made herself abandon her emotional reaction and think rationally, analyze the situation the way she had learned on the job. She would not have pegged Rachael as an abuser or Lunella as a victim, but she had been in law enforcement long enough to know that outward appearances were usually deceptive. Households had secrets. People did crazy shit behind closed doors. However, she had become a witness to what could only be regarded as a physical assault. That meant she was involved in her official capacity as sheriff. She would have to speak to Lunella when she was certain they would not be overheard.

"Yes, ma'am," Lunella replied diffidently to Rachael. Her gaze shifted to Annalee. "Are you ready to go?"

Annalee's gut clenched, but she answered smoothly, "Sure. I've got everything I need for now. Mrs. Skinner, please thank your husband for me. I appreciate his cooperation."

Rachael nodded, making no reply. Although it went against the grain to turn her back on a known abuser, Annalee exited, following Lunella out of the house.

Once they were headed down the trail, Annalee put a hand on Lunella's arm, halting her. "Hey, how are you doing?" she asked, pitching her voice soft.

"I'm fine." Lunella gave her a smile that seemed genuine. The mark on her cheek had already faded to a slight pink.

"Do you want to press charges?" Annalee waited until Lunella made the expected protest, then continued, "If you don't press charges, the abuse will never end. I know you're scared, but look, there won't even be a discussion of jail time for your aunt. The D.A. won't ask for that on a first offense. She'll get court ordered anger management sessions. She'll learn to control... Oh, honey, don't cry. I'm going to help you, I promise. It'll be okay..."

To Annalee's consternation, Lunella's shoulders started shaking and she covered her face with both hands, making distressing sounds. When Lunella looked up at last, her eyes were sparkling and she was grinning, not crying as Annalee had feared. "Anger m-m-management?" she wheezed, obviously finding the notion hilarious.

Annalee waited. Lunella might be having hysterics; after all, people had weird stress reactions sometimes. But the woman continued to giggle, making noises like a broken bellows until she was red as a beet. Annalee was beginning to feel somewhat embarrassed, like she had made a wrong call despite the slap she witnessed. Nevertheless, she remained patient, figuring she would get an explanation eventually.

At last, Lunella wound down, a hand curled over her ribcage. "Oh, I ain't had fun like that in a long time," she said between gasps. "Whoo! Hurts like a sumbitch."

"Mind telling me what's so funny?" Annalee asked, vaguely resentful. She hated feeling as if she was being laughed at, although she knew Lunella was not mocking her.

Lunella stood a bit straighter, though she still clutched her sore ribs. She wiped her face with the heel of her free hand. "Just the idea of Aunt Rachael... Hee-hee-hee..."

"Don't start up again or we'll be here all day." Annalee tried for a stern tone. It was a serious issue, damn it. "Really...what's so funny about domestic abuse?"

"S'not what you think," Lunella said. She was clearly making an effort to address Annalee's concern. "You don't understand our family, the way things work. I was...I was out of line, I guess you'd say." Her smile became sly. "Do you like me?"

The question took Annalee aback. "Well, I...I don't..." she stammered.

"It's okay. Honestly, I like you, too. Really I do. I like you a lot." Lunella leaned forward. Before Annalee could move away, put a little distance between them, make a protest, for God's sake...Lunella's mouth was on hers.

She tried not to encourage the kiss but Lunella was insistent, and Annalee did nothing to discourage it either. Lunella reached up and tilted her head to the exact right angle to apply gentle little licks along her lips. Goosebumps rose tingling on her skin from neck to knees. This was good, so incredibly good. Their bodies fit together with seamless perfection. Lunella was making breathy, happy-sounding noises, pressing herself against Annalee, a hand on her hip and the other hand squeezing her buttock. Against her common sense, against her good judgment, Annalee responded, turning pliant in the embrace, her mouth opening to admit Lunella's tongue.

She arched into the solid warmth of Lunella's body, her nipples tightening, rubbing almost painfully against her cotton undershirt. The heat of desire pooled low in her belly. Annalee moaned, the sound startled out of her as Lunella nipped at her throat, nuzzling and dragging kisses over the line of her jaw. This had happened in the dream, she recalled, then her mind went muzzy, details slipping away as she was captivated by what was happening here and now.

Raising shaking hands, Annalee cupped the side of Lunella's face, her thumb smoothing over the cheek that Rachael had slapped. Her hand dipped lower, until she could feel the steady flutter of Lunella's pulse at the base of her throat. Tremors ran through her, a series of incredibly intense shocks that tingled outward from her spine and upward from the boiling slickness between her legs.

The kiss suddenly turned wilder, more desperate, fueled by the mysterious alchemy of lust and pure want. Letting out a surprisingly loud snarl, Lunella grabbed Annalee and crushed their mouths together, their teeth clashing. It felt like Lunella was trying to devour her alive. Annalee surrendered, begging silently for more. Heady sensation rushed through her, leaving her oblivious to almost everything except the intense, bruising force of

Lunella's mouth on hers. She felt as though a fist clenched her heart in a brutal rhythm.

Lunella broke the kiss, then ran her lips over Annalee's cheeks, her temples, the sensitive spot behind her ear. No tongue, no wetness, just a series of soft sweet pressures that made the hairs on Annalee's body stand on end. Annalee moaned low in her throat, followed by a stuttering gasp as sharp teeth grazed her throat, the pain combined with a pleasure so incredible, she could only clutch at Lunella's flannel-clad shoulders and hang on.

She could feel herself coming alive, every nerve waking, straining towards the light like a new green shoot emerging from the earth.

A bird called loudly in a tree above their heads — *whip-poor-will! whip-poor-will!* — and it was like ice water poured over her. Annalee pulled away, panting and lightheaded. Wiping her palm across her mouth, she watched Lunella, who was staring back at her with huge flake-gold eyes. She could not speak. The words would not come.

"Mine," Lunella said, not at all out of breath.

Annalee gasped for air. She was not sure if it was a trick of the light or her vision, but Lunella's outline became fuzzy. She could have sworn the woman's face sharpened, the bones shifting beneath her skin. Uncertainty replaced desire. This was too much like the dream, when a wolf had replaced her imaginary human lover.

"I am not yours," Annalee whispered. "I am *not* yours," she repeated more strongly, then winced when Lunella's wordless growl reverberated loudly between them. Annalee shuddered. The woman sounded like an animal. It was not really frightening; she could read protectiveness and possession in the sound, and that worried her.

She did not know Lunella, but her feelings were more powerful than she would have expected had she given herself permission to fantasize about it. *What's the old joke about two lesbians and a U-Haul?* Annalee thought. *Shit, we ain't even had a first date yet.*

Lunella took a step forward, holding out her hand. When Annalee did not take it, she said quietly, "I won't hurt you."

"That's not what I'm afraid of," Annalee replied, louder and more tartly than she intended. Lunella looked hurt and a little lost, so she added, "I'm not...look, you're an attractive woman, very attractive. I won't deny that. And yes, I'm attracted to you."

"Good." Lunella came another step toward her, smirking.

Annalee took two paces backwards. "But I can't act on that attraction. Damn it, I'm the sheriff! Your uncle is a suspect in a murder investigation. It's a conflict of interest for one, and for another...I just can't. Okay? I can't do this with you."

"Why not?" Lunella sounded genuinely curious, not defensive at all. Annalee considered that a good sign. Maybe this wouldn't turn ugly.

"Because I'm an elected official in a county where gays and lesbians don't officially exist," Annalee told her bluntly. "If they do, they're expected to stay in the closet, not flaunt themselves in public where they might offend the sensibilities of good solid citizens."

"*Those* people," Lunella scoffed.

"Yes, goddamn it. This isn't the big city, honey. I have to work with people like that every day. They have to respect my badge and my office, and they sure won't do that if they can't respect me as a person. It isn't right and it sure as hell isn't fair, but it *is* reality." Annalee inhaled, a deep breath that did nothing to ease the constriction in her chest. "I wouldn't be able to do my job and keep the peace. I'm not...I'm not ready to give that up."

Lunella's gaze was steady. "Like your father."

The statement was so unexpected, Annalee could only blurt, "What?"

"He...he knew things. Secrets. And he didn't want to *not* do his job, either." Now it was Lunella's turn to step backwards, off the trail and into the bracken beneath the trees. "Alexander Dempsey was one of those secrets," she went on. Her expression was stricken and slightly sick, as if she had revealed something huge, something devastating. "What Aunt Rachael said is true — this is about our survival, and that includes you. It'll always include you, 'cause you're mine, no matter what you think." With that, Lunella turned around and vanished into the forest, swallowed by the undergrowth in less than an eye-blink.

Frustration made Annalee want to ball up her fists and scream, but instead she muttered, "Fuck, fuck, fuckity-fuck-fuck!" Another deep breath, exhaled with force, and she felt no better or any less confused.

Ezra had mentioned someone named Dempsey, calling the man a parasite worse than Lassiter. Lunella said this Alexander Dempsey fellow was a secret, a secret that Annalee's father had known. Had her father lost his life because of some secret? Because of Dempsey? Was her father's death connected somehow to Lassiter's? What did Rachael and Lunella mean when they talked about their family's survival?

So many questions and damned few answers were forthcoming.

It was akin to being frozen between one heartbeat and the next, waiting for something to happen so life could continue at its normal pace. The investigation was being pulled into a murky direction, where motives and players remained unclear.

Annalee jammed her hat on her head and set off down the trail, headed toward the gate. Murder seemed to be only one of her problems.

"Mine," Lunella had insisted.

Part of Annalee wanted desperately to respond, "Yours," but she could not. She dared not. Lunella's embrace, the fevered kisses, the dizzying sensation of belonging that had felt so natural, so right...Annalee could not forget any of it, no matter how hard she tried.

A sudden savage fury bubbled up inside her, and she bit the inside of her cheek until she tasted blood. Restraining herself from throwing a punch at a nearby tree, she stomped down the trail, every footstep taking her further away from what she wanted.

Taking her away from Lunella.

## Chapter THREE

The following morning in her office, Annalee stared at her computer, waiting for the search she had initiated on John Delano Lassiter aka Shadrach Rafferty to be completed. After what felt like years — during which time she drank half a cup of coffee, scalding her tongue, and ate a stale cheese Danish from the vending machine — the printer started spewing pages. Annalee squinted at the printout, thinking she was going to need reading glasses soon or get herself a pair of longer arms.

Noah came into her office after a perfunctory rap on the door frame. "Good morning," he said. "How'd it go at Uncle Ezra's?"

Annalee glanced up. The deputy's relieved expression irritated her. What had he expected, that she would end up lost in the woods and eaten by bears? Damn it, she did not need a babysitter. "Everything's fine," she replied curtly. "Got a possible lead."

"Aunt Rachael called me last night," Noah offered. "She said to thank you for helping Bear."

"That's mighty kind of her, I'm sure." Annalee finished her coffee and shuffled the printer pages into the correct order. She did not want to think about the Skinners at the moment; anything that reminded her of Lunella was unwelcome unless it pertained to the case. Her lips still tingled with the sense memory of being kissed, and the surface of her skin was tender, as if she had been bruised without showing a mark. If she dwelled on the exhilarating moments she had spent in Lunella's arms, if she allowed herself to regret her decision... But she would not let that happen.

"Listen, Shadrach Rafferty..." Annalee began, focusing on business to stave off an impending funk.

"Who?" Noah shifted from his weight foot to foot, and after she glared at him, finally flopped down in the chair opposite her desk.

"Shadrach Rafferty is the man John Delano Lassiter used to be." Annalee scanned the pages, taking in the details of Lassiter's past. "After his parents divorced, he and his mother went to live with her family, meaning the Skinners. He was raised as Ezra's brother."

Noah nodded. "Skinners stick together, thick and thin."

"Well, there was a falling out of some kind between him and your Uncle Ezra," Annalee told him. "You know anything about that?"

"Way before my time."

"Ezra told me there was an accident and Lassiter almost died, and after that there was bad blood between them," Annalee said. "Don't know exactly what happened, and Ezra ain't talking. As for Lassiter, he disappeared from the county records in '68, when he was sixteen, and doesn't turn up again until '72, when he was arrested in Atlanta on felony theft and fraud charges. Seems Lassiter turned into a con artist, running scams from New York to Miami. Got a history of fraud, theft, occasional assault — a genuine revolving-door inmate.

"Then in '98, Lassiter was serving a nickel term for fraud and firearms possession, mostly at the prison farm over in Baldwin. He got religion while he was inside, and I guess later he hooked up with Alexander Dempsey."

"Who's Dempsey?"

"Some doctor, used to work at a company called Transgenic. We need to find out if Augusta P.D. has any information on Dempsey. By the way, Lassiter legally changed his name after he got out of Baldwin." Annalee put the papers into a file marked HOMICIDE: RAFFERTY, SHADRACH aka LASSITER, JOHN DELANO.

"You got anything else?" Noah asked.

"Plenty of questions." She tossed the file into the PENDING box. "You'd best put in that call to Augusta today. Know anybody over there?"

Noah nodded. "Yeah, couple of guys. I'll put in the request, see if I can get any info on Dempsey expedited."

"Sounds like a plan to me."

Without preamble, Minnie Hawkins sailed into the office. The heavyset, middle-aged woman wore a leopard-print blouse with a deep décolletage, paired with a knee-length hot-pink skirt and matching pumps. Her backcombed hair was high and bubble-shaped, almost a beehive, dyed henna-red and sporting a few spit curls at her temples.

"Hey, Sheriff, you forgot your messages when you came in this morning," Minnie drawled, fanning a sheaf of flimsy yellow note-papers. Her fingernails were long and painted glossy scarlet, the same color as her lipstick.

"Thanks," Annalee said, taking the small pile. A thought struck her as Minnie turned to go. She asked on impulse, "Wait a sec...you've lived here all your life, right?"

"Born and raised," Minnie replied, swiveling back around to face the desk. Annalee could have sworn the woman's vast bosom lagged a split-second behind the rest of her body.

"You ever hear of a Shadrach Rafferty?" she asked.

Minnie pursed her lips. "Shadrach Rafferty... Yeah, sure, one of the Skinners' cousins. That sure brings back some memories."

Annalee made a shooing motion at Noah, who understood and quickly scrambled out of the chair. "Please sit down, Minnie, and tell me all about it," she said, a thread of elation buoying her mood. If there was any scandal in Daredevil County that Minnie Hawkins didn't know about, it wasn't worth knowing, even the ones that were decades old.

"All right, let me see..." Minnie frowned in thought as she took a seat. "I'd just had my daughter, Chloe. Lord, that was a labor of love, let me tell you! Thirty-two hours worth. My regular doctor was on vacation in Hawaii, and I had this young intern who didn't even look old enough to shave regular! That boy was the spitting image of my sister's boy, you know, the Joshua who went to Duke on scholarship and married the Marshall girl. So can you imagine me laying there, everything below the waist on display to God and the curious, with a doctor who looked like my nephew crouched between my legs! Like to have put a quiver in my liver, I tell you, and I don't have to say it twice. Anyhow, my sister-in-law came over from Murfreesboro to help, and she got bit by a king snake. Good heavens! She lost her nerve and went completely to pieces, bless her heart. Had to be given a knock-out shot."

"Shadrach Rafferty?" Annalee prompted, hoping to get the woman back on track.

"I was getting to that," Minnie admonished, shooting Annalee a disapproving glance from behind the cat's eye glasses perched on her nose.

"Sorry, sorry," Annalee said, holding up her hands in a conciliatory gesture.

Minnie made a moue and went on, settling into the chair like a plump hen on her nest. "As I was saying, after my brother Jimmy finally showed his face at the hospital with a bucket of fried chicken but without the biscuits, and I gave him what-for, though he really can't be blamed since his elevator don't always stop on every floor, bless his heart, for which I blame our cousin Jeanette for hitting him with a whiffle ball when he was five years old."

Annalee blinked. She was accustomed to Minnie's seemingly unstoppable floods of information, but that did not mean she was able to assimilate everything in a single gulp. A look at Noah's glazed expression told her there would be no help from that quarter. She would have to try and pick out the relevant facts on the fly. Asking Minnie to confine herself to the subject of Lassiter aka Rafferty would be futile.

"Anyhow, I remember the ambulance brought in a boy who'd been attacked by a dog," Minnie said, lacing her fingers over the rounded bulge of her belly. The color of her fingernail polish clashed horribly with the skirt's hot pink hue. "Shadrach Rafferty, his name was at the time, though I hear tell that he changed it to Reverend Lassiter. I will never forget that day at the hospital. The boy must've been about sixteen. Had some pretty bad bites, poor kid. Bleeding like a stuck pig. I figured it was somebody's hunting dog what done it, you know, 'cause they can be vicious. Good Lord, my second cousin-by-marriage, Zeke — he's a devoted deer hunter, you know — his little girl just missed being mauled by one of his pit bulls, and would have been hurt bad or maybe even killed 'cept she was saved by the grace of God and his wife Susan, who swings a mean five-iron.

"So to get back to what I was saying...at the hospital, Shadrach kept claiming it was his cousin Ezra what done it. He said that they'd had a fight over a girl and Ezra'd bit him. Well, everybody knows Shadrach's cousins are the Skinners, and while they may not be the handsomest folks in the county, they ain't exactly dogs!" she chuckled.

"What happened?" Annalee asked.

"Far as I can recall, Shadrach got about fifty stitches and a course of rabies shots."

"Anything else?"

"Shadrach quit school right before graduation and hightailed it out of here, away from Daredevil County. Don't know where he went or what he did after that."

"Okay, Minnie, thanks. I appreciate it." There was another piece to add to the puzzle. Annalee was about to update her notes on the computer when Minnie cleared her throat.

"Ezra Skinner ended up marrying Rachael Dupres, you know," Minnie said. It was clear that having started a cozy chat, she had no intention of being dismissed yet, not until she had dispensed every morsel of information at her command. Noah's soft groan was ignored. "I heard it was a very nice wedding," Minnie continued. "The reception was over to the Youth Center that used to be on Caldwell Street in Lingerville. You remember it? Sure you do. The Parsons owned the place. They used to have kiddie roller skating disco parties before those Yankees opened the indoor ice rink in Fort Noble and stole their business."

The first sentence finally registered. Annalee's head whipped up so fast, her vertebrae cracked painfully. "What?" she asked, wincing and rubbing her sore neck. "I mean, who did Ezra Skinner marry?" she clarified.

Minnie looked smug. "Rachael Dupres, a transfer student from somewhere Up North... Canada, I think. Yeah, she was one of them foreign exchange students. Mind you, I wouldn't blame Ezra and Shadrach for fighting over her. She was a real pretty girl back then. Real pretty. Her and Ezra got married right after graduation."

"Thanks, Minnie, that helps a lot. I appreciate it," Annalee said. After Minnie gave her a triumphant grin and walked out of the office, she turned to Noah and said, "Aunt Rachael's from Canada."

"I guess so." Noah flushed under her steady regard. "Look, all this stuff is old news, I guess. Maybe my momma knows about it, but if she does, she never told it to me."

"I'm not accusing you of anything," Annalee assured him. "So Lassiter got bit by a dog as a teenager, and he got bit by another dog just before he died. Coincidence?"

"Could be."

Annalee rubbed the side of her nose, sighing. It was not easy making a coherent whole out of scattered bits of information. "Okay, when they were young men, Ezra and Lassiter fought over a girl. That's the source of the bad blood. But what brought Lassiter back here?"

"Too bad we can't ask him," Noah commented. "I don't think his widow would tell us, even if we could get past her lawyer."

"That reminds me...how'd we do on Lassiter's shotguns?"

"We got the report from Ballistics this morning. None of the shotguns are the murder weapon; they're all clean."

"Well, I don't have enough evidence to get a search warrant for Ezra Skinner's home, so that's out." Annalee rifled through the messages that Minnie had given her; nothing was urgent. "Call the people you know in Augusta. If we can find out more about Alexander Dempsey or Transgenic or both, maybe we'll figure out why Lassiter came home."

"Which may give us the killer's motive. Gotcha." Noah jerked his thumb at the door. "I'll make that call, then I gotta run out to the Fullerton place."

"Bailey Fullerton?"

"Yeah, the familiar nuisance call. Same old, same old."

"Do tell."

"One of his pigs got into Mrs. McInerney's garden, and she's raising Cain on account of her prize-winning tomatoes got et. Says she's gonna kill the pig, and Fullerton is threatening to fill her butt full of buckshot if she lays a pinkie on his porker."

Annalee smirked. Eulalia McInerney and Bailey Fullerton were the two most stubborn, anti-social neighbors in the county; scarcely a month went by without some kind of trouble stirred up between them. Settling the dispute was going to require the wisdom of Solomon, but she reckoned Noah was smart enough to handle it. "You settle that without either of them calling me to complain, and I'll buy you the best steak dinner in town."

"You got yourself a deal."

After Noah left, Annalee returned a few telephone calls. Around eleven o'clock, Noah's contact in the Augusta P.D. came through, sending a fax containing Alexander Dempsey's criminal record, which amounted to a whole lot of nothing. Just as she finished perusing the file, Deputy Cynthia Starbuck rapped on the door frame and entered the office.

"I heard you needed some information on Transgenic," Cynthia said, pushing stray locks of her frizzy brown hair out of her eyes. "My sister's husband's brother-in-law worked at Transgenic for a while, couple of years back."

"What do they do over there?" Annalee asked, waving at Cynthia to take a seat.

"From what Elliot told me when I e-mailed him, Transgenic is a biological technology company. You know, them people that mess around with DNA? Like the goats they put spider genes into, so they make spider silk in their milk."

"Transgenic crosses goats with spiders?" Annalee shuddered. She hated spiders.

"Not necessarily that, but stuff like that. Genetic engineering. That's what they do." Cynthia slouched down in the chair, nibbling her thumbnail. "Elliot said Dempsey was head of Transgenic's Research & Development section till he screwed the pooch."

"What'd he do?"

"He was working on a human longevity project. I guess he was trying to figure out how people could live pretty much forever, which is against God's will as far as I'm concerned. Anyhow, I was told that Dempsey did some unauthorized drug trials using homeless people in Huntswell as experimental subjects. A couple of them died as a result. The company paid Dempsey off to keep his mouth shut, and pressured him to confess to the deaths to avoid the publicity of a trial. Dempsey did time for manslaughter, reduced sentence, early parole for good behavior. He got out about six years ago."

Annalee exhaled a frustrated breath. "Why the hell isn't Dempsey's manslaughter conviction in his records? I couldn't find so much as a parking violation."

"According to Elliot, the records were sealed; that was part of Dempsey's deal with the Huntswell D.A.'s office. Dempsey did the court mandated time, and he's pretty much unemployable in the science sector. His line of work, your reputation is everything. Nobody'd have him these days, not any lab of any note, and he'd never get any funding. I reckon the D.A. figured the deal was safe to make."

"Dumb ass district attorneys and their dumb ass deals," Annalee muttered. "So where'd Dempsey serve his time?"

"Prison farm in Baldwin."

An alarm bell began to ring inside Annalee's mind. She double-checked Lassiter's record. "Our victim did time in Baldwin. That must be where they met."

"And you want to hear something else weird? I did an Internet search on Baldwin last night. That particular farm was being used as a testing ground for a strain of new high-yield crops developed by Cutshall Agricultural, and Abner Cutshall happened to be on the Parole Board at the time. He's the one who recommended Dempsey's early release."

Annalee closed the files and set them aside. "You know, I think it's about time I went and had a little talk with Abner Cutshall."

Cynthia stood. "Want some company?"

"Sure, why not? I call shotgun."

The drive out to Cutshall's mansion was made in silence. Cynthia was not a chatterbox by any means and saved her concentration for driving. Not that Annalee minded; she was busy mulling over Lunella. The strength of her attraction remained unabated. She could still smell the woman's unique scent, still feel the powerful body pressed against hers. The ghost of Lunella's caresses lingered on her skin. Annalee ached for her; it was a physical pain centered behind her breastbone, more acute with every breath she took. To enter into any kind of relationship would be impossible for all the reasons she had already stated, but in spite of her earlier resolve, she could not help wishing things were otherwise.

Arriving at Cutshall's antebellum-style mansion brought her focus back to the case. Cutshall owned thirty acres of prime real estate outside of Huntswell; he had a private fishing pond, stable, golf course, tennis court, and helicopter pad. A separate garage stored his collection of vintage automobiles. When Cynthia brought the patrol car to a halt in the curving gravel drive, Annalee noted the colorful banners and bunches of balloons decorating the columned front porch. One banner proclaimed: HAPPY BIRTHDAY AMY!

She groaned. "Shit, it's Cutshall's granddaughter's birthday."

Cynthia shut off the ignition. As soon as the engine stopped running, so did the air conditioning; the atmosphere in the car immediately became stuffy. "I'm sure the old man can spare us a couple of minutes. Maybe even a piece of cake, you ask nice enough," she said.

Annalee gave Cynthia the stink-eye and opened the door, letting in a blast of hot air that smelled like recently cut grass with a hint of horse manure, the scent of a rich man's country home. "Don't make me regret bringing you along, Deputy. Behave."

They went around the side of the house, following the sounds of shrieking children. The backyard had been turned into a little girl's fantasy playground complete with a castle-shaped bounce house, beribboned ponies to ride, pastel ballerinas with fairy wings passing out candy and favors, strolling jugglers, a puppet show, more balloons, and a buffet table covered with hamburgers, hot dogs, chicken legs, potato salad, cupcakes, ice cream and Jell-O. What appeared to be a horde of screaming, hyperactive children ran around the place. In the midst of the noisy chaos was the Great Man himself, Mr. Abner Cutshall.

In appearance, Cutshall was the epitome of the kindly old grandfather. He had the fluffy silver hair, the indulgent smile, the round-lensed spectacles perched on his nose. He was dressed in slacks, a button-down shirt, and a knitted vest in spite of the warm weather. The clothing did not quite disguise his body's fragility.

At the moment, Cutshall was listening to a red-haired child in a pink princess gown who was sobbing some incoherent complaint to him. As Cynthia and Annalee approached, he patted the girl's shoulder and held a pristine white handkerchief to her snot-streaked face.

"Now, Amy, honey, blow your nose and stop crying. Robbie Harris may be yanking your pigtails today, but tomorrow he'll be stealing kisses," Cutshall said indulgently.

"Ew! That's gross, Papaw!" Amy cried. She blew her nose, then ran away screaming at the top of her lungs, "Robbie's got cooties! Robbie's got cooties!"

Cutshall shook his head, dropping the soiled handkerchief on the ground. It was flicked up by a person in a monkey costume carrying a scoop and a bucket half-filled with trash and pony droppings. Spotting Cynthia and Annalee, Cutshall straightened, sucked in a wet-sounding breath and wheezed it out again. "Sheriff, what can I do for you?" He sounded cold and polite, a far cry from the doting granddaddy.

"Do you have a minute to spare, Mr. Cutshall?" Annalee removed her hat as a gesture of the respect she did not feel. "I'd like to talk to you about Reverend Lassiter."

He grunted, "It's about damned time. Come on into the house; I can't hear myself think with all the hoo-hah out here. Jesus Christ, I swear there was less consternation on Omaha Beach."

Cutshall led the way to his home office, a cool space dominated by a big burl-walnut desk. There was a portable oxygen tank nearby. Annalee had heard the Great Man was struggling with a pulmonary disease; last year, he had also been diagnosed with Type II diabetes. *Money can't buy good health, and that's no lie,* she thought.

French doors behind the desk let in a haze of sunlight as well as the muted roar of Amy's party in full swing. Cutshall settled down at the desk and took off his glasses, gesturing towards a leather sofa pushed against the wall.

"What can I do for you?" he repeated, his voice raspy, punctuated by heavy inhalations of breath. "You may want to bear in mind that I'm not inclined to do you any favors, Sheriff, not since your office denied my very reasonable request to be allowed custody of the reverend's body."

"I am sorry about that, sir," Annalee said, forcing herself to maintain a façade of professional calm. She truly despised Cutshall. The man was a hypocrite, mouthing pieties in public while doing his greedy best behind the scenes to accumulate as much wealth as possible, no matter who he hurt along the way. "An autopsy was necessary, given the death was not accidental or due to natural causes. Furthermore, we're under no obligation to release the body to you," she took some satisfaction in telling him. "His next-of-kin is his wife."

Cutshall's glance was sharp. He frowned; his lips were the color of raw liver. "I'm a sick old man and I have little time to waste. Cut to the chase."

"We've recently uncovered information that John Lassiter was an alias. The victim's real name was Shadrach Rafferty, a known con man with quite a criminal record." If Cutshall wanted blunt, Annalee would give it to him with both barrels.

He leaned forward slightly, resting an elbow on the desk blotter. His hands were liver-spotted, the knuckles swollen with arthritis. "Is this a blackmail attempt?"

"Not at all, sir. That would be against the law, as I'm sure you know." *Trust Cutshall to make a wrong-headed assumption,* Annalee thought. "I take it you didn't know Lassiter's true identity?" she asked.

"No, I did not." Cutshall sat back, grimacing. "Despite anything he may have done in his past, Sheriff, the reverend was a good man. He was strong in the Lord."

"Ever heard of Dr. Alexander Dempsey?"

Cutshall hesitated a second too long in answering, which was how Annalee knew he was lying when he replied, "Never heard of the fellow."

*Interesting. Why would Cutshall lie about that?* "Are you sure?" she asked him. "He used to work at Transgenic in Augusta, one of those bio-tech companies."

"I think I know my own mind," Cutshall grumbled testily. "Is there anything else?"

Annalee sat up and fixed him with a glare of her own. "You were on the Parole Board that took care of inmates at the prison farm in Baldwin, is that correct?"

"Sheriff, do we need to dance around here?" Cutshall sounded irritated. "I'd like to rejoin my granddaughter's birthday party some time today."

"Just answer the question, sir."

"You know good and goddamned well that I was on the Parole Board. It's part of my public record of service."

"Then I'm surprised you never heard of Alexander Dempsey, since he gained early release from Baldwin on your recommendation. Do you recall him now?"

Cutshall did not flinch. He slapped the flat of his hands on the desk top, looking angry. "Am I expected to know every two-bit criminal in Daredevil County?" He broke off and coughed, a sound that was thick and ropy. She waited for him to put the oxygen tank's nasal cannula over his ears and adjust the prongs in his nostrils. Some color returned to his face.

"I doubt Dempsey would be classified as a two-bit criminal, Mr. Cutshall," Annalee said after Cutshall's breathing steadied.

"He was a geneticist working on human longevity. Killed a couple of homeless men in Huntswell with his experiments. I figure he met Lassiter on the prison farm since they were there at the same time serving their sentences."

"Am I being accused of something here?"

"No, sir. Not at all." Annalee got to her feet, motioning for Cynthia to follow her lead. She had aggravated him long enough, but could not resist a parting shot. "I'm going to be asking the judge to issue a subpoena for the Church of the Honey in the Rock's membership records. If I find Alexander Dempsey listed as a member..." She left the threat unuttered.

Cutshall glared at her a moment longer. She waited him out, wondering which way the man was going to jump. At last, he said slowly, reluctantly, as if every word were being dragged out of his mouth, "Yes, now that I've given the matter some thought, I do believe Dr. Dempsey is a member of our congregation."

"I see. Thank you, sir." Annalee was careful to keep any hint of triumph out of her tone. She paused on her way to the door. "Are you his sponsor, Mr. Cutshall? I just find it hard to under-stand how a man like Dempsey — a man who has been basically unemployed for six years — could afford membership in your church, which I understand has a very exclusive congregation."

"The House of God is open to all those who seek the truth," Cutshall said with such mock piousness, it made Annalee itch to slap him.

"Were you aware that Lassiter was related to the Skinners?" Annalee asked, reining in her temper. "That he and Ezra Skinner fought over a girl in the past?"

"The reverend did not share that much of himself with us."

Annalee noted the slight hesitation. Cutshall was lying again. She asked, "Was this fight the reason he so often denounced the Skinners in the pulpit?"

Cutshall replied impatiently, "Our conversation is over, She-riff."

"I want to speak to Alexander Dempsey. Do you have his address? Phone number?"

"I do not."

"Who's your church secretary?"

"I'm tired of your interrogation tactics, Sheriff Crow. If you want to know anything else, get in touch with my lawyer. In the meantime, I'm telling you to get off my property."

Annalee squared her shoulders. "Let's be clear about this, Mr. Cutshall. Dr. Dempsey is wanted for questioning in a murder. I believe you have knowledge of his whereabouts. You may play golf with Judge Gill, but he can't help when I arrest you for obstruction and interfering in a homicide investigation. I would not like to do that, sir. I would not like to have to put handcuffs on you and take you away from your sweet little granddaughter's party."

Cutshall's mouth worked spasmodically, as if he was chewing on blasphemies. Finally he spat, "I'll have your badge."

"I'm a legally elected county official, sir. You're welcome to try." Annalee was a good poker player; she knew when to up the ante. She turned to Cynthia. "Head on out to the car and get on the radio, see if you can raise somebody from the *Daredevil Trumpet* or the *Huntswell Star*. The arrest of Mr. Abner Cutshall is bound to be news."

Cynthia was not a bad poker player herself. She clearly understood the value of a bluff. "Yes, ma'am," she said crisply. "You want me to contact the TV news people, too?"

"The more the merrier, Deputy."

Cutshall let Cynthia get almost to the door before he said, "I won't forget this, Sheriff." His eyes were cold and gray and filled with frustrated fury.

"I don't expect you to," Annalee replied. There was something terrifyingly liberating about burning one's bridges. Hell, she was not just burning this particular bridge — she had soaked the struts in gasoline and nitroglycerin, strapped C4 and dynamite to the supports, and dropped Fat Man and Little Boy on it for good measure. Cutshall had not supported her election campaign, but he had not opposed it, either. He had remained planted firmly on the fence. Now she had made Cutshall her enemy and would have to watch her step. The first mistake she made, the first 'i' left undotted or 't' left uncrossed, and he would be leading the pack demanding her firing, if not an outright tar-and-feathering.

"Try the Sheridan Apartments on James Street," Cutshall said. "And Sheriff Crow? I *will* be keeping my eye on you."

"I'd expect no less from a tax-paying citizen," Annalee said blandly. She collected Cynthia and chivvied her to the patrol car, moving at a not-quite trot.

"Put the lights and siren on and get the lead out, Deputy," she said, sliding into the passenger side. "I'll bet Cutshall is on the phone right now, warning Dempsey to get the hell out of Dodge." She had barely enough time to buckle her seatbelt before Cynthia revved the engine and sent the patrol car careening out of Cutshall's driveway, the tires spewing gravel. It was only a few moments before they were on the highway headed towards town.

"Outta my way, damn it," Cynthia muttered as she stomped on the accelerator, jerking the steering wheel at the same time so the patrol car just missed clipping the bumper of a station wagon. Annalee held on for dear life as they swerved from lane to lane, passing slower vehicles. Scenes from the *Dukes of Hazard* flashed through her mind, intercut with images from the classic driver's ed. scare flick, *Blood on the Highway*. Cynthia's driving also brought back memories of hot pursuits, few of them pleasant.

With her free hand, Annalee snatched up the radio mic and called Dispatch for back-up, asking for Noah's unit to be sent to the location.

James Street was on the other side of Huntswell. Even with Cynthia doing her best NASCAR race impersonation, it took a good half hour to arrive at the Sheridan Apartments. The last quarter-mile, Annalee flicked off the siren and lights, not wanting to spook Dempsey if by some miracle he was still at home.

Noah's patrol car was parked in front of the manager's office. Annalee went inside, wrinkling her nose at the strong smells of peppermint schnapps, stale cigarette smoke, and the unmistakable sweet-sour odor of marijuana. There was no visible evidence of drug use, however, and the manager, Mrs. Davies — an irascible old lady who kept her portable television's sound at full volume so she would not miss a moment of her soaps no matter where she puttered in the office — was known to suffer from glaucoma. Annalee said nothing about the lingering, distinct fragrance. She was not without compassion. As long as she did not actually catch Mrs. Davies smoking pot, she would ignore it.

Noah was waiting for them. "Dempsey's in 408," he said.

"Do we know if he's to home?" Annalee asked.

Mrs. Davies was sitting at her desk, her gaze fixed on the portable set's flickering screen. She popped a bonbon into her mouth and mumbled around it, "He left about thirty minutes ago, you know."

Annalee could barely hear the manager over the soap opera histrionics blasting from the television speakers. "Did you see Dempsey leave?" she asked, raising her voice.

"Mr. Dempsey's car's always parked right out there in front of the office so's I can watch it through my window during the day," Mrs. Davies explained, munching another bonbon. The bulk of her attention never wavered from the show. "Drives one of them fancy BMW cars, though I've often said he ought to buy American. Boy's always worried about thieves, bless his heart, and about dings and dents. Men and their love affairs with automobiles. I swear, if a man could procreate with a car, he would."

"Did he say where he was going?"

"I'm not his mother, Sheriff," Mrs. Davies rasped. "I'm just the landlady. You want to know where he gets off to, I reckon you'd better ask him yourself."

"Yes, ma'am. Thank you for your help. If you see or hear from Dempsey, please don't tell him anything, just call my office."

Mrs. Davies flapped a hand in answer.

Annalee thanked the woman again and left the office. Once outside in the parking lot, she said, "All right...Noah, you hook up with that assistant D.A.... What's her name?"

"Miz Terrill," Noah said.

"Sherry Terrill, right, and get a search warrant for Dempsey's place."

"What are we looking for?"

"How 'bout the shotgun that killed Lassiter? There ought to be probable cause for a warrant, considering the link between the victim and Dempsey, and Dempsey's on the run."

"Allegedly on the run," Noah corrected. "It's all circumstantial."

Annalee rolled her eyes. "Po-tay-to, po-tah-to. Let Terrill argue justification in front of a judge. Far as my office is concerned, Dempsey's a homicide suspect, wanted for questioning in connection with the death of John Lassiter." To Cynthia, she said, "Go upstairs; keep an eye on his door. I'll call for CSU."

Assistant D.A. Terrill managed to procure the warrant in record time, having it couriered to them by a state police trooper. As soon as the paper was in her hand, Annalee led Noah upstairs to the fourth floor. Mrs. Davies had given them the master passkey, so there was no need to beat down the apartment door. Annalee left the CSU techs in the corridor while she and Noah cleared the scene.

The two bedroom apartment was obsessively clean and tidy; even the stack of magazines on the coffee table was neatly arranged with the corners aligned. Annalee called out, "Police! We have a warrant!" There was no answer. She and Noah checked all the rooms. The décor was neutral throughout, off-white and tan, and there were no personal touches visible — no photographs, no kitschy vacation souvenirs, no art, not even a stereo, but there was a sleek computer system that looked as if it had cost more than a few bucks.

Noah eyed the computer in clear envy. "Wish I could afford one of those."

"Well, the county's seizure of property law won't cover it, I'm afraid. Maybe we could get the hard drive examined by our techs, see if it turns up any leads on Dempsey's whereabouts from his files." Annalee holstered her weapon. "Let's get CSU in here to do their job." She moved out of the apartment, letting the technicians take over the search for evidence.

No shotgun was found, but the techs did turn up an expensive leather-bound Bible stamped with 'Church of the Honey in the Rock' in gilt on the inside cover. The discovery provided further confirmation Dempsey was a member of the elite congregation. Since he was not a millionaire, influential businessman, or local political power broker, she assumed he must have something of value to offer. His skills as a geneticist, perhaps? How the hell did that fit with the known facts? Annalee shook her head. Speculation would only go so far.

"The refrigerator's not got much in it," Noah reported. "Couple of cans of Mountain Dew, piece of cheese, ketchup, coffee beans, leftover pizza from Pasquali's. Kitchen trash has been emptied. There was a cheap lockbox in the bedroom closet."

"Anything in it?" Annalee asked, knowing somebody would have picked the lock or pried the box's lid open.

He shrugged. "Empty as a church on Monday, except for a .38 Beretta."

Annalee nodded, considering her options. "Okay, send the Beretta to Ballistics, see if anything comes up in IBIS. Maybe we can scare up a lead. Say, is there a common area where the building residents dump their trash? Dumpster around the side? If so, somebody's gonna have to find the bag that came from this apartment. Could be something in it that'll help us find Dempsey, or understand what the hell is going on around here."

Noah snagged a technician and passed on the message.

CSU departed the scene with the computer's hard drive, an external drive, a collection of CDs, and a handful of USB sticks and Flash drives that had been hidden in hollowed-out books, all of it scheduled to be sent to the computer forensics lab in Huntswell. They also took with them a large collection of trash bags from the ground floor dumpster.

Annalee told Noah to put out an APB on Alexander Dempsey. She went on, "I want you and Jeeter to contact as many members of the church's congregation as you can get hold of. See if they know where Dempsey might be hiding, the names of his associates, suppliers, sponsors, family, or friends. You have my blessing to threaten the good people of the Honey in the Rock with an obstruction charge if they won't talk. I'll bet Assistant D.A. Terrill has arrest warrants just burning a hole in her pocket."

"Anything else?"

"Flag Dempsey's credit cards. Send an alert to the airport in Huntswell, but also to all the private airfields, the train and bus stations," Annalee said.

"Roadblocks?"

"Our budget can't afford the man hours necessary to cover the whole of the county. Besides, I bet Cutshall is Dempsey's sugar daddy. I don't think he'll go too far from his source of income. In fact, I think Dempsey's probably hiding out at the church."

"But we can't prove it."

"Not to a judge's satisfaction, damn it, not unless we can show Dempsey's actually there. We can't get a search warrant or use thermal imaging, and I doubt we'd get permission for a wiretap, but we've got other options. Deputy Starbuck!" Annalee called on sighting the woman. "I've got just the job for you."

Cynthia was given the task of coordinating a stake-out at the church. Annalee planned to bring in the other deputies in rotating shifts, keeping the church under surveillance twenty-four hours a day until the case broke. That much, her office could afford. If Dempsey had gone to ground in the church, she believed he would eventually have to come up for air. One confirmed sighting was all it would take to get the warrant she needed.

"Okay, so that'll be Rourke, Gilchrist, Petrie, and Ames on days," Annalee said to Cynthia, who was scribbling a list on a notepad. "Try to bring in Foster, too, as an alternate..." She broke off when her cell phone rang. "Hold that thought, Starbuck."

Annalee checked the caller I.D. The call was originating from her office's switchboard. "Crow here."

Minnie Hawkins's voice came through. "Sheriff, sorry; couldn't raise you on the radio. We've got a report of a DB out by mile marker sixty-two on the Ateeska side of the Lauder extension road. Couple of fishermen called it in. Sounds pretty gruesome from the description. CSU and M.E. are en route."

"I'm on it." Annalee closed the phone. "We've got a body," she said to Cynthia.

"Another one?" Cynthia frowned. "That's quite a bumper crop."

"You coordinate the stake-out; get with Noah if you have questions. I'll handle the DB. I expect to see a progress report on my desk when I get back to the office."

"No problem."

"If there's a break in the case, call me."

Cynthia nodded and made shooing motions at her. "I'll handle it, don't worry."

Annalee would have preferred staying in Dempsey's apartment and supervising, but she trusted her deputies to do the job properly.

The drive out to mile marker sixty-two proved to be a long déjà vu moment for Annalee. She had taken the same route just the day before, traveling out to the Skinner's place to question Ezra about Lassiter. That recollection brought her mind circling back to Lunella. The feel of the woman, the taste of her mouth, the golden flash of her eyes, her deep-throated sexy growl... Annalee snorted. She was getting downright obsessive about somebody she barely knew. *Maybe I just need to get laid.* That might be the ticket. Go to Atlanta for a weekend, hit the clubs and bars, find Ms. Right Now and party hard. Get it out of her system.

*Shit, who am I kidding?* Annalee rubbed her jaw and groaned. She did not really want meaningless sex with a stranger. She wanted Lunella Skinner, damn it.

"I am so, so very screwed," she muttered, suddenly recalling the confrontation between Lunella and Rachael at the house, and the way Lunella had said, "Mine", as if claiming her. The memory sparked another. In the erotic dream, she had also heard a voice, and with a start she realized that the dream voice sounded a hell of a lot like Lunella, sexy growl and all. After a moment's consideration, she chuckled at her own foolishness. It was clear that her desire for Lunella was making her remember the dream incorrectly.

Dr. Betty Vernon was already at the scene when Annalee arrived. The woman's dark skin was sheened with sweat, glistening in the strong sunlight that bathed the area like poured honey. There was precious little shade at this point on the Ateeska, just a few cottonwoods straggling beside the riverbank. The water was dark green and seemed quiet, the surface disturbed by subtle ripples of turbulence. A cloud of tiny flies swarmed through the air. Annalee closed her mouth, held her breath and batted them away from her face.

"I'm hoping to write this one up as a unique case study for the *Journal of Forensic Medicine and Pathology*," Betty said as Annalee picked her way carefully down the side of the embankment, trying not to break an ankle or lose her balance.

"How so, Doc?" The humid heat was like being hit in the face with a steaming wet mop. Annalee had to work not to gasp.

"You'd better see for yourself. If I told you, you'd think I was pulling your leg."

Annalee went over to the body. At first, she was not certain of the sex of the horribly deformed corpse, but the lack of male genitalia clued her that the victim was female. There was no clothing, just a few dirty tatters of cloth around the neck and wrists. The victim's dirt-smeared skin was drawn tight over lumpy bones, so tight every tendon and the knobs of the vertebrae stood out in sharp relief. The fingernails and toenails were quite long and encrusted with filth. The face was the worst aspect, more animal than human — the nose was flat, the lower and upper jaws pushed forward grotesquely, showing oversize canines. The thickly tufted eyebrows ran together in a single caterpillar line that stretched almost to the temples.

She had never seen anything like it in her life, yet she could have sworn the victim was familiar. Another sense of déjà vu shivered through her. Try as she might, though, Annalee could not reconcile this victim's features with any of the faces she dredged out of her memory. Surely she could not have forgotten a woman who looked like that! Had it not been for the presence of the medical examiner and other law enforcement officers, she might have thought there was a hidden camera somewhere.

"I can't tell you how surprised I am to find such profound maxillo-mandibular deformity," Betty said, squatting beside the corpse and pointing a purple nitrile-gloved finger. "It's quite rare, even unique, in my opinion, although I'm not sure if the abnormalities are the result of a tumor or birth defect. This poor woman had to be in considerable pain."

"Time of death?" Annalee asked.

"No rigor to speak of, the liver temp's ninety-six degrees, it's a very warm day, and the vitreous humor is clear, so I'd say possibly within the last three hours."

"Cause?"

"There aren't any obvious injuries. We'll know more after the autopsy. I can tell you that lividity suggests the victim was killed elsewhere and her body transported here, and there are also abrasions on the heels."

"Shit. The killer held her by the arms and dragged her," Annalee said, mopping sweat from her face with her shirt sleeve. "That makes this the secondary crime scene. We still have to find the primary."

Betty stood up. "I'll try to find out if any local doctors were treating a patient with these deformities. That should make identifying her somewhat easier."

"Sheriff! Over here!" called a CSU technician.

Annalee had almost turned to go when she saw Betty lifting a lock of matted hair away from the side of the victim's head. A startlingly bright gold eye stared at her from the deformed face. The sick feeling in Annalee's stomach increased.

The technician waving at her from about ten yards away had found a dead animal. A wolf, as it proved, but not one of the pale-coated wolves that populated Malingering Deep. This animal's coat was brindled black and silver. Its lips were drawn back from teeth that seemed far too small and too blunt for a predator's muzzle. Checking the corpse, Annalee found little sign of insect activity and decided the kill must be fairly fresh. Perhaps the wolf had died around the same time as their other victim. If so, why hadn't the hunter reported finding a woman's body?

Annalee knelt down and ruffled through the fur, finding at least a dozen small wounds in the chest and head, none of which seemed damaging enough to have caused death. "Looks like shotgun pellets," she said. "From the spread, I'd guess the weapon was fired at a distance of twenty yards or so."

"Yeah, I found a pellet in the forest litter." The technician held out an evidence bag.

The pellet seemed to be highly polished steel... *But the color's not quite right*, Annalee thought. She handed the bag back to the tech. "I don't know if this is connected to our murder victim, but bag the wolf and take it to the morgue as well," she told him. Her cell phone rang and she answered the call. It was Noah.

"We just started the first shift of the church stake-out," he reported. "Nothing much going on except for one thing."

"What's that?" Annalee tried to tune out a nearby cicada's enthusiastic resonant buzz.

"The basement door around the back of the church is busted."

"And?"

"Looks like the damage was done from the inside, like somebody in an all-fired hurry tore his way out of the basement."

"Any witnesses?"

"Not so far, sorry."

"Okay, let's keep our eyes peeled. Canvass the area, find out if anybody saw anything." She looked at her watch. The crime scene here was in good hands and progressing well. "My stomach thinks my throat's been cut," she told Noah, "so I'm headed over to Double Pete's for dinner. I suggest you, Jeeter, and Cynthia eat while you can, maybe go home and get a shower. We're going to be pulling some long days till this is over."

"The dead body...we know him?"

"Her. No identity yet, no cause of death. Got a dead wolf at the scene, too."

The abrupt silence on the other end of the call made her nerves crawl. Finally, Noah asked, his voice cracking, "A wolf? You sure?"

"Not one of the Deep wolves," Annalee reassured him, even as she wondered why she felt the need to do so. How had she known that was his concern? "The fur's colored wrong," she said. "Black and silver, not white."

"Thank God," he breathed.

Annalee coughed self-consciously. "Um, you heard anything from Lunella?"

"Such as?" Now he sounded amused.

"Nothing," she mumbled. Was she fourteen years old? Would she start passing notes next? *Check the first box if you like me, the second box if you don't. Christ!* "Look, you got anything from the church members yet?" she asked, making herself return to business.

"We've tracked down four members so far, have another six on the list. Ain't nobody knows nothing."

"No surprise there. You ought to get in touch with Jane Darnell," Annalee said, suddenly remembering her hairdresser's cousin. "She's the church's cleaning lady. I'll bet she can give you more contact information."

"Jane Darnell, right. Anything else?"

"I'll keep you in the loop." Annalee snapped the phone shut.

Leaving Betty and the CSU technicians to their work, Annalee drove to Double Pete's, a diner in Brightbrook. The half-pound blue plate special hamburger was greasy and delicious, flavored with onions and mustard. The platter came with fries, coleslaw, and Pete Hollander's homemade green tomato relish. After dinner, she debated having a slice of the diner's famous "mile-high" lemon meringue pie for dessert, but feeling that her uniform pants might be getting a tad tight around the waist, settled for a cup of frozen vanilla yogurt topped with fresh fruit. She asked Pete to pack her some end slices of roast beef to go, meaning it as a treat for her cat, since Mongo would eat a brick if it was wrapped in meat.

By the time she returned home, it was close to dusk. Annalee was tired; she wanted nothing more than to sit down and spend a couple of mindless hours in front of the television. She walked up the porch steps and stopped at the top, puzzled. Usually, Mongo was right beside the door waiting for her, but there was no sign of the Maine coon cat.

"Hey, Mongo!" she called, rattling her house keys. "I've got roast beef! Come and get it, kitty... Come on, don't be shy."

There was no answering meow. Annalee went to the door and found it swung open under her touch. The door was unlocked.

Her muscles immediately tightened with a painful tension born of anticipation and apprehension. Her neck twanged under the strain. She dropped the bag and key ring, and drew her service weapon. Nudging the door further open with her hip, she hollered, "Police! If you're armed, drop your weapon and show me your hands!"

No one replied. There were no gun shots, and she could not hear anyone moving around inside. Nevertheless, Annalee raised her voice and called out, "I am authorized to use deadly force if you do not exit with your hands in plain sight!"

This was her home; she had a tactical advantage as she knew where all the furniture and light switches were. Rather than stay silhouetted against the doorway and continue to be an obvious target, Annalee crouched and scuttled over to the living room sofa, where she was greeted with a loud and very aggrieved meow. She tried to shush the indignant cat without giving away her position, but Mongo was having none of it. He yowled and bumped her with his head, demanding attention or possibly the roast beef that was still in the bag on the porch.

"Damn it, will you quit that, you demented fuck-nut." Annalee pushed Mongo away. She cocked her head, listening as hard as she could, but unless the erstwhile housebreaker played the tuba or blew an air horn, she could not have heard him over the cat's loud rumbling purr and near continuous meows. For such a big animal, Mongo had a voice as high-pitched as a castrato, which he was, but his soprano yowls never ceased to amaze her. At last, after several tense minutes during which nothing happened, Annalee holstered her weapon and straightened from her crouch, willing her pulse to return to normal.

She clicked on a lamp. The living room looked the same as usual; nothing seemed out of place. Moving to the kitchen, trying to avoid stepping on the cat winding around her ankles, she found the same thing. Had she simply forgotten to lock the door when she left that morning? Annalee tried to remember but came up blank. In her defense, locking doors and windows was an ingrained habit. She had seen the results of breaking and entering too many times, had interviewed too many victims who felt violated and afraid, not to take care of her own home's security. Still, she supposed anyone could suffer a momentary lapse.

Going upstairs, she found nothing amiss, no signs of an intruder. *Guess I'm getting senile already*, she thought after doing a search of the bathroom. Mongo was wailing downstairs, so she went back down to the living room, picked up the diner bag and took it to the kitchen. Leaving the cat to gobble his roast beef treat, she walked outside to the backyard.

The dense line of trees was the same, the greens and browns turning smoky gray as evening approached. Overhead, the first stars were glimmering, Orion the Hunter sprawled to the east. Her gaze sought and found the Big Dipper constellation; she followed the "handle" which pointed to the brilliant speck of light that was Arcturus. The moon was a milk-white crescent, bright as new minted silver against clouds dyed plum and indigo by the faint twilight. Annalee inhaled deeply, her spirits settling as peace stole over her.

Suddenly, she frowned. One thing was marring the perfection of the moment, but she did not know what was missing. It was on the tip of her tongue. The more she considered the matter, the more elusive the information she was chasing became. Frustrated, Annalee blew out a breath and raked a hand through her hair, and just like that, she knew.

No wolf.

She had only seen the animal once in her backyard, a pale watchful presence with haunting gold eyes. Why did she miss it now? Why did she feel so lonely? It made no sense. Her attraction to Lunella was enough of a problem; she did not need to develop a weird obsession with the local wildlife on top of that.

Annalee sighed. All these years of resisting temptation had caught up with her. She was too tired for any more self examination and besides, thinking about what she wanted and could not have was depressing. An hour or two watching dumb-ass procedural dramas on the idiot box sounded good. Turning around to return to the house, she caught sight of the back door at the edge of her vision, then as she completed the turn, what she saw caused a sickening jolt of dread to freeze her in mid-step, her belly tightening in a painful cramp.

Someone had drawn a crude target in red paint on the door's surface. In the center of the target was a dead crow, its glossy wings spread wide. Nails driven through the wings held it in place. To her shock, Annalee realized the bird was still alive. Its beak was open and it was breathing in shallow, panting inhalations, fine tremors quivering its feathers.

She started to shake, and had to sit down on the top step quickly, wiping her mouth over and over with the palm of her hand, trying to control her rising gorge. Despite having seen many examples of man's inhumanity to his fellow creatures in her career, this act of barbaric cruelty was truly one of the most horrifying, no less so because it was a violation that struck at the heart of her home. After a few moments, Annalee decided it was time to get up and do what needed to be done to end the crow's suffering. Not permitting herself to delay any further, she snapped the bird's neck, killing it instantly.

A childhood rhyme about crows ran through her mind:

> One for sorrow, two for joy,
> Three for a girl, four for a boy,
> Five for silver, six for gold,
> Seven for a secret never to be told.

Who had nailed this abomination to her back door? She was certain it was meant as a threat. There were any number of people who might have cause, she thought. One of the Ricketts, perhaps, desiring vengeance against her for the death of Barabbas, or for her role in breaking up their gambling ring. Several of the men in that family, including Cleophus and his two brothers, were in jail awaiting trial on a variety of charges, but there were still plenty of their relations who could have done it.

What about her investigation into Lassiter's murder? Could the killer be trying to warn her off because she was getting too close? Annalee considered the Gunns as suspects, too, since she was sure one of them had killed her father. At the Pro Shop the other day, Titus had insinuated as much, and she did not think the old man had been blowing smoke up her ass.

She felt weary, a tiredness that settled over her like the heaviest mantle imaginable, muffling her senses and weighing her down. Moving slowly, Annalee went into the house to fetch the equipment she needed to pry out the nails, remove the bird's body, and clean up her door. There was no point reporting it to the police. The second a file was opened on an incident like this, the press would be camped at her office demanding statements, and there would be public speculation ranging from maniac stalker to Satanic ritual. That kind of grief she did not need, not when there was already so much going on in her life.

Tomorrow, she would go on with her duties, and not permit this monstrous attempt at intimidation to prevent her from doing her duty.

Tonight, she could only hope the dead crow — and her father, another dead Crow — would not feature in her nightmares.

## Chapter FOUR

By the following afternoon, Dempsey was still a no-show at the church, but Annalee continued to pin her hopes on the surveillance teams. Leaving Noah in charge of the office, she took a patrol car out, intending to go over to the morgue and see about the deformed victim from the day before. She was not in the mood for company, so she drove alone.

As predicted, her sleep had been troubled by a nightmare, but not of birds or crows. Instead, Annalee had seen a pale wolf-skin nailed flat to her back door. The head was attached to the pelt, the wolf's golden eyes glittering at her, awake and aware, filled with a loneliness and longing that clawed at her heart. *Mine.* She had woken up wiping tears from her cheeks, her chest aching, her throat raw, wishing Lunella Skinner was there, which was seven kinds of crazy, no matter how miserable she felt at oh-shit-thirty in the morning.

After checking into the morgue, she made the long awful walk down the corridor. Annalee found Betty Vernon in the main autopsy room, standing by a stainless steel sink and knocking back a shot of whiskey. A half-empty bottle of Jack Daniels was near her elbow. The sight of the medical examiner drinking hard liquor during the day was so shocking, Annalee halted in her tracks, gaping. Betty lowered the glass and grimaced at her.

"Join me?" she asked.

"The hell? When did you start drinking on the job?" Annalee demanded.

"Since I got *that* in my morgue." Betty pointed at the first autopsy table, where the dead wolf was strapped down on its back, stiffened legs in the air. Flaps of hairy flesh and the rib cage were peeled back to expose the animal's body cavity. The grotesquely deformed female victim was on the second table, her naked body looking pitiful under the harsh fluorescent lights. She, too, had already been opened for a post mortem examination.

Annalee reached out and took the empty glass away from Betty, hoping the woman would not start chug-a-lugging whiskey straight out of the bottle. "You want to tell me what's going on, or do I have to stand here and guess?"

"That thing shouldn't exist." Betty indicated the dead wolf a second time. "Its organs are...wrong." The last word was pronounced faintly. She shook her head and added, "You have no idea, Sheriff. No idea at all."

"Just tell me."

Betty sighed. "There are medical details you won't understand, but the gastrointestinal tract, the muscles of the bladder neck...let's say that if I didn't know better, if I wasn't certain I could detect any tampering with the corpse, I'd swear this was a prank."

"How so?"

"Bottom line and without resorting to a lot of jargon, that thing may grossly resemble a wolf of the *Canis lupus* variety, but inside, it's more *Homo sapiens* than canine. The apparent hypodontia — that's the poorly developed and undersized teeth — is actually normal for an adult human male, thirty-two teeth plus scars on the gums from past wisdom teeth removal. And then there's the blood, which is human, too. Type A, in fact."

Annalee's gut clenched; she felt like taking a drink herself. "Are you sure?"

"The differences between the two species are significant, Sheriff. I triple-checked my findings. Besides, how many wolves do you know who've had their wisdom teeth surgically extracted?" Betty closed her eyes and sighed before opening them again. She looked tired.

"This isn't a joke." Annalee made it a statement rather than a question.

Betty's mouth thinned to a grim line and she crossed her arms over her chest. "Apart from the other evidence of just how wrong this is, the stomach contents contained filet mignon, baked potato with butter and sour cream, and creamed spinach, as well as the better part of a bottle of red wine, and bourbon and coffee."

"O-o-o-okay," Annalee replied, her astonishment increasing. "Looks like our wolf ate a damned fine dinner at T-Bones in Odom." It was a pricy, upscale steak house famous for its creamed spinach side dish. T-Bones motto was "Rare steaks well done". Her father had taken her there for a celebratory dinner when she graduated from the academy. "I wonder if our victim put it on his American Express platinum card," she quipped.

Betty ignored Annalee's feeble attempt at humor. "I also found irregular, enlarged alveolar spaces of black emphysematous lung tissue, and small bronchogenic carcinomas. Looks like our wolf smoked at least a pack a day."

Annalee breathed, "Jesus Christ on a bicycle."

"I don't think He has much to do with this."

"Don't bogart the whiskey, woman. Gimme that." Annalee grabbed the Jack Daniels bottle when Betty offered it and took a swig. It burned going down her throat, but the mellow heat soon settled to a comfortable glow in her belly. She wondered when she had been dropped into an episode of the *Twilight Zone*. "Anything else you want to tell me?" she asked, dreading the answer. Any more weirdness and she might snap.

"Our female victim's stomach contents were similar to the wolf's, except she had a salad with French dressing instead of creamed spinach, and a lot more bourbon. She also has the beginnings of cirrhosis. Her blood alcohol level was twice the legal limit."

"What killed her?"

"A massive stroke. I estimate her age at over fifty, but her arteries were clear, no sign of carotid occlusion. No diabetes, no heart conditions, no vasculitis. As far as I can tell, her blood pressure simply sky-rocketed, causing a rupture in the artery. It would've been like being shot in the head at close range...there was no warning and she wouldn't have felt a thing. She literally dropped dead. I haven't been able to determine *why* her blood pressure rose so rapidly. There are drugs, of course, but her tox screen came back negative."

"And the wolf?"

"That one's...it's even odder, if possible. God, I need another drink. Stuff like this is only supposed to happen to Mulder and Scully." Betty picked up a kidney-shaped metal pan. There were several small round balls rolling around in it. "Shotgun pellets made of silver."

"You're shitting me," Annalee said flatly.

"'Fraid not. None of the pellets penetrated very far into the wolf's body, and did not damage any of its internal organs. Near as I can tell, the wolf suffered an acute anaphylactic reaction after being shot. Death was due to breathing obstruction. The throat swelled shut."

Annalee felt her eyes growing rounder. "It was allergic to the silver?"

"Yes, I believe so." Betty walked across the room and put the pan down on the counter next to the sink. The metallic clink of steel on steel sounded very loud in the otherwise quiet morgue. "These pellets are consistent with the ones that I retrieved from Lassiter's throat wound, by the way. Sheriff, I've seen some things in my time that would curl your hair, but this takes the cake. I'm not sure if I'm losing my mind or if I've wandered onto a movie set."

"You're not alone. I'm freaking out, too." Annalee spotted a gleam of white in an evidence bag. "What's that?"

"String of cultured pearls. I found it around the female victim's neck. They're real, all right." Betty smiled for the first time since Annalee had entered the morgue. "You rub 'em on your teeth. The plastic fakes feel smooth, but real pearls are slightly rough." She waited a beat for Annalee to gulp before adding, "Of course, that's not a good idea when the pearls in question have been in contact with a biological hazard like a human corpse, so I applied another test to determine the pearls' authenticity. Whoever she was, our victim had money, or access to significant sums, in order to be able to afford that piece of jewelry."

Annalee stood stock still, stunned. Real pearls...that detail brought a memory slamming home. Shit! She knew exactly where she had recently seen a woman wearing a string of pearls. In her mind's eye, she saw them glimmering discreetly against lavender cashmere. It was an impossible thought, a thought that made her mind shudder away in revulsion and disbelief, and yet... A horrible suspicion dawned.

"Listen, if I authorize the expense from my discretionary fund, will you rush DNA results for the female victim and the wolf?" Annalee asked.

Betty's gaze was direct and unsettling. "Now why would I do that?"

"Because I said so, damn it." Annalee shoved the Jack Daniels bottle back on the counter. "Sorry. Just rush the results, okay? Call me as soon as you get 'em."

"It'll take a couple of days for the state lab to process."

"Soon as the results are in, you call me." Annalee had to make herself clear. "You call me first, yeah? Nobody else. And hold off on that article you're planning to write."

As Annalee turned to go, Betty stopped her. "What is it?" she asked accusingly. "Why do you want me to test the wolf's DNA? What the hell do you know?"

"I can't talk about it now, maybe later. Christ, just do it, okay? Get it done and call me." Annalee shrugged Betty off and continued out of the morgue, needing air and open spaces. On her way to the car, she wondered what other spitballs she was going to have to deal with today. *So this is what being the ground floor tenant in a two-story outhouse is like.* She took out her cell phone and called the Crime Scene Unit.

"Hey, Wally, I need to know what evidence was picked up at the Ateeska River scene yesterday," she said when the call was answered by the day shift supervisor.

"You mean the gargoyle lady? Sorry, that's what the techs are calling the vic," Wallace Cumberland replied in a nasal drawl. "Lemme grab the report... Okay. Some pieces of cloth — pure Mongolian cashmere, very high end, we're trying to trace the dye lot to the manufacturer; half-empty pack of Dunhill cigarettes, which is rare in this neck of the woods, you'd have to agree, since most folks around here dip snuff; an 18-karat white gold cigarette lighter with the initials A.M.T.; a Patek watch; a man's shirt, trousers, and jacket — Saville Row tailored and probably cost more than a lowly peon like me makes in a month. Looks like the lighter I mentioned was found in the coat pocket. No wallet or I.D. Whoever belonged to the clothing didn't even leave lint in the trouser pockets. Clean as a whistle. The clothing was found near the scene, the lighter and Dunhills about a hundred yards away under a blackberry bush. No idea if the items are related to your victim. There were prints on the lighter and the cigarette pack; we're running them through AFIS."

"Do me a favor, Wally...you got computer access where you're sitting?" Annalee blinked sweat out of her eyes. She could not believe she was doing this. The notion was absolute lunacy. She was half tempted to disconnect the call and forget what Betty had told her, or at least pretend to forget. Nevertheless, she had seen the evidence. There was doubt, yes, but there was also a little part of her that believed it *might* be true.

"Yeah. Shoot," Wallace replied.

"I need info on a lawyer out of Atlanta, Aiden Thompson."

The sound of clicking keys filtered through the phone. In the background, Annalee could make out muted music playing. It was some kind of ethnic thing, full of drums, high-pitched flutes, and twanging string instruments. Getting in the patrol car, she winced as her butt made contact with the scorching leather seat. The steering wheel proved too hot to touch, as she discovered when she had to snatch her hand back or risk first-degree burns. She left the door wide open, hoping to catch a breeze and relieve some of the oven-like temperature, but the air was still, as dead as her great-uncle Hammond. The heat coming off the parking lot asphalt made her want to start shedding clothes. Instead, she sweated, held the phone to her ear and waited for Wallace to finish his search.

"Aiden Thompson, senior partner at Thompson, Thompson, Camp, and McElwee," Wallace muttered at last. "Here we go...what do you need to know?"

"First off, does he have a middle name?"

More keyboard clicking. "Yep, it's Marshall."

Annalee closed her eyes, remembering the initials on the lighter. "Thompson's an officer of the court, which means his fingerprints are on file with the Criminal Justice Department. You've got access, right?"

"Sheriff, I've got an all-season pass to every database you can name and then some. So you're thinking the lighter belongs to this Thompson guy, huh? Let's find out."

*When hearing hoofbeats, think horses, not zebras.* That was the problem with law enforcement training, she thought; it left you completely unprepared for stuff that did not make logical sense. It could not deal with things that shouldn't exist, like Old Lady Shelby's ghost-baby, heard wailing in her home's basement during summer thunderstorms. Annalee did not necessarily believe in life after death, but she had heard the ghost-baby herself, searched the basement and found no rational explanation for the uncanny wails.

Now she was wondering if the wolf they had found — the animal with human blood and human teeth and human organs — had once been a lawyer from Atlanta.

"We've got a hit," Wallace said. "The fingerprint's a match. Should we put out an APB on Thompson? We can prove he was at the scene; he may be a material witness."

"Yeah, get in touch with my office and tell Deputy Whitlock to issue the APB as soon as possible. Thanks, Wally. I'll get back to you." Annalee disconnected the call and let her head fall back against the seat rest. In a couple of days, the DNA results would be in and all hell was going to break loose if the wolf's DNA matched Thompson's.

She had a suspicion that DNA from the deformed woman was going to match Ruth Lassiter. Ruth and Aiden had looked very cozy together the other day. What the hell happened to them? How had they become so...so changed? Annalee felt like vomiting when she recalled the dead woman's disfigurement.

Dempsey had to be the key. It appeared he was messing around with DNA, a modern day Frankenstein playing God with people's genes, turning them into monsters. He was as crazy as a shit-house rat, and she was fairly certain he was being bankrolled by Cutshall, who was old and sick and no doubt felt mortality nipping at his heels. Christian belief in "God's golden shore" aside, an arrogant man like Cutshall had to resent his body's betrayal. He was probably clinging to the hope of a cure for the destructive effects of aging. Annalee closed the car door and turned on the ignition, letting the air conditioner blast until a stream of chilled air hit her sweaty skin.

She called Noah and asked after he answered, "Did we get statements from those two fishermen who called in the dead body on the Ateeska River yesterday?"

"Yeah, but they didn't see much. On the other hand, we found a witness who swears they saw a monster at the church."

Annalee sat up so quickly, her knees knocked against the steering wheel. She ignored the brief pain. "Who? What did they see?"

"You know Dennis Dooley? Runs the chicken farm east of Hallelujah Ridge?"

"The one they call 'Cock-a-Doodle' Dooley?"

"Uh-huh. Seems he was delivering a load of eggs to the restaurant next door. Saw a monster bust out of the church's basement. Said no way it was human. His description is kind of a match to our female vic. A man came out of the church in pursuit, shot the thing with a tranquilizer dart and dragged it back inside. The shooter's description matches Dempsey."

"Can we get a warrant to search the church?" she asked, knowing the answer.

Noah's laugh was bitter. "Not from any God-fearing judge in this county, not unless we've got a smoking gun. Even then, I wouldn't bet on it."

"One witness won't do." Annalee curled her lip in disgust. "Okay, keep up surveillance on the church. Soon as Dempsey pokes the tip of his nose out of the door, you bring him in, even if you have to enter the church to do it. Sighting a suspect wanted for questioning should be probable cause enough to stand in court."

"Got it, boss. What are you going to do?"

She knew what she *had* to do, but Annalee did not want to pay another visit to the Skinners. Not yet. Her gut told her the Skinner family was mixed up in this somehow, even Lunella was in it up to her neck, and she did not have the strength to face them. To face her.

Eyes the color of flake gold.

Annalee groaned.

"Hey, you okay?" Noah asked.

"Oh!" Annalee had forgotten she was still on a call. "Look, I'm headed back to the office. Have those witness statements ready for me."

"Gotcha."

The remainder of the day was the usual routine, apart from the on-going stakeout at the Church of the Honey in the Rock. Annalee kept busy with paperwork, trying to distract herself. She wanted to avoid thinking about Dempsey, about the twisted corpse of Ruth Lassiter, and the thing she was afraid Aiden Thompson had become.

Annalee stared blankly at the computer screen. One word kept popping into her head with the same annoying regularity as the blinking cursor.

Werewolf.

Obviously, she had seen too many movies.

People transforming into monsters... There was nothing supernatural going on in Daredevil County, no full moon, no occult curses. This was science gone bad, the stuff of nightmares and conspiracy theories. It was the sort of thing some black-hat government organization might be accused of perpetrating, experimenting illegally with recombinant DNA to create a super-soldier or some such other nonsense. A nice plot for a novelist, perhaps, or a television show, but she suspected the reality was far less elaborate.

Without warning, a yawn split her face, widening until her jaw ached. A troubled night always left her tired. Annalee took a sip from her mug, grimacing at the bitter flavor of cold coffee. It was stuffy and humid inside the office despite the air conditioning; she desperately wanted fresh air, and her ass was going numb from sitting. Annalee glanced at her watch and saw with some surprise that it was getting close to five o'clock. She stood up, stretched until her vertebrae popped loudly, and walked out of her office.

"I'm taking the SUV out to the Skinner place," she told Minnie, going behind the reception desk to retrieve the keys. The trip was impromptu, born of an impulse. If she saw Lunella, perhaps she would be able to get the woman out of her system. Surely Lunella could not be as desirable as memory insisted! Once the rose-colored glasses were off, Annalee would cease to burn for the woman. "I'll be out of range for a couple of hours."

Minnie nodded, most of her attention focused on the portable DVD player propped near her phone. She was watching a classic soap opera, *The Edge of Night*. Annalee remembered seeing that as a kid on her grandmother's black-and-white set, back in the pre-cable days. The memory made her feel old.

Driving out to the Lauder extension road, Annalee tuned the radio to a classic country station and turned the volume up, hoping to keep her mind occupied with music for a little while. The interior of the SUV was chill and damp from the air conditioning, which did nothing to dry the sweat on her skin. She took off her sunglasses when she went off-road down the trail that led to the Skinner property.

When she reached the gate, Annalee parked and got out of the vehicle. She stood there for a minute, stretching out the kinks, inhaling the forest's earthy smells, grateful to be out of the stifling confines of the office. In her experience, law enforcement was three kinds of butt-work — sitting on her butt doing paperwork, sitting on her butt in a patrol car, and sitting on her butt interviewing witnesses and suspects. *I should probably add sitting on my butt eating rubber chicken at state-sponsored events.*

Annalee was halfway over the gate when a distant howl caught her attention, followed by the unmistakable report of a shotgun. The sound sent a chill racing up her spine to explode inside her skull, a panic signal that sent her scrambling down to the ground. It might be hunters, but instinct insisted otherwise and her brain agreed. She took off running, her shoes thumping on the earth. Her blood rushed cold through her veins, but hot coals lodged under her ribcage, and every mouthful of air seemed superheated more by urgency than temperature. By the time she finally reached the house, Annalee was breathing hard, the muscles in her legs cramping, dark spots swimming in the edges of her vision.

She saw nothing out of place in the yard, no vehicles missing, but the front door of the house hung from a single hinge. *Jesus. That can't be good.* Going up the steps cautiously but quickly, trying to control her panting, Annalee noted high velocity blood splatter. More blood was smeared in a wet trail that led through the doorway. *Drag marks.* Someone had been shot, then taken inside. She had passed no one on the trail. That could mean the shooter was still in the house, or they were on foot in the forest, getting away.

Assuming the worst case scenario — that the shooter remained on the scene — she drew her .38, trying to force her body to move past the slight vertigo and breathlessness the effort of getting here had cost her. The situation could turn real ugly, real fast, and she had no way of calling for backup. Of course, she could return to the SUV and try the radio, but she dismissed that option. People, possibly including Lunella, were in trouble now, right this minute. Returning later might be too late. Her nerves tingled, her senses sharpened as she became more acutely aware of her surroundings. There was a faint murmur of voices coming from inside the house. One voice rose above the rest.

"I have to go after them! I have to! Aunt Rachael, don't..."

It was Lunella.

Hesitating no longer, Annalee went in, keeping her step light although her heart was pounding fast and furious. "Hey, y'all, it's Sheriff Crow," she called loudly, making sure her tone was casual. "Everybody all right in here?"

After a pause, Lunella appeared from the direction of the kitchen. She seemed distraught, her hair hanging in pale tangles around her face, a bruised swelling on her cheekbone. "Oh, God...you can't...no, please, you have to go," she stammered. "You can't be here."

"Who got shot?" Annalee asked. Relief that Lunella was unharmed swept through her in a dizzying wave, but she did not holster her weapon yet. She lowered her voice, pitching it so that only Lunella could hear her. "If there's somebody in the house, just nod, okay?"

Lunella let out a strangled sob and shook her head.

Annalee was holstering her gun when Lunella's knees buckled. She grabbed the woman before she could collapse. "Talk to me, honey," Annalee pleaded, searching Lunella's expression for any clue, the least goddamned hint as to what was going on. "Tell me what happened here. Please, I want to help. I can help if you just talk to me."

"It's Bear," Lunella said. Her eyes were huge, the brown irises sparkling with golden flecks of color. "They took Bear."

"Who?"

"The Gunns." Lunella's fingernails dug into Annalee's biceps, perilously close to drawing blood.

She ignored the twinge. "Are they still in the house?"

"No, no, they left. Took off with him into the woods."

"Did you or your uncle or aunt shoot at them?"

"Uncle Ezra tried to stop them. They shot him." Lunella's voice dropped to a bare whisper and she shuddered. "They shot him."

*Shit. Okay, that changes things somewhat.* Annalee swung Lunella around, grunting with the effort, and managed to get her seated on the leather sofa without dropping her. "Stay there," she said, pointing a finger to emphasize the command. Unlike the other weirdness, *this* she could deal with — a hopefully non-fatal shooting incident with witnesses. Annalee moved to the back of the living room and through a door into the kitchen, where she found Ezra laid out on a wooden table, his shirt open, a dozen bleeding wounds visible on his hairy chest. Rachael was bent over him with a pair of tweezers in her hand.

"There's no cell signal out here," Annalee said after a moment, projecting calm in an emergency as she had been taught. Rachael seemed to be in a state of shock. Certainly, her current behavior made her an unstable element whose behavior could not be predicted. As far as Annalee was concerned, folks who were normal in the head did not perform crude surgery on the kitchen table as if the clock had turned back a century or two.

Annalee added, "Why don't you put those tweezers away? We can stop the bleeding with pressure until the paramedics get here. You got towels, right? We'll do that, then I'll drive back to the highway to call 911 and have an ambulance dispatched." She was running through the plan in her head: take one of the Skinners' pick-ups to the gate, transfer to the SUV, haul ass back to the highway. If she put the accelerator down and did not babysit the alignment, she could be in contact in less than ten minutes.

Ezra's face was gray; he was sweating heavily and panting, the red curl of his tongue protruding from his mouth. Rachael did not acknowledge Annalee's presence or answer any of her questions. Nibbling her bottom lip in concentration, she dug the tweezers into one of the wounds, making Ezra bite off a scream. His muscles went rigid, his back arched, and he gripped the edges of the table until the wood creaked.

"Jesus Christ!" Annalee went to stop Rachael and froze when the woman bared her teeth and growled. "What the hell's going on?" Annalee cried, appalled.

"Get out of here!" Rachael literally snapped, biting off each word. She twisted the tweezers in the wound, her probing accompanied by a spurt of dark blood. Ezra bellowed in agony, the tendons standing out in his neck. When Rachael withdrew the instrument, it was gripping a shotgun pellet. Silver metal gleamed through the liquid scarlet sheen that coated it.

"Look, Mrs. Skinner, your husband needs medical attention." Annalee shifted around the table, trying to see if any of the man's wounds showed signs of an arterial bleed. She thought she detected a discoloration that signaled significant gunpowder residue on his skin, which did not jibe with the dispersed shotgun pattern; the wounds were too far apart for the shooter to have been standing any closer than thirty yards away by her estimation. She tried to catch Rachael's eye and said, "Ezra could have internal bleeding."

"I said, leave us be!" Rachael snarled.

Lunella stumbled into the kitchen. "Let Aunt Rachael alone," she said to Annalee. "Please, don't interfere. You don't understand. Ezra can't... She has to get them all out or he'll be poisoned."

Rachael dropped the pellet on the floor. There were several there already, mired in little pools of drying crimson. Sweat glistened along her hairline, a sheen of white in the sunlight coming through the kitchen window above the sink. A droplet shivered on the end of her nose, winking like a diamond as it fell off.

A small lump writhed under Ezra's skin, drawing Annalee's attention. She took an involuntary step backwards, her stomach convulsing as she was assailed by instant nausea. Her hand fell on the butt of her gun as another quivering lump surfaced on the man's body. She had seen a rat inside a corpse once, making similar movements as it ate its way through the abdominal cavity. Ezra moaned, the sound raising goosebumps on her forearms.

"What the fuck?" Annalee could not help blurting.

Lunella grimaced. "I told you...he's being poisoned by the silver."

While Annalee watched, a greenish-black line branched out from an oozing pellet wound on Ezra's belly, running towards his ribcage. Dirty yellow, foul-smelling pus began to leak out of the small hole. Rachael stabbed the tweezers into the wound while Ezra's eyes rolled back to show the whites. Annalee had never seen or heard of a reaction like that to being shot. This was something else, something beyond her experience.

"The hospital can't help him, only Aunt Rachael can. She's his mate," Lunella insisted. "Come on, please; let her do what needs to be done. Ezra will be fine once she gets the silver out. He'll be able to heal."

Annalee turned and took hold of Lunella's arm. "Tell me everything," she said through gritted teeth, suddenly furious, "and I mean everything!" Nothing made sense. She was not going to be jerked around any more. She wanted answers and she was going to have them, damn it! "Talk to me, Lunella."

"The Gunns were working for Lassiter, now they're working for Dempsey, and he works for Abner Cutshall," Lunella got out in a gasp.

It was not exactly what Annalee wanted to hear at the moment. She shook Lunella's arm a little, willing her to be more forthcoming.

Rachael's growl renewed — a sound like thunder, filled with threat, the promise of hurt. Lunella turned to her aunt, although she did not pull out of Annalee's grasp. "Anna's mine! She deserves to be told," Lunella said, trembling but defiant. "I'm going to tell her everything, no matter what you say."

"Go on, then," Rachael replied, her focus returning to Ezra, who was shivering and whining low in his throat. Another pellet wound was leaking pus. "Do what you want, girl. Please yourself. I don't have time to stop you, so on your head be it."

Lunella looked as if she might throw up from sheer nerves. Nevertheless, she pulled Annalee out of the kitchen, back to the living room. The door closed behind them, cutting off Ezra's soft whimpers. Annalee maintained her grip on Lunella.

"We're different from other people, us Skinners, I mean," Lunella began, her expression beseeching Annalee to understand. "We can...some of us can...turn, you know? From human to wolf. No, listen to me...you wanted to know, and I'm tellin' you."

"I'm listening," Annalee said grimly. That might actually explain a lot, as insane as the notion sounded. She was going to keep an open mind, but that did not mean letting her brains slide out of her ear.

"Maybe I should show you instead." Lunella stripped off her clothes, yanking her shirt over her head and unbuttoning her jeans, kicking them off in a few seconds while Annalee stared, her mouth falling open at what seemed like an acre of smooth, lightly tanned flesh exposed to her view. Her mind was temporarily derailed by Lunella's breasts, which were small and firm, the nipples dusky pink, crinkling as they were exposed to the air. Her waist and hips formed a nearly straight line with very little feminine dip before melding into strong thighs and calves. She was husky, but Annalee got the impression of dense bone structure and heavy muscles under a thin padding of fat.

"Lunella, what are you do...oh, crap." Annalee broke off as the woman's whole outline suddenly shimmered, sparkling like dust motes in a sunbeam. Lunella shrank vertically and expanded horizontally, her image blurring to mist. Annalee blinked, her rational mind insisting this was a hallucination, while the rest of her struggled to understand how and why. In a few seconds, Lunella the human female was gone, replaced by a blond-coated wolf that shook herself vigorously, fluffing out her furry ruff. The wolf glanced up at Annalee, her black-lipped muzzle parting in what was unmistakably a canine smile.

She had seen this same wolf in her dreams.

Annalee's chest was burning. It took her a moment to realize she was holding her breath. She let it come shuddering out. The wolf — no, Lunella — was pressed against her shins, whining. Hardly able to believe what she was seeing was true, Annalee put out a shaking hand. Lunella's fur was soft, like glossy silk under her fingers. The wolf's tongue was wet and equally soft. Lunella lapped at Annalee's wrist, showing an impressive array of sharp teeth. Annalee was somewhat surprised to find that she was not afraid.

Lunella's outline shimmered again, and she returned to her human form. She seemed completely unselfconscious about her nudity. "Bear's my brother," she said, rising from her crouch. "He don't like to turn. He'd rather stay wolf. There's some like that in the family."

"How? How do you do it?" It was the only question Annalee could think to ask. She was as much stunned by the revelation of Lunella's change as by the woman's nude body. Wrenching her gaze away from the nest of darker blond curls at the juncture of Lunella's thighs, she waited for an answer that would help her understand.

Lunella started shrugging on her clothes. "Just that's the way it's always been."

"Then how come you don't get along with Noah Whitlock?" Annalee asked, recovering her wits sufficiently to recall Lunella's apparent animosity towards her deputy. "He's your cousin."

"Yeah, but ain't none of us trust the law that much. Would you? Knowing what we are, would you trust a guy in a sheriff's department uniform?" Lunella bent down to pick up her shirt and her breasts stirred provocatively. "Besides, Noah's like Bear 'cept the opposite, you know? He can't change from skin to fur. His momma wanted him kept out of family stuff when he was young on account of that, and he went to some private school over in Ogee, so he's just not that close kin to us. And when he was twelve, he spied on me when I was skinny-dipping over by the old quarry, and he caught me changing into fur, and totally freaked out, and ran into the pond and nearly drowned, the dumb ass. I was grounded for a month."

Annalee carefully did not roll her eyes. Family feuds did not need to make sense; they just existed. It was as it was. "Lassiter's mother was a Skinner," she said, trying to make connections on the murder case. She needed something logical to cling to, a distraction to help smooth out the jangled mess of her nerves.

"Yeah, he didn't have the gift. That happens sometimes, too. He was jealous of Uncle Ezra, 'specially after Aunt Rachael was sent down from Canada to join our pack. Grandma Naomi was grooming Rachael to be alpha bitch when she stepped down, was plannin' for her to marry Ezra, but Lassiter hated it. He wanted Rachael for himself. He tried to get her to run away with him, but him and Ezra had a dominance fight. Lassiter lost."

"Lassiter went away, then he came back years later. Why?"

"Dempsey." Lunella's upper lip curled and gold flickered in her eyes. "The gift's in our genes, whatever the hell that means. We live longer than regular folks, heal a lot faster...that's why they hired the Gunns to put live traps on our land. Lassiter knew what we are, and he betrayed us, he told Dempsey. We try to find all the traps, but the Gunns are good at poaching, s'why they got Bear. He's not... Bear's forgotten some human stuff, maybe he can't change no more. We have to save him, Annalee. They got him. They got him!"

*Right. Abduction of a minor. Attempted murder.* Annalee hiked up her thick leather belt, feeling as if she was girding her loins for battle. "You know where Dempsey is?"

"Cutshall's place, I think."

"All right. Let me call for backup..."

"You can't."

"Honey, I can arrest Dempsey for kidnapping and... Oh." Annalee remembered Bear was a wolf from a family of werewolves. No way could she make *that* charge stick. She could bring Dempsey in as suspect in Lassiter's murder, but that would likely expose his work to too many people. The situation had to be handled discreetly, at least until she knew that the Skinners, Lunella especially, were protected, their secret kept safe. Visions of government laboratories, youth-greedy politicians with big budgets and few morals, and vivisection experiments by cold scientists sprang to vivid life in her mind's eye. Annalee swallowed. The thought of Lunella strapped down on a table... She remembered the dead wolf in the morgue, its rigor-stiffened legs splayed in the air, and almost gagged.

"Come on," Annalee said after a pause. *Screw it; you only live once.* "We'll go out there to Cutshall's place and play it by ear."

Lunella took a deep breath, several expressions chasing across her face one by one — relief, terror, tender affection, fierce protectiveness. "You'll help us?" she asked uncertainly, looking at the floor. Her gaze swept up to meet Annalee's. "You don't mind?"

In answer, Annalee stroked her thumb over Lunella's upper lip, remembering how it had felt to kiss her, to lose herself in the other woman's embrace. The sweetly painful throb of her heart had not altered with this new facet. Her acceptance of Lunella as a werewolf came easily, perhaps aided by her dreams.

It struck Annalee that her self-denial, her excuses, her doubts had been for nothing. Maybe it would never work between her and Lunella. Maybe any relationship they tried to develop would go seriously to hell in a couple of months, the break up punctuated by thrown dishes, tears, screaming matches, and slashed tires. Maybe Annalee would be run out of town by a torch-bearing mob. Maybe the world would end tomorrow.

Maybe she ought to get her head out of her ass and surrender to the inevitable.

It occurred to her that this unusual romance was swift and sudden, unexpected, and likely to blow up in her face, but she had to take a chance on happiness at some point. Now seemed as good a time as any to try a relationship. If she lost her badge because she was outed as a lesbian, so be it. She would make sure the ones responsible for her father's death paid, whether she was sheriff or not. For now, it was a thrill to be wanted, to know that Lunella desired her above any others. Annalee looked into Lunella's eyes and read the hope there, the slowly dawning realization that her affection would not be rejected.

"You win," Annalee murmured, leaning in to rest her forehead against Lunella's. "I'll rent the damned U-haul."

Lunella kissed her gently, a brush of mouth against mouth that was the most erotic touch Annalee had ever felt in her life. Something broke inside of her, filling her with a wave of tenderness. She pulled away with great reluctance, shivering.

"We'd better get going," Annalee whispered against Lunella's lips.

Lunella's inhalation was more of a gasp, but she nodded and took a step back. Her gaze was hazy, drugged. She ducked back into the kitchen, the door closing behind her. When she returned, the softer emotions in her expression had been replaced by resolution and what Annalee interpreted as a good dose of guilt.

*Aunt Rachael,* Annalee assigned guilt automatically. *Nobody like a mother or mother-substitute to manipulate the right buttons. Wonder what's going on there?*

"I'm ready," Lunella said.

"How's Ezra?"

"He'll heal. Aunt Rachael got the silver pellets out."

As Lunella moved past her, Annalee could not resist pulling her in for another soft, sweet kiss, hoping to erase the frown tugging her mouth down at the corners. She felt Lunella stiffen. Breaking off the kiss, Annalee glanced up and met Rachael's steady gaze. The woman had an impressive scowl on her face. Rachael said nothing; she stood there with her arms crossed over her chest, motionless and silent and judgmental. Annalee wanted to stick her tongue out like a defiant child. Instead, she guided Lunella to the ruin of the front door. Whatever Rachael's problem was, it would keep until after Bear was rescued.

On the drive to Cutshall's mansion, Lunella clicked off the radio, ending some country music singer's yodeling wail about a lost lover. The sun had fallen behind the high ridge of the tree line, allowing magenta-tinged twilight to creep over the ground. In the darkness, Lunella was reduced to a silhouette in the passenger seat until a reflection of the SUV's headlights off a road sign caught her eyes, making them glow like honey amber and gilt for a brief second.

"Your daddy knew about us," Lunella said out of the blue.

Annalee jerked the wheel in surprise, sending the SUV skidding onto the shoulder of the road. She fought the grip of the dusty soil, then managed to shift the vehicle back onto the road, grateful for the tires' bite on the asphalt surface. After sitting in silence a moment, trying to regain her composure, Annalee cleared her throat and asked, "What?"

"Uncle Ezra and your daddy went to high school together. Kind of like you and me." Lunella's voice was soft. The lack of light made it impossible to read her expression. "He knew about the change, about how we are. He tried to stop Lassiter."

"You know who killed my father?" Annalee gripped the wheel so hard, her hands ached. A renewed surge of grief was tempered by rage — at those who had done the killing and at the ones who had shielded the murderer with their silence.

"I wanted to tell you."

"I know, honey. I know." Annalee tried to push back the anger. She was not really mad at Lunella. "Just tell me now."

Lunella touched her thigh, fingertips stroking lightly. "It was one of the Gunns who pulled the trigger, one of Titus' boys, Dewey maybe, but we think Lassiter ordered it done." She sighed. "I'd better start at the beginning. Jesus, what a mess!"

"You can say that again." Annalee kept her gaze on the road by force of will.

"Look, I know what you're thinking." Lunella sounded bitter. "You think it's our fault he got killed."

"No. Daddy was a lawman. He made his choice." Annalee patted Lunella's hand in what she hoped was a comforting way. "What happened?"

"I don't know, not everything. Uncle Ezra went to talk to your father when Lassiter took Bear the first time. I guess Dempsey was doin' experiments or something, he needed Bear's blood. They put a silver collar on Bear so's he couldn't change from fur to skin even if he wanted to — that was Lassiter's doing, he knew what silver does to us."

That explained the canine hair caught in the links of the necklace. "Lassiter took some silver stuff that turned his skin gray," Annalee said. "I forget what the M.E. called it."

"Yeah. That's how Johnny burned his mouth, biting him."

Annalee thought about the nips on the dead man's shins, and the nasty, raw-looking rash around Johnny Skinner's mouth. "Was that before or after he shot Lassiter?"

"No, you still don't understand. They took Bear. Your daddy went to straighten that out and they killed him, they dumped his body in the forest for us to find. It was a warning. Lassiter...he ain't right in the head, Annalee. Him and Dempsey, they got some crazy idea about living forever, and they think we've got the secret, and they don't care who they kill. Poor Bear...they were hurting him. He couldn't tell me what all went on, he's got no words, but I found scars on his body. Dempsey was cutting him, cutting him open..." Lunella's hand clenched into a fist. "He's my brother. Blood is blood and kin is kin."

"Tell me what happened at Yellow Jacket Pond." When Lunella continued to hesitate, Annalee went on, "It's not like I'm going to arrest anybody at this point. I can't, honey. If I arrest your uncle or anybody else connected to the killing, your secret's bound to get out."

"But you're the sheriff."

"My concern here is justice." Annalee watched the road, feeling the weight of the badge pinned to her chest. "I understand how feuds get started. I was bred in the hills, too. Whatever happens..." She paused, trying to decide how to articulate her feelings. Fierce resolution stiffened her spine. "It ends here. No matter what happens, the whole thing — the Skinners, the Gunns, Dempsey's experiments — it's going to end now, I swear."

"How can you—"

"Trust me." Annalee risked a glance toward the passenger side. Lunella was still in shadow, unreadable but not unreachable. "Please, just trust me. I will *not* let you come to harm. You hear me? I'm going to protect you and your kin, and do what needs to be done." She pulled off her badge and tossed it over her shoulder into the back seat. "Tonight, I'm not the sheriff of Daredevil County. Tonight, I'm plain ol' Annalee Crow."

"There's not a thing that's plain or old about you," Lunella replied, a hint of laughter in her voice.

Despite the seriousness of the situation, Annalee smiled. "So...you were telling me about the pond?" she prompted.

Lunella sighed again, her levity vanishing. "Dempsey wanted...he wanted a subject that he could communicate with, you know? Bear ain't got words but he understands a lot, and I guess it wasn't enough. Lassiter talked to Uncle Ezra, said he'd exchange Bear for somebody else, like me or one of the younger boys. Aunt Rachael was so pissed, I thought she was gonna have a stroke. Anyhow, me and Matthew, Mark, and Luke went out to the pond in fur, while Uncle Ezra and Johnny went there in skin to meet Lassiter. Johnny was bait, yeah? We wouldn't have let anything happen to him, none of us. We just wanted to get Bear back.

"You should've heard that bastard Lassiter, talkin' like we was just a step above the animals, or maybe lower than that. He said we was cursed by God. Said we ought to be grateful — grateful! — that our curse was gonna help righteous Christian folk like Cutshall and the rest of his congregation. They're all wastes of air, you ask me."

"I take it the meeting went bad."

"You'd be right about that." Lunella fell silent a moment, then went on, "Johnny don't have a lot of control yet. He went nuts when he smelled Bear's blood. Lassiter had Bear in a cage. He was hurting. He'd been cut and burned, and Johnny... Look, it's hard to keep hold on the change when you're young. That's why we mostly live apart. A man gets killed by a wolf in the woods, it's an accident. Man gets killed by a wolf in the city, everybody gets riled, asks questions, starts poking around. It's safer to stay hidden."

"Johnny killed Lassiter." This was actually not shocking to Annalee. Apart from the details, all murders were the same — the deliberate taking of a life for one reason or another. Some reasons were justifiable, others not so much.

"Not exactly. Johnny bit Lassiter, and Lassiter panicked and ran, which was about the worst thing he could've done."

Running would trigger a predator's chase instinct. *Stupid bastard never had a chance*, Annalee thought. Technically, she was not supposed to be happy when a citizen was murdered, but she could not help feeling some satisfaction that Lassiter had gotten what he deserved. Kidnapping what amounted to an incompetent minor, even if that minor was in the form of a wolf, and allowing said minor to be tortured, all in the name of helping a bunch of rich old people stay alive...it was sickening. Dempsey was shaping up as a second Josef Mengele. Annalee's jaw went tight. *Not on my watch, goddamn it.*

"Uncle Ezra turned and killed him, took out his throat." Lunella's statement came out low, almost a whisper. "I used the shotgun after, so nobody could tell he'd been bit."

"The M.E. said the edges of the wound looked a little irregular," Annalee commented, proud that her tone betrayed none of the faint sense of horror she felt at the thought of her girlfriend's uncle killing a man by tearing apart the victim's carotid artery with his teeth.

Silence fell between them again, broken when Annalee's curiosity prompted her to ask, "That was you at the pond, wasn't it? The day we found Lassiter's body. I saw a wolf."

"Uh-huh."

"And at Lassiter's house."

"I have to protect you."

"Yeah, honey; you did that when you killed Barabbas Ricketts."

"He was gonna shoot you!" Lunella exclaimed.

"I'm not arguing, or accusing you of doing wrong, or anything like that," Annalee said mildly. "I just hope you understand that if every idiot who threatens me gets killed by a wolf, people are gonna talk. You want to end up dodging silver bullets the rest of your life?"

Lunella's answering growl was deep, pitched low enough to create an answering vibration in Annalee's body. She squirmed, gooseflesh rising.

"I am not going to stand by and let you get hurt," Lunella said. "You're mine!"

When Lunella said that in such a possessive tone of voice, Annalee felt a strong inclination to roll over and beg. "Yes, I'm yours," she replied, "but you've got to—"

Annalee nearly lost control of the SUV when Lunella slithered across the seat, grabbed her and forced her head around. As Lunella's lips captured hers, Annalee applied the brakes, bringing the vehicle to a coasting halt, thanking God there was no traffic.

Lunella kissed her, lapping at her mouth. Caught in an awkward position, Annalee ignored the twinge in her neck and strained to return the kiss, using her tongue to chase the unique mélange of flavors that meant "Lunella" to her. She was not aware of whimpering until Lunella pulled away, then she felt teeth nipping the side of her throat.

"Mine," Lunella whispered, biting harder.

It was painful but at the same time, Annalee felt a staggering surge of arousal. Her inner muscles clenched, a sweet ache that had her clutching the steering wheel in a white-knuckled grip. Lunella released her just before the bite would have broken the skin, leaving that area of her flesh sensitized and throbbing. Annalee struggled to catch her breath. Lunella nuzzled Annalee's face, snuffling and rubbing cheek-to-cheek. The motions reminded her of Mongo demanding attention, and she realized Lunella was scent-marking her.

"Just don't pee on me," Annalee murmured.

Lunella's startled snort of laughter was muffled by her neck. "Sorry."

Annalee inhaled deeply and let it out slowly, her body easing. "No, it's okay. I'll have to remember to cover up the hickey. What brought that on, anyway?" Even as she asked, the answer came to her. "I'm yours," she stated, amazed anew when Lunella let out a soft whimper, her eyes huge and glimmering soft gold.

"You keep saying that, we're gonna get arrested for public indecency," Lunella said, moving back to the passenger side with obvious reluctance.

"It's an instinct thing, yeah? A wolf thing?"

Lunella's reply was clipped. "It's a *you* thing. Now get going; I won't tell you twice."

"Yes, ma'am." Annalee shook herself mentally and sent the SUV back on its course.

Once she had calmed down enough to think rationally, Annalee turned the case over in her mind. She believed Ruth Lassiter and Aiden Thompson had gotten some kind of experimental gene therapy treatment from Dempsey. The debacle with Lassiter's murder and Dempsey being wanted as a suspect had likely put enormous pressure on the project; perhaps the widow and the lawyer had demanded they receive treatment in case Dempsey was caught and arrested. Well, whatever Dempsey was doing, he still hadn't perfected his recipe, judging from the less-than-stellar results.

"Who killed Aiden Thompson and Ruth Lassiter?" Annalee asked. "We found their bodies yesterday by the Ateeska River, near your place."

"No idea. None of us," Lunella answered defensively.

"Hush, honey. I wasn't accusing anybody of anything. After tonight, I reckon none of us are going to be without sin." Annalee made the turn-off onto the highway, cutting between a Volvo and a Ford truck. She did not turn on the flashing lights and siren that would have cleared her path because one, she was not on official police business, and two, she did not want to give Cutshall an early warning of her presence.

After twenty minutes in traffic, Annalee spotted the long driveway that led to the antebellum mansion and turned the vehicle onto it, tires crunching on the gravel. She clicked off the headlights, navigating by the moon. "Lunella, you got any idea where Dempsey might be hiding out?" she asked. "Cutshall's got thirty acres around the house and a shit-load of out-buildings where he could stash a fugitive away."

When there was no answer from Lunella, Annalee slowed the SUV and brought it to a halt on the side of the driveway, parking beneath the spreading branches of a peach tree. As soon as the SUV stopped, she flicked on the interior light, squinting until her eyes adjusted to the brightness. It was worth the risk of detection to be able to see Lunella's face.

Lunella was huddled against the passenger-side door, her legs drawn up on the seat. She was looking at Annalee with a hopeless fear that made Annalee feel faintly sick. "I can find them, I think," she said, "but I'd have to...you know, sniff them out."

At first, Annalee was nonplussed, then she remembered. *My girlfriend's a werewolf. Gives new meaning to the phrase "that time of the month". Nope. No way. Not going there.*

"Uh, sure, yeah, of course, good plan." Annalee stumbled over the rush of words that spilled out of her stupid mouth. Scratching her eyebrow, she tried again, needing to soothe Lunella's fear of being rejected. She understood that, at least. "I don't...I don't mind, honey. The other part of you. Hairy, okay; scary, not so much. You're kind of cute, you know? Cuddly." The instant she said it, she flushed in embarrassment. *Geez, Crow, dorky much?*

A bright red blush crept up Lunella's neck to stain her cheeks, and she grinned, wide and slightly goofy. "Yeah? You think I'm cute?"

"Uh-huh." Annalee had to grin back, some of the tension draining from her muscles. "Cuter than a sack full of puppies, matter of fact." She winced, thinking that the phrase might not be taken as a compliment by a woman who could become a wolf at will.

Instead of being offended, Lunella just scooted closer and planted a kiss on Annalee's cheek. "Thank you," she said softly, her gaze luminous with affection.

Annalee was torn between wanting to haul Lunella in for a more serious kiss, and knowing there was no more time for shenanigans. She settled for cupping the side of Lunella's face. "I like you," she said. "I like you a lot."

"Same here, 'cept I love you, Annalee Crow." Lunella leaned in again and gently bit Annalee's bottom lip. "I chose you as my mate a long time ago. That'd be hard enough for my family to swallow if you were a human male, but Aunt Rachael...she was expectin' me to take over as alpha bitch, and you can't lead the pack if you don't breed. That's why I was sent to Canada. Aunt Rachael hoped I'd grow out of it, choose a male mate, but I never stopped wanting you, loving you. Waiting for you to see me, to want me, to choose me. I came back for you. Now you're mine."

"Why me?" Annalee asked the question without thinking, and immediately felt like the world's neediest high-maintenance girlfriend. "I mean, how long have you known?"

"I think I was born in love with you," Lunella replied with appealing shyness, glancing sidelong at her. "But in school, that's when I really knew you were mine."

*This can't be real.* Annalee's palms dampened with nervous sweat. *What am I getting into?* It was a cherished fantasy of hers, to be with someone who smiled at her like *they* had gotten lucky, and now it had happened. She wanted Lunella, sure, and she liked her, but everything was moving so fast between them, it was frightening.

"We don't really know anything about each other," Annalee protested, even as she mentally berated herself for sounding so whiny. "We haven't spent time together. I mean, a year when we were kids at the same school and... How do you know I'm the one?" The clock was ticking. She needed to get her head back into the case, find Dempsey and rescue Bear, but she could not make herself stop this insanity.

"I swear, Annalee Crow, you're as obstinate as a mule!" Lunella frowned. "I know who my mate is, and that's you. You're mine."

"What if I don't want to be yours?" Annalee asked quietly.

Instead of being hurt, Lunella pinned her with a topaz-bright gaze and said, "You're mine. Wiggle all you want, you know I'm right. You've dreamed us together."

"Wait...you know about my dreams?" Annalee found the notion hot, but also somewhat embarrassing.

Lunella nodded. "It happens when mates find each other. You didn't realize it back then 'cause we was kids, but I knew. So did Aunt Rachael."

"So you're responsible for those—"

"Yeah, kind of." Lunella ducked her head shyly. "Did you like it?"

Annalee scrambled to make sense of what the other woman was telling her. "So we were...you know, really together? In my dreams?"

"Uh-huh."

"And you got sent to Canada after graduation, which is why I stopped having them."

"Uh-huh."

"But when you came back, I had another one."

Lunella gave her a smug smirk. "Uh-huh."

"And that makes us mates?" Annalee asked weakly. "Honey, I'm not sure—"

"Look, when we touch each other, you don't feel weak and alone 'cause I'm not just using you to get off," Lunella said, looking at her intently. "I love you. Those women you went with in the city, they could touch your body but they never, ever touched any other part of you, did they? That's the difference. I'll take care of all your parts, every one, and I'll never stop till the day I die. We mate for life, you know."

That level of devotion left Annalee breathless. What reply could she possibly make to such a declaration? *Wolves mate for life.* The prospect should have been terrifying, but Annalee just felt warm, as if she had stepped from a rainstorm into summer sunshine. She understood that Lunella would forgive every sin she committed and would never, ever reject her, no matter what. She was beloved.

It was insane. It was impossible. There were so many reasons not to do this, Annalee could not list them all. Lunella was looking at her, and the love she read in the other woman's face made her heart flutter.

"Fine," Annalee said breathlessly. "You can take care of my parts."

Giving Annalee an approving smile, Lunella shucked out of her clothes, her outline shimmering as she changed to her other form.

Between one heartbeat and the next, a wolf was crouched on the seat next to her, showing a brief gleam of teeth. Annalee took a careful look at the animal, seeking the familiar, and found Lunella's eyes laughing back at her from the furry face. Finally, Annalee plunged both hands into the thick ruff and scratched, letting the surreality of the moment wash over and through her. *This is my girlfriend. This is my mate.* Saying it in her mind was not as weird as she feared. Lunella whined and pushed her cold wet nose against Annalee's wrist, obviously seeking comfort.

"Yeah, yeah, it's okay," Annalee said, responding to Lunella's distress, read in the flattening of ears against the wolf's broad skull, and the droop of the plumed tail. "I'm okay, really, I swear," she continued. "Not that I want to stick my tongue in your mouth right now, 'cause I'd have to arrest myself, and I'm not that way inclined anyhow, but I'm not freaking out any more either. Honest. It's cool."

Lunella's ears went up and her tail whisked through the air twice. The sound she made was not quite a bark, but it was extremely loud in the confines of the SUV.

"Ease up, there; no need to shout," Annalee said, her ears ringing. "Come on, let's go find your brother, kick Dempsey's ass, get this over with, go home, and canoodle."

She opened the driver's side door and slid out of the vehicle, waiting for Lunella to follow. Once the wolf was on the ground, Annalee was able to discern just how startlingly huge Lunella was in her fur-form, at least three times bigger than an average Arctic wolf. She had not been in the right frame of mind to notice Lunella's size back at the Skinner house. A tidbit from a high school science class flitted through her mind — the law of conservation of mass. Lunella's form may have changed, but no matter her shape, her mass would have to remain constant since matter could not be gained or lost in the transition from human to wolf.

*No wonder Lunella's super-sized when she's got her fur coat on, and I'd better keep my pie-hole shut about that,* Annalee thought. *Telling your girlfriend her outfit makes her look larger than life is probably a good way to end up banished to the sofa.*

Annalee retrieved her flashlight from the SUV, the solid weight of it reassuring. While Lunella cast around, her head low, her nose questing for scent, Annalee glanced in the direction of the mansion. In the night at this distance, little could be seen of the house except a vague outline and several yellow rectangles of light that indicated windows. The nighttime hush was broken by the rhythmic buzz of cicadas, the scrabble of Lunella's paws on the gravel, the call of a whippoorwill.

A shiver traveled cold down Annalee's spine.

She almost stumbled when Lunella was suddenly there, pressing against her shins. "You got something?" Annalee asked.

In answer, Lunella rubbed her head against Annalee's knee in a distinct up-and-down motion.

"Okay, you take point, I got your six," Annalee said, flicking on the flashlight.

Lunella huffed and started walking, her pace quick but within Annalee's limitations. Annalee concentrated on the bushy tail swinging just ahead of her, sweeping her flashlight's bright white beam over the ground to avoid falling over roots or stepping into holes as they left the driveway and continued over the grounds. Lunella stopped, nudged her, and disappeared, swallowed by the darkness in a split second. Annalee clicked off the flashlight and stayed where she was, waiting for the wolf to reappear. Every sound dug under her skin, twanging her nerves — a breeze rattling through tree branches, the soft rush of owl's wings swooping just above her head. After what seemed like an eternity, but was probably only a minute or two, she felt a cold wet muzzle thrust into her free hand.

Turning on the flashlight, she politely avoided shining it into Lunella's eyes. "Well?" she whispered. When Lunella gave her a disgusted look, she realized the stupidity of expecting a verbal answer and tried to formulate a better question. "You got a bead on Bear?"

Lunella nodded.

Annalee did not think Cutshall had hired guards on the property, but her police-trained instincts were pinging furiously for attention. The last thing she needed was to get shot for trespassing, or get caught by a security guard. That would make the local headlines for certain, and likely prompt an inquiry from the Commissioner which had the potential to damage not only herself, but the Skinners, too. Such a debacle had to be avoided at all costs.

"Anybody else around?" Annalee asked.

A shake of the head this time, the thick ruff taking on a dandelion fluffiness that tempted Annalee to run her fingers through it. She resisted, however, limiting herself to a single light stroke skimming the surface of the wolf's fur.

With Lunella again taking the lead, Annalee was soon standing outside a structure that she identified as a barn. Cutshall bred racehorses as well as keeping a couple of ponies for the grandchildren, so this was either the stable or hay storage. The door opened on well-oiled hinges without a creak, leaving Annalee thanking God for WD-40.

Inside, there were the expected bales of hay, neatly stacked; sacks of animal food of various kinds; bins and barrels and buckets; racks of riding gear; a collection of miscellaneous farm equipment. No horses. Lunella stuck her nose behind Annalee's knee and shoved.

"Hey!" Annalee regained her balance by windmilling her arms. She swung the flashlight around, the beam illuminating Lunella's hindquarters. The wolf was pawing at the floor, pushing loose straw away from what proved to be a trapdoor with a metal ring in the center. Annalee knelt, playing the light over the door's surface before pulling on the ring. The door opened; bits of straw and dust floated in the air, glinting in the flashlight's beam. Glancing into the hole, Annalee saw a set of narrow steps.

She looked at Lunella. "That's pretty steep...can you manage?"

Lunella nodded, the motion stiff and jerky, obviously unnatural to her current form. Annalee could not help a gasp when the wolf started down the stairs, accompanied by a muted clicking sound. Checking a tread for signs of stress before starting down herself, Annalee found marks in the wood that were definitely claw-like. She hoped Lunella had not damaged the seat upholstery in the SUV; that would be a bitch to explain on the Repairs to Vehicles authorization form.

She had to turn off the flashlight and tuck it into her belt loop, needing both hands to help guide her way down the stairs, which were not only narrow but steep enough to make her calf muscles burn from the acute angle. The air was clammy and unpleasant, tickling like spiderwebs against her face. She counted twenty-two steps to the bottom, which was a bare concrete floor. Annalee checked the corners of the ceiling and the nearby walls for the telltale lights of security or alarm systems and found nothing. If Dempsey was here, it seemed he was confident about not being caught, or perhaps he was too far gone to care.

Lunella's growl caught her attention. Annalee put the flashlight on, keeping the beam tilted towards the floor. The wolf was standing rigidly in place, the hair along her spine raised in a clear threat display. Annalee touched the butt of her gun. She listened intently, but heard nothing apart from Lunella's growling, which was increasing in volume.

She risked putting a hand on Lunella's head, not wanting to startle her. "Show me where Bear's being held," she said, pitching her voice low. "We'll take him home."

Lunella shivered but obeyed, adopting a stiff-legged pace that spoke eloquently of her distress and barely controlled rage. Annalee walked at Lunella's side, resting her palm against the wolf's back while they moved in tandem. A dim light shone at the end of the corridor, growing brighter as they came closer. Annalee clicked off the flashlight and tucked it into her belt loop, drawing her service weapon instead. She hoped she would not be forced to use it...*but whatever Dempsey's doing, it ends tonight.*

Annalee heard a man's voice coming from around the corner and halted, listening.

"Stupid, stupid, stupid!" the man ranted. His voice was unfamiliar to her, his accent no slurred southern drawl but sharp and staccato, somewhat nasal, definitely originating from Up North. She supposed the speaker was Dempsey. "I told them not to take the serum," he shouted. "I told them it wasn't ready. I need more time, damn it!"

There were shuffling sounds, then the man continued more calmly, "Need more silver soon. Mmm, yes, I'm sure that doesn't hurt anymore. Just be still and let it happen." Another pause that lasted a few heartbeats. When he spoke again, his tone was fretful. "Where the hell is Cutshall? I need that helicopter. Have to get out of here..."

Lunella's snarl was thunderous and shocking in its intensity. The wolf whipped around the corner, fangs bared, ruff standing out like a lion's mane. Annalee made a snatch at Lunella's tail, missed, and skidded after her, entering the room in a half-crouch, her .38 held in front of her.

The first thing she saw was Lunella darting at a man, her jaws snapping. The man managed to dodge the bite and lunged towards a shotgun leaning against a stainless steel examination table. Annalee hollered, "Police! Surrender your weapon! Do it now!"

Distracted, he turned in her direction. She caught a snapshot glimpse of his face — an average looking guy, early forties, brunette hair thinning back from a high forehead, no visible distinguishing marks. His mouth was open so wide in surprise, she could see the gray amalgam fillings in his back molars. He screamed when Lunella took advantage of his momentary paralysis to rip into his leg above the knee, tearing a slash in his jeans and the flesh beneath. Blood spurted, speckling her fur with crimson, dying her muzzle red.

Annalee felt like she was losing control of the situation. She tamped down the urge to panic and said, "Lunella, stop! Stop it right now! Get away from him!"

Growling horribly, Lunella backed away, but not very far.

Dempsey — it had to be Dempsey, there was no other explanation — was edging toward the shotgun. Annalee aimed her weapon at him. "Don't go there, sir. I mean it."

"I'm...I'm defending myself," he gasped, "against that...the animal."

She dug into her pants pocket and pulled out a bandana. Tossing it at him, she said, "Tie that around your wound and step away from the shotgun. It's loaded with silver, right?"

Dempsey's eyes went huge behind his gold-rimmed glasses. "How'd you know?" he whispered, pressing the bandana to the slash in his leg.

"I know everything, Mr. Dempsey." It was not the whole truth, but Annalee knew that admitting she remained in the dark about some aspects of the case would not be productive. Her father had taught her to always portray herself as omniscient; many suspects were compelled to tell their story if they believed the police already had the answers.

"It's Doctor, not Mister, and I doubt you're as knowledgeable as you claim," Dempsey called her bluff. "You know about the creatures, certainly, since you've got one there, but the rest..." He gave her an unpleasant smirk.

Annalee controlled her shudder. Dempsey gave off an air of unwholesomeness, and his smile was a sharp thing, ready to slice. She would bet he was the type who tortured pets and set fires just to find out what happened next. "Why don't you prove me wrong?"

Lunella's not-quite bark was insistent. Annalee carefully shifted part of her attention to the wolf, keeping her gun aimed at Dempsey, who was still lingering too close to the shotgun for her to be easy about it. Lunella was moving to another part of the room — the laboratory, she corrected herself, since the space was jam-packed with scientific equipment she figured had cost Abner Cutshall a good chunk of his net worth. She could also make out a series of cages lined up along the back wall, big enough to contain a wolf as large as Lunella.

The thought of Lunella being confined sent an uncontrollable rush of anger through her, and Annalee's finger tightened on the trigger of the .38. She pushed down the urge to eliminate the threat Dempsey represented. Exactly what she was going to do with him, she had not decided, but shooting him out of hand was not an option. *Not yet anyway*, she thought grimly.

Stopping beside a cage, Lunella pawed at the door. Annalee took a step to the side to get a better view and realized the cage was not empty; it contained a pale-furred form—Bear, she supposed. She tracked the dark red plastic line that snaked out between the bars to an IV pouch on a stand, the pouch approximately half-filled with blood. Catching a movement in the corner of her eye, she shifted to cover Dempsey with her weapon.

"I told you, don't go there," she said to him. "Put that shotgun out of your mind. I *will* shoot you, and I *will* claim self-defense. You think I don't have a throw-down gun in my car? You think I can't close this case any damned way I please?" Again, what she said was not strictly true, but it made for an effective threat. "This is my jurisdiction, not Abner Cutshall's. He can't protect you if he's under a grand jury investigation himself."

"Listen to me, you have to listen to me," Dempsey said, sounding desperate. Blood was leaking past his knuckles where he had his hand clamped against the wound in his leg. "I need him; I need more of them. The creatures...they're the key to immortality. Surely you can see that! They're just animals, and the benefits to humankind—"

"Bubba, you're just about a cunt hair shy of full-tilt boogie insane," Annalee said, shaking her head in disgust. "People are people, no matter what they look like or what they believe in. Your kind of thinking built the concentration camps and gas chambers, and I am *not* going to allow you to do the same in my county. Besides, ain't nobody supposed to live forever, least of all rich bastards who're afraid of dying 'cause they know they did a lot wrong and not much right on this earth. Money can't buy salvation."

"You don't know what you're talking about," he sneered. "God created man with built-in obsolescence, but I can change that."

"Put your hands behind your head and turn around. Do it, Dempsey. I ain't gonna ask nice again. Don't be stupid. Hands behind your neck, and we'll all just walk away from here, have us a little talk down at the sheriff's office." She may have left her badge in the SUV — and wasn't that a gesture as useless as tits on a boar hog, because she was still wearing her uniform — but she had not gotten rid of the pair of handcuffs hanging on her belt.

Annalee unhooked the cuffs one-handed. Dempsey was obeying, his hands drifting upwards in a gesture of surrender. Lunella's claws clicked on the concrete floor, telling her the wolf's position, which was near to her right. *Okay, this is going to be a piece of cake,* Annalee thought, holstering her revolver as she reached for Dempsey's wrist. She needed both hands to secure the suspect.

Without warning, Dempsey dived for the shotgun, snatching it up by the stock, turning and firing almost in a single motion. Annalee realized she was not hit and fumbled her .38 out of the holster, internally chiding herself for not taking more precautions. Rattled by the ear-splitting boom of the shotgun's discharge, she got off a single shot, winging Dempsey in the upper arm. He dropped the shotgun and ran, headed toward the back of the laboratory. Annalee was about to pursue him when she heard a low moan.

Lunella had been caught by the shotgun blast.

## Chapter FIVE

It was as if someone had pulled the plug on her anger, sending it whirling away to be replaced by a fear that left a rusty iron taste in her mouth. Annalee cursed and fell to her knees beside the stricken wolf. "Oh, shit, honey, what's he done to you?" She remembered Ezra in agony from silver poisoning, the writhing lumps in his body, the foul-smelling pus, and she had to repress a shudder. Dempsey was getting away — the sumbitch had obviously considered Lunella more dangerous than an armed law enforcement officer, considering he had had a choice of targets — but Annalee remained where she was.

Lunella shivered, her forepaws scrabbling futilely as Annalee performed a quick examination. Dempsey had fired at an oblique angle, thank God. If Lunella had taken the full brunt of the blast in the head at close range, she would probably be dead. It looked as if a half-dozen pellets or so were embedded in the wolf's sharp muzzle; there were a couple of bleeding nicks in one of the upstanding ears, and a deep graze perilously close to an almond-shaped eye that burned gold. Annalee knew Lunella must be in serious pain, so she kept her movements deliberate, not sure if Lunella might forget herself and snap.

"All right, let's see what we can do here," Annalee murmured, retrieving a folding knife from her pants pocket. Lunella's answering yelp was shrill. "Calm down, I'm going to have to dig the pellets out before... Hey, can you change? You know, back to human?"

The wolf struggled to get up. Heedless of the danger of being bitten, Annalee dropped the knife and flung an arm around Lunella's neck to stop her. "Honey, you got to stay still!"

Lunella wriggled, panting harshly. Her breath hit the side of Annalee's face; it smelled sweet, like Coca-Cola and vanilla extract. Annalee tried to hang on to the squirming wolf, getting a mouthful of fur for her trouble, then Lunella twisted and broke free. She made it half-way to the cage that contained Bear before she collapsed, whining softly.

Annalee's knees were bruised and aching. Getting up, she went over to Lunella and squatted, ignoring further protests from her abused joints. "Listen, I need to take care of those silver pellets," she said. "You know they're poisoning you. Hold on and let me..." Annalee squeaked when Lunella turned her head and took hold of her calf, the sharp-toothed jaws closing carefully but firmly.

"Uh, honey, you want to..." *Not bite my leg off* was what she almost said, but thought better of it. "I can't do anything for you like this," Annalee said. "Let go of my leg."

Lunella braced her paws on the floor and pulled her head back, very nearly knocking Annalee on her ass. The huge razor-sharp canines pierced the cloth of her uniform trousers; she could feel them pressing into her flesh, denting but not breaking the skin. Not yet. Annalee repressed the instinct to pull away, knowing she might be badly injured if she did.

She stayed perfectly still and said in as calm a tone as she could muster, "Honey, you need to let me go so I can help you."

Instead, Lunella pulled again. Annalee inhaled. This was not good. Lunella growled, sounding frustrated and irritated, out of patience. Annalee put a hand on her muzzle, feeling the swelling, the poisoned heat running through the wolf's blood. Lunella's nose was hot and dry, as if she was feverish. At last, Lunella released her grip on Annalee's leg, only to roll over on her belly and attempt to crawl to Bear's cage.

Annalee sighed. "You want to be there so bad, let me help, goddamn it." She rolled to her feet, then bent and grabbed Lunella just above the forepaws. Putting some power into it, she dragged the wolf across the floor, trying to be as gentle as possible while hauling a not inconsiderable weight. Her back muscles screamed with the effort.

"Damn, girl, you're solid," she muttered.

Lunella's grumbling little growl seemed like the wolfish equivalent of "fuck you", so Annalee smiled, kept her mouth shut and heaved until Lunella was in front of Bear's cage. As soon as she was in range, Lunella snapped at the IV line.

"Quit that! He might need... Oh, wait a second." Annalee realized the IV had been set up to drain Bear's blood, not replace it. The bag was about three-quarters full. She stuck her hand through the bars, peeled the tape off his shaved foreleg, and managed to remove the large bore needle, having no idea how to reverse the flow or if it would even be safe to do so, considering the risk of air embolism. Bear slept on, unmoved and unmoving, apparently drugged unconscious. Annalee turned back to Lunella.

"Are you going to let me get those pellets out now?" she asked.

Lunella closed her eyes and relaxed, except for a very slight quiver in her pale ruff.

Annalee retrieved her knife. Taking a deep breath, she knelt next to Lunella's head — Christ, her knees! The concrete was killing her knees! — and after wiping the blade on her pants and wishing she had antiseptic, she used the point to dig out the first pellet. Lunella held still, letting out a long rusty whine through her nose. A mixture of blood and dirty yellow pus ran freely down her muzzle. Annalee continued digging at the silver pellets that were lodged beneath the skin, working as quickly as she dared. At least there were no grotesquely writhing lumps to distract her, just the slipperiness of blood on her fingers, the smell of it mingled with the stink of her own fear, acrid and thick. Every soft pained sound Lunella made struck her to the heart. Finally, the last pellet popped free. Annalee threw it into the corner.

"Honey, I think they're all out. You hear me?" Annalee patted the broad skull; the fur was spiked and sticky with drying blood.

Like an answer to her prayers, the wolf's form shimmered, elongating and thinning to mist. An after-image hung in the air for a second, resolving into a naked female figure prone on the floor. Lunella lay there panting, several scabbed wounds marring her face, but she was the most beautiful woman in the world as far as Annalee was concerned.

"Bear..." Lunella whispered, reaching out a hand to touch the caged wolf's paw.

"We're going to break him out, I promise," Annalee said. "Can you stand up?"

Lunella's skin was slick with sweat; tendrils of pale hair stuck to her face, which was tinged slightly green. There were bruised-looking pouches under her eyes. Nevertheless, she heaved herself to her feet with Annalee's help. Annalee stretched, trying to relax her knotted muscles, while Lunella tugged on the cage door. It was fastened with a padlock. Bear did not stir. Lunella pulled harder, her teeth set in a snarl.

"Hang on! Hang on!" Annalee cried out, grabbing Lunella's arm. Her grip slipped and she nearly fell. She yanked herself upright and pain flared across her ribs, the familiar hurt of muscles stretched beyond their limits. Annalee managed a backwards step and forced down the heartfelt desire to curl up in the corner and cry like a little girl.

"Look," she said, "we need the key, or a crowbar, or a bolt cutter. Lunella! Focus, honey." Annalee tried really hard not to betray how much her side was hurting, like a lick of hot lightning wrapped around her ribcage. "Key, crowbar, bolt cutter. Yeah?"

Lunella heaved a sigh. "Key, crowbar, bolt cutter. Got it." She glanced at Annalee and frowned. "Sit down before you fall down."

"I'm good to go."

"No, you're not. I can tell you're in pain." Lunella took Annalee's arm and guided her across the laboratory, gently pushing her into a chair. "Stay put."

*How sad it is*, Annalee thought, watching Lunella puttering around, searching inside drawers and cabinets, *that I'm too hurt and too tired to appreciate a naked woman right now, especially when she bends over like that. Hubba frickin' hubba.*

About five minutes later, Lunella located bolt cutters, which she used to snip the padlock off the cage door. Bear remained unconscious, even when Lunella shook him. It was obvious that he was not going to walk out of there. Annalee's knees gave an almighty twinge at the thought of hauling his heavy carcass up the ladder. *Wait a second.* Dempsey had not run off in the direction of the corridor; he had gone the opposite way. Either he was lurking in the lab, which she found preposterous, or there was a second exit. Annalee went to check while Lunella remained crouched beside Bear, crooning to him.

Annalee found an elevator and would have done a dance of joy if the pulled muscles in her side had allowed it. As it was, Annalee backtracked as swiftly as she could, eager to tell Lunella the good news. She quickened her steps when the muffled sound of weeping came to her. Lunella was stretched out on the floor, her upper body wedged into the cage with Bear. Her face was buried in her brother's fur and she was crying.

"What's wrong?" Annalee asked, panic fluttering in her chest. "C'mon, talk to me."

"He's dying." Clutching handfuls of Bear's wheaten coat, Lunella turned her head to look at Annalee. "He's dying and I can't help him."

"Isn't there anything you can do?"

"He'd have to change. That's the only way." Lunella scooted out of the cage, her bare ass wriggling in a way that would have been enticing had matters not been so dire. She dashed tears away with the back of her hand. "When we change...it's kind of like a do-over. I don't know why, that's just the way of things. We don't heal at once," she indicated the scabs on her face, "but we do heal a lot, real quick. Faster than humans. Not with silver inside, though. It's a poison that keeps us the same shape till it's removed. Bear ain't changed to skin in years, and he's lost too much blood. I can't reach him."

Annalee noticed the wolf's eyes were half-open. "Can he hear you?"

"I'm not sure. Maybe, maybe not."

"Talk to him, honey. Do your best." Annalee spared a thought to jogging back to the SUV and calling for an emergency veterinarian to be dispatched to the location. When she mentioned the idea to Lunella, she got an emphatic refusal.

"We have to get him out of here," Lunella insisted. "We have to get him home; he don't have much time. Maybe Aunt Rachael can do something."

"Okay, that's not going to be a picnic, but I think we can manage. There's an elevator to the top..." Annalee paused, thinking. "We'll have to rig a travois and drag him out, 'cause I'm pretty sure neither of us can carry him for very long."

Lunella nodded, looking grim and sad, and about a half-second from putting her fist through a wall. "If nothing else, he'll die free, not caged like an animal."

"From your mouth to God's ears," Annalee said, bending to plant a brief kiss on Lunella's bare shoulder. "But I hope nobody's dying tonight."

It was Annalee's turn to make a tour, gathering the things they needed to jury-rig a way of getting Bear to the surface. It seemed as if Dempsey had been staying in the laboratory instead of the church; she found empty fast-food wrappers and pizza boxes, a pile of dirty laundry and a cot with several blankets folded at the foot. She brought the cot and blankets back to Lunella, then spent a few minutes using the miniature saw-blade on her knife to remove the cot's back legs. Between them, she and Lunella managed to wrestle Bear onto the makeshift travois and strap him in with torn strips of blanket. Her side ached like a bastard, but she would be damned if she'd sit back and let Lunella do all the work.

Dragging the travois to the elevator was not as easy as it sounded; the thing did not corner well by any stretch of the imagination, and the rough stumps of the sawed-off legs sometimes snagged on a bump on the concrete floor. Annalee was sweating heavily and in considerable pain from the strain. When they reached the elevator, she almost wept in relief, deliberately not thinking about the hard slog ahead, having to drag that goddamned travois over grass and earth and Hell's half-acre when they got to the surface.

In the elevator headed up, up, up, Lunella shot Annalee a look from beneath lowered brows. "I told you I know you're in pain," she said. "What did you do?"

Feeling stubborn and pissed off that Dempsey had gotten away, Annalee shook her head. "I'm fine," she lied.

"I can smell it on you," Lunella went on, still giving her the stink-eye.

Annalee straightened, stifling a gasp as her side cramped. "You can smell me?" she asked, horrified by the notion. She had put on deodorant after showering that morning, but... *hey*, she thought with a touch of resentment, *it's been a strenuous day. So I'm not daisy-fresh any more. Cut me some slack here.*

"Yes," Lunella huffed impatiently. "I can smell lots of things, even in skin. Like I can tell by your scent if you're in pain, or if you're happy, or if you're excited...you know."

A memory burst into the forefront of her mind — the first time she had visited the Skinner place, walking down the trail with Lunella, entertaining lustful thoughts as she watched the woman's amazing denim-covered behind swaying back and forth in front of her, within touching distance. "So you can tell when I'm..."

"Uh-huh."

Annalee felt a blush heating her cheeks. "Oh."

Lunella moved closer, pressing her nude body against Annalee's uninjured side. "You're my mate." She reached up and touched a lock of hair that had come loose from Annalee's braid. "I'm tuned to you. So, is it broken?"

"Huh?" Annalee wished she could stop the dumb-ass things coming out of her mouth.

"Your rib...is it broken?"

"No, just pulled a muscle."

Lunella nodded. "Better let me haul the travois alone."

"But you're—"

"Fast healer, remember? The silver's out and I'm feeling much better."

The elevator coasted to a smooth stop with no alerting *ting* to tell them they had reached their destination. Annalee's pride did not let her like being made to feel useless, but she had to admit Lunella was right. The woman was in much better shape at the moment.

The doors slid open and the first thing Annalee saw was the muzzle of a gun.

The next couple of seconds passed in an adrenaline-fueled blur.

Annalee started to draw her .38. Training had her pivoting to present a smaller target even as her vision re-focused on the person behind the gun — male, red hair, green eyes, the black swirl of a tribal tattoo on his neck. The gun was a Beretta semi-automatic. Her mind supplied the facts: there were seventeen 9mm rounds in the clip, one in the chamber. Not as much stopping power as a .45, but deadly at close range.

Lunella's snarl echoed off the elevator's metal walls, clanging inside Annalee's skull.

The red-haired man's finger tightened on the trigger.

Several shots split the air, momentarily deafening her.

The gunman fell forward into the elevator, his Beretta clattering into a corner near Annalee's foot. She kicked the gun away from his outstretched hand, and covered the man with her sidearm. He was face-down in the boneless sprawl of unconsciousness or death. The elevator doors tried to close but bounced off his legs and rolled back.

Annalee's body was zinging with flight-or-fight energy. Impossible as it was, she felt as if her hair was standing on end in a porcupine bristle and her heart was lodged behind her tongue. She gripped her .38 and waited for the shooter. The enemy of her enemy was not necessarily her friend, especially in these uncertain times.

Noah Whitlock appeared, his expression grave and furious, the rims of his nostrils pinched white. "You couldn't have called for backup?" he complained. To Annalee's momentary fascination, Noah's eyes glinted gold in a manner that was becoming familiar.

Lunella shouldered past him, unconcerned about her nudity. Her skin was streaked with blood and sweat, patched with grit from the floor. The scabs on her face were crusty dry, looked disturbingly like pork rind scraps, and were already starting to flake off, revealing pink new skin beneath. "Dempsey...have you seen him?" she asked.

"Nope." Noah holstered his weapon. "You okay?" he asked Annalee.

"Shit, Whitlock, your timing could be better, but not by much," Annalee replied, trying to catch her breath. She had never lost bowel control before, but she had come close to hollering for fresh brown trousers. "Who's this asshole?"

"I spotted a black Hummer when I was coming in to the property," Noah said, bending to check the gunman's pulse — a formality, Annalee thought, since the redheaded man was clearly as dead as a department store dummy, and unlikely to rise till Judgment Day.

Noah straightened. "There were two men inside the Hummer, driver and passenger. This guy was the one riding shotgun. Some other guy joined them — male, Caucasian, about six feet, average weight, gold-rimmed glasses, a limp. I followed redhead here."

Lunella growled and pushed a shock of blond hair off her forehead, a jerky movement eloquent with impatience. "They're getting away," she snapped. Her gaze was focused somewhere beyond the immediate area.

Annalee stepped out of the elevator. "I think our redheaded friend was sent to get rid of witnesses, maybe retrieve stuff from Dempsey's lab. I heard Dempsey mumbling about a serum. Bet that's what he gave Rachael Lassiter and Aiden Thompson."

"Jesus." Noah looked sickened. "How's Bear?"

"We need to get him out of here," Lunella replied, walking back into the elevator. "You move that trash out of my way first." She indicated the dead gunman.

Annalee had no objection to Lunella taking charge for the moment and Noah did not question his cousin. He bent, took hold of the dead man's ankles, and dragged the body out of sight. Annalee had to thrust her arm between the doors to prevent them from closing.

When Noah returned, he and Lunella managed to drag Bear's travois out of the elevator while Annalee stood guard. Bear was semi-conscious now, making little soprano puppy whines. Lunella shushed him, stroking his fur. She grabbed her side of the travois and nodded at Noah. "Let's go," she said shortly.

Annalee wanted to kiss Lunella, to comfort her, but settled for a pat on the woman's solidly muscled shoulder she hoped was reassuring. She walked ahead of Noah and Lunella, taking point since the adrenaline had worn off already, leaving her tired, stiff, and aching. She was not sure she could summon the necessary strength to haul the travois, especially now there was a second pair of hands to help.

The elevator had deposited them at the back of Cutshall's stable. The odors of manure and hay scratched at Annalee's throat. A single overhead light was burning, a piss-yellow bulb that gave just enough illumination to navigate by, but the stalls on either side were cast in deep shadow. As they proceeded, a horse let out a series of angry sounding squeals and began kicking its stall door, an infuriated pounding soon echoed by the other horses. Even the ponies joined in, clattering their hooves and raising a racket.

"What the hell is that about?" Annalee asked, raising her voice to be heard.

"It's us," Lunella replied, her teeth bared in what was emphatically not a grin. "Me n' Noah. Horses are prey animals. They smell us and they're afraid."

Annalee narrowed her eyes. "You told me Noah couldn't change."

"Don't matter none. He's still got the blood."

"He's standing right here," Noah said, sounding bitter.

In that instant, Annalee could see exactly how it had been for the lonesome young boy, different from everyone else but not different enough to be embraced by his kin. He had belonged fully to neither world. Lunella and her family had not treated Noah very well, but he had still come out here to help. Which reminded her...

"How the heck did you know where we were?" she asked him.

Noah shrugged and shifted his grip on the travois pole. "Uncle Ezra called me, told me what kind of crazy shit y'all were doing." A horse poked its head over the stall door and tried to bite him. He shifted out of range. "Figured I'd better check it out."

Lunella gave him a tiny approving smile. "Good to see you, cuz."

He flushed. "C'mon, or do you want the whole household to know we're trespassing?"

By the time they exited the stable, Annalee had the beginnings of a spectacular headache. She breathed the night air, drawing it deep into her lungs. Overhead, a moon the color of buttermilk had risen above the ridge line. "Where're you parked?" she asked Noah.

"Hard by the old wishing well."

That was closer than her SUV, if she was remembering the lay of Cutshall's property correctly. "All right...here's what we're going to do," Annalee said. "Noah, you take Lunella and Bear back home, by which I mean to the Skinner place. I'm headed out to the church, which is where I reckon I'll find Dempsey."

Both Lunella and Noah began to speak, their simultaneous protests rendering their words unintelligible. Annalee held up a hand for silence. "No arguments," she said, drawing on her authority as sheriff. "Bear needs medical attention and Dempsey needs to be stopped. We can't do everything together. We're going to have to split up. It makes sense."

Lunella was still shaking her head. "I'll go with you to the church," she said, a mulish expression on her face.

"I don't think so, honey. Listen, you need to go with your...your brother," Annalee said, stumbling slightly over a sentence her brain insisted was too impossible to contemplate. "He needs you, and we sure can't stand here jawing over it all damned night."

As if on cue, Bear made a particularly pitiful whimper. Lunella's head whipped around and she stared at the wolf on the travois, clearly conflicted. Finally her shoulders slumped. "Yeah, okay, I'll take him home. He needs Aunt Rachael."

Noah opened his mouth but snapped it shut when Annalee anticipated him. "Lunella can't do this alone. You go with her," she said, batting away a mosquito whining shrilly in her ear. "I don't care about what happened when you folks were twelve years old. Get over it. When you're done, if you haven't heard from me otherwise, I'll see you at the church."

And that was that, as far as she was concerned. Annalee lingered only long enough to see Lunella and Noah disappear into the darkness, dragging the travois between them. She wasted no time finding her SUV. Lunella's clothes were on the front passenger seat where she had left them. Annalee scooped up the T-shirt and pressed her nose to the fabric, which was richly impregnated with Lunella's musky scent. She inhaled the familiar bittersweet fragrance, feeling some of the tension coiled in her belly beginning to relax. Allowing herself only a moment's indulgence, she put the shirt aside and started the engine.

There was business to be done.

The drive to the Church of the Honey in the Rock was uneventful, giving her a welcome opportunity to compose herself. Downtown Brightbrook was not that far from Cutshall's property, about twenty minutes in normal traffic, but this late at night there was virtually no one else on the road. The real action, Annalee knew, would be over in Lingerville at the bars and illegal cock fights, the movie theater, and the lone dance club offering two-for-one longnecks. She watched the accelerator needle edge over the speed limit and did not care. Any passing patrolman would assume she was responding to a call.

The church was located next to a family style restaurant named Twinkle's that served the worst country-fried steak in the county in Annalee's opinion, and their mashed potatoes were instant, another grievous sin. The church building had once been a Quik-E-Print shop until the owner was arrested by her father for counterfeiting Green Cards and passports. There was no steeple, no bell, just a squat concrete block structure with huge, street-facing windows. The interior was shielded from casual view by thick white and blue curtains. One of the windows had discreet gold lettering painted on the wide pane — *Church of the Honey in the Rock, Rev. J. Lassiter, attendance by appointment only.*

Annalee parked the SUV at the curb next to a black Hummer — the vehicle seen by Noah Whitlock, she assumed — and cautiously approached the front door. She had no search warrant and therefore no official standing; she did not even have probable cause. Then again, she had no intention of bringing the matter to court if it could be helped. Exactly what she was going to do to Dempsey, she had no idea. An arrest would mean putting paperwork into the system. Once that happened, there was nothing to stop the entire story from getting out. It would only take one curious reporter to ferret out some inconvenient facts and the werewolves of Daredevil County would be exposed to the public. She was not going to let that happen, but she was not going to do nothing, either.

First things first: get hold of Dempsey.

Annalee pulled out her flashlight. As she recalled from a brief stint of working for the Quik-E printer before she went to the police academy, there was a narrow alley between the church and the restaurant that led to a rear area which could not be seen from the street. Behind the church was a plot of heat-withered grass that backed onto a stand of hickory trees, technically part of the city's Grover Makepeace Public Park. Annalee progressed as silently as possible, leaving the flashlight's beam off since she found the moonlight sufficient for now. She passed the shattered basement door. Someone had tidied up the splinters and nailed a few boards over the hole, but something — likely Ruth Lassiter, her body and mind twisted by Dempsey's serum — had really busted the hell out of it.

The back door with its chipped and faded paint was intact and, when Annalee tested the knob, proved to be unlocked. She opened the door and slipped inside, finding herself in a tiny kitchenette with a single cabinet, a sink, and a mini-refrigerator. A dim light beckoned to her from the next room, a square space with three rows of folding chairs and a carpeted dais with a carved oak pulpit. A large gilt cross hung on the wall. The air had the stale feeling of a house left uninhabited or neglected.

Annalee was operating on instinct, letting that guide her through an empty room adjoining the church hall and to a door. Pressing her ear against the panel, she could detect a faint mutter of voices. They seemed to be coming from far away, so she believed they might be in the basement. It was impossible to identify how many people were there; more than one, certainly. Dempsey, and who else? Maybe the Hummer's driver? Someone unknown?

Putting away the flashlight and drawing her weapon, Annalee paused a moment. Her heart was thump-thump-thumping in her chest with such force, she was surprised the wild beating was not audible. This was exactly the sort of situation that made a law enforcement officer's sphincter pucker. She did not dare call for backup — what would she tell her other deputies? That a mad scientist was using werewolf DNA to turn rich folks into mutants? She would be lucky to escape being confined to a rubber room and treated to a strict regimen of anti-psychotics. Waiting for Noah was equally problematic. He might come in the next five minutes or the next five hours, too late to capture Dempsey if the man fled the scene. Furthermore, an unknown number of potential assailants still hid in what she assumed was the basement or a sub-level of the building. She had no way of knowing if they were armed and/or prepared to resist. Dempsey had already tried to shoot Lunella, which in her mind indicated he was dangerous and desperate.

Seconds ticked past as she waited for her gut to tell her what to do.

At last, Annalee eased the door open. The voices became more audible, but she still could not make out the conversation. She was able to identify Dempsey and Abner Cutshall as the main participants in what sounded like an argument. To her surprise, it seemed that Deuteronomy Cutshall, Abner's journalist son, was also down there. Ron's relationship with his father was shaky at best, everybody knew that. What was he doing at the church?

She quietly picked her way down the stairs, aided by the light shining at the bottom. When she was halfway there, she stopped and crouched, peering under the banister at the men below, who had their backs to the staircase. Annalee held her .38 in front of her, the grip adhering to her sweaty palm. She licked her salty upper lip and settled in to watch and listen, ready to react when it became necessary.

"You've had months!" Cutshall wheezed. He paused to take a hit from the portable oxygen cylinder next to him. In the weak illumination, he appeared insubstantial and ghost-like, halfway into the next world. "Months, Mr. Dempsey, to perfect your serum," he continued more loudly. "My corporation has provided you with not only the necessary funds but also the research subjects you required, and at great physical and financial risk, I might add. I've been very generous; it isn't wise to disappoint me."

"But sir, we're just not ready." Dempsey sounded weary. He had a thick blood-spotted bandage tied around his leg over his jeans.

Cutshall interrupted. "You need to concentrate on perfecting your formula."

"Without a research subject—"

This time, it was Ron who cut the scientist off. "You'll do as you're told, Dr. Dempsey. He who pays the piper calls the tune."

"That's my boy," Cutshall said approvingly, taking another deep sucking breath of oxygen. "I knew I could count on you, Deuteronomy."

Ron curled his hand around Dempsey's bicep, squeezing hard enough to make the doctor wince. "Do you have copies of your research notes?" he asked.

"Of course." Dempsey dug a flash card out of his shirt pocket. "I record everything and back up my files twice daily."

"Good. Then you'll have no difficulty continuing your work in another laboratory." Cutshall gestured at Ron, who went over and helped him sit down in a chair. "I don't have much time left, Dr. Dempsey, so don't waste any of it. I'll order the Gunns to capture two of the creatures for you after the sheriff's been eliminated. Will that be sufficient?"

Dempsey rubbed his face. He looked frustrated and tired. "Mr. Cutshall, I'm still working on controlling the mutation. Delivering the morphogens that affect normal tissue differentials isn't a problem, but until I'm able to... Well, it's a technical problem that will take time to solve." He shrugged and swept a hand through the air. "Do you want to wind up like Ruth Lassiter and that lawyer friend of hers?"

"Why did you inject them, anyway?" Ron asked.

"Because they threatened me." Dempsey's expression was petulant. "That lawyer, Mr. Thompson, he was very offensive. Very offensive, sir. I told him the serum wasn't perfected yet. I told him he should ask Mr. Cutshall for permission, but Thompson wouldn't listen. Mrs. Lassiter said she deserved the serum since her husband had been murdered by the creatures, and she wouldn't listen to me! I tried to warn her. I tried to warn them both."

Ron grimaced. "So she turned into a...a thing?"

"As I said, the mutation isn't controllable yet. They both suffered a terminal genetic alteration. Mrs. Lassiter escaped. I was able to subdue her with a tranquilizer dart, but she died. Mr. Thompson...he attacked me. I shot him with silver." Dempsey's eyes narrowed. "Unlike the creatures I've been studying, Mr. Thompson was not merely inconvenienced by the silver but actually appeared to suffer an acute anaphylactic reaction that killed him."

"For a genius scientist, you're a damned-fool incompetent," Cutshall muttered. "Dumping the bodies by the river... You could have done a better job of concealing your mistakes. They were found by fishermen, for God's sake! Now the sheriff's involved."

Dempsey stiffened. "I'd planned on disposing of the remains in the river."

"And when you were seen, you ran away like a coward and left your mess behind." Ron snorted. "Next time, let the real men do the important jobs, Dr. Dempsey. You'd better stick to your lab equipment and research subjects."

Cutshall held up a trembling, liver-spotted hand and Ron fell silent "We'll meet Titus Gunn and his boys at their hunting shack, just as I've scheduled," the old man said. "From there, we'll head for the airport."

"Why do we have to go out there?" Dempsey asked. "Why not straight to the airport?"

"That snake Titus only deals in cash and only deals with my father," Ron said. "He don't trust telephones. Now shut up and quit acting like you've got a say, 'cause you don't."

"Ron, my boy, have you heard from Harrison?" Cutshall asked.

Ron grimaced. "When I went to pick up the doctor at the barn, he told me there was a creature running loose in the lab with a woman cop. I told Harrison to take care of them. He ought to be waiting at the house. Sorry I didn't tell you before."

"A woman cop?" Cutshall's gaze cut to Dempsey. "Who?"

"Dunno, some female in a uniform."

"Was it the sheriff?"

"I don't know."

"Call the house right now and find Harrison." Cutshall directed the sharp-voiced command to his son.

Ron pulled out a cell phone and made the call. After a few moments, he snapped the phone closed and shook his head. "The housekeeper hasn't seen him," he reported.

"Damn it." Cutshall sucked oxygen before he continued. "We've got to hurry, gentlemen. If the sheriff survived her encounter with Harrison, I can almost guarantee she's on her way over here. That woman's as stubborn as her father."

"The Gunns can take care of Crow, same as they did her daddy," Ron said. He ran his fingers through his red hair, making it stand up in messy improbable clumps on his head. "The SUV's out front. Let's go."

Annalee knew the time had come to act. She stood up, aiming her gun at Dempsey. "I'm afraid that you gentlemen will be coming with me," she said loudly.

Only Dempsey appeared startled. He turned, his hand flying up to cover his mouth. Abner Cutshall merely gave her a cold-fish stare, while Ron...

Ron spun around and pulled the trigger of the gun he was holding, the gun that she had not seen or anticipated.

Her hip flared with pain and she thought, *Shit, I'm hit,* just as her blood began burning, a rush of heat that circled her heart and pumped through her limbs. The steady beat of her pulse slowed, a deliberate banging against her eardrums. Annalee glanced at her burning hip and made out the black-feathered tip of a dart sticking out of her tan uniform pants. She raised her .38, but the muzzle was wavering too much for her to fire off a shot. It fell from her nerveless hand. Lightless black crept around the edges of her vision, turning everything fuzzy. Her knees buckled and she fell forward, thinking, *This is gonna hurt like a mother-fu—*

Bump-bump-bump!

The world spun over and over in snatches of images and flashes of red-tinged darkness accompanied by sickening lurches as she tumbled down the stairs. Her head, her elbow, her knee, her shoulder, her uninjured hip cracked against the treads, bright sparks of pain in the skin-tingling flush of adrenaline and endorphins. A final bone-rattling thud and Annalee was sprawled face up on the floor, staring at a bare low-wattage bulb hanging from the ceiling. Her chest was rising and falling, but there was not enough air to fill her lungs. Her tongue was thick in her mouth. She fought to stay conscious.

Cutshall stood over her, a silver-haired vulture hunched and waiting for his prey to succumb. His mouth curved in a wintry, close-lipped smile. "You should have minded your own business, but I suppose like father, like daughter," he wheezed.

Annalee slid into oblivion without so much as a sigh.

When she awoke, the smells of earth and fetid decay were in her nostrils.

Annalee groaned, summoning the strength to roll over on her back. Her body ached, but it was a general sort of unspecified hurt that spoke of bruises and stiffness, not violations. She scrabbled automatically at her holster but it was empty; her gun was gone. Peeling her sticky eyelids apart, she glanced around and saw various species of trees, brush, a slice of late afternoon sunlight in a sky the color of a robin's egg. She was in a forest, which meant Malingering Deep, and from the sun's position it seemed she had lost nearly a day.

From a short distance, she heard men's voices raised, catcalling and screeching, as well as the crackling thunder of guns being fired.

"Gonna get you, Sheriff!"

"Better run, bitch, less'n you can outrun a bullet!"

It was the Gunns.

A surge of panicked energy put her on her feet where she swayed in place, trying not to throw up from the lingering effects of the tranquilizer Ron Cutshall had shot her with, that rat bastard. Her head felt like a balloon, loosely tethered and floating at least a foot above her neck. It was difficult to think through the fog. Nevertheless, self-preservation sent Annalee stumbling forward, prey in flight from the hunters.

Her utility belt had been stripped, Annalee discovered as she went along, her head slowly clearing, but she still had a folding knife in her pocket. However, with no compass, no GPS and no idea of her exact location, she could literally wander for years without making it out of the forest. On the other hand, standing still and waiting for the Gunns to murder her was not an option either. Annalee's only hope was to elude the hunters as long as possible, giving Noah time to realize she was missing and put together a search party. Lunella would find her, she was certain. She just had to stay alive long enough for that to happen.

A gunshot sounded close, too close. Annalee increased her speed, urging her body to move despite her stiffness and the queasiness in her stomach.

Branches slapped at her face and neck, snagging her clothing when she broke into a shambling run. Her hair had come loose from its pins. The strands stuck to her sweaty face and became entangled in. thin branches only to be yanked free as she continued to flee from her pursuers, who from the sound of things were gaining on her. Titus Gunn and his boys were not bothering to stalk quietly through the woods; they wanted her to know they were there, gleefully sporting until they brought her down.

It was not long before hot knives stabbed under her ribs. Each breath was a laboring torment, and her sweaty shirt stuck to her skin. On the next step, Annalee skidded uncontrollably on a patch of slimy dead leaves and managed to catch herself on a fallen log, part of a lightning-shattered hickory trunk that was a good four feet in circumference. When she pushed herself upright, a piece of loose bark luminescent with mold sloughed off, making her lose her balance. She fell, landing badly and getting the wind knocked out of her. Sparks whirled in her vision. She wondered if this was how her father had died.

Annalee heard something moving through the nearby brush and thought it was likely a hunter, one of the Gunns. She needed to hide, and there was no time to think, only to act. Scooting into a shallow hollow beneath the log, she prayed her uniform's tan color would help her blend in with the forest floor, which was covered with the rotting remnants of last autumn's fallen leaves. The sun was going down fast, darkness bleeding into the sky. The lack of light would help conceal her, too. She tried to curl up, to make herself a smaller target. Once, when she was little, her father had let her hold a baby rabbit; she could recall the frantic pace of its heartbeat, the vibration drumming against her fingertips. She felt like that baby rabbit now, terrified into paralysis, waiting for something awful to happen.

A man moved clear of the undergrowth, walking near her hiding place. She could only see his feet and legs as he walked — faded jeans and old leather boots worn supple — but she figured he was a Gunn. It wasn't deer season, and the tourist hunters who came to the Deep were usually clad in new Gore-Tex boots and crisp camouflage gear, with fragrant pine-and-moss scent wafers pinned here and there to mask their human odors. Annalee risked a peek, trying not to make a sound when she shifted. The man had oily black hair, acne-scarred skin, mean eyes set close together. A silver scar on his upper lip and long sideburns that came to the angle of his jaw identified him as Jethro Gunn, Titus' oldest grandson.

Jethro paused, one boot slightly raised in a way that reminded her of the wolf in her backyard. Annalee closed her eyes. *Lunella.* A wave of longing made her tear ducts burn, but she was glad Lunella was not there. The thought of her girlfriend — Jesus, her *mate* — being run down like an animal made her burn in another way. She was angry...no, she was furious. Furious at herself for getting caught, furious with the Gunns who were hunting her for sport and for Abner Cutshall's money, furious at the hypocritical Great Man for his greed, his sickness, his willingness to destroy any obstacle in his quest for life eternal in this world, screw the next. Cutshall was trading his heavenly reward for more secular gains.

She hoped they all burned in Hell.

The wild green odor of the woods gave way to the sharp scent of urine. She realized Jethro was pissing against the log, a stream that splattered on her face, hot and reeking. She closed her mouth tightly, willing herself to stillness, even though her first inclination was to jump up and pound the asshole into the ground like a tent peg. Jethro grunted loudly, squirting out a few more short jets before the urine stream tapered off to droplets. He stepped away, quickly disappearing from her view. Annalee forced herself to wait several minutes before clawing her way out from under the log, her skin crawling with the need to cleanse Jethro's stink off. She scrubbed her cheeks with her shirt sleeve, needing to erase the smell and scorching feel of his urine, not caring she was smearing dirt all over herself.

A loud crash sounded to her right, followed by a man cursing.

Annalee was off again in a scramble, picking a direction away from Jethro and the unknown male. The Gunn boys were not the best hunters in Daredevil County, thank God. They tended to use traps for their poaching and did not possess much in the way of trail skills, otherwise they would have been able to track her progress through the forest more easily. It helped that she was trying to be careful not to leave any too-obvious signs, like torn bits of clothing, but the heavy undergrowth in places she could not avoid made that difficult.

She heard a loud metallic click first, then a split-second later came a shattering pain in her leg. Annalee's choked scream was part surprise, part agony. She reached down, clenching her teeth against a whimper, and found she had been caught in a leg-hold trap. There were no pointed steel teeth to bite into her flesh, but the trap's tight grip was excruciatingly painful, especially where it pressed against her shin. Remembering what had happened when Bear was caught in a similar trap, she managed to kneel on her good leg, biting back another scream when a fresh wave of agony rose to engulf her. The world tilted and whirled in a sickening way, and she had to swallow back a flood of bile. She fumbled around, found the spring levers on either side and compressed them, releasing her leg from the trap.

"Over here!" shouted a Gunn.

There was no time to spend even a single precious moment checking her leg for injuries. She was pretty certain it was not broken; that would have to be good enough. Annalee limped away as fast as she could, needing to put as much distance as possible between herself and her pursuers. It was almost dark, the forest swathed in deepening gray; soon, she would have to find a place to hide. The Gunn boys would probably remain in the Deep overnight. Would they make a camp or continue hunting her with flashlights? Either scenario seemed likely. There were enough of them to make either option feasible.

After a while, Annalee paused behind a tree, pressing her back against the rough bark. The temperature had dropped, leaving the air cool enough to make her shiver. She felt as though she was covered in a layer of greasy sweat and filth. Her mouth was dry, her lips cracked, and she would have sold her soul for a drink of water. There was a current of jittery energy running through her that only served to make her more exhausted. Her leg really hurt, a throbbing ache emanating from the bone. Annalee wiped the back of her hand over her chin and tried to summon the strength to go on.

Her head snapped up when she heard a howl, long and full-throated — not human, but wolf. A sobbing spiraling pack-song split the night. Annalee almost collapsed in relief. She did not recognize Lunella's "voice", but at least it had to be one of the Skinners. Deciding that shouting to catch the wolf's attention was perhaps the worst idea ever, she absently rubbed her aching side while debating what to do. Backtrack, trying to avoid the Gunns? The Deep was too big...she would never be able to pinpoint the wolf's location. Stay where she was and let the wolf come to her? This particular area was too exposed, and she doubted the Gunns would stop actively hunting her just because they heard a wolf howl.

The best thing, Annalee concluded, was to stick to her original plan: find a place to hide and stay put. Lunella knew her scent, and she reckoned so did Rachael, Ezra, Bear, and perhaps other Skinners as well. If she could stay hidden and safe...

Her bad leg throbbing, Annalee chose a new direction and staggered onwards, wishing for a beer, an aspirin, and ten minutes parked in the Barcalounger in front of the television. Uncertain watery moonlight filtered through the treetops, but there was not enough illumination to see properly, as evidenced when she wandered into a blackberry bush about five minutes later. Extricating herself from the grasping thorns was an exercise in patience and stinging pain. In spite of her care, her shirt was ripped in several places by the time she worked her way free. She scrubbed at a particularly cruel laceration on her arm and continued on her way, pacing herself deliberately, straining her eyes to penetrate the shadows for a secluded spot where she could lick her wounds in peace, so to speak, and wait for dawn.

A cold gun muzzle shoved against the side of her head made her gasp.

"What have we got here?" Titus Gunn's dry-as-dust chuckle drew her upright, clinging to a tree trunk for support when her knees threatened to buckle.

Annalee tried to calculate the odds of drawing her pocket knife before he pulled the trigger. Titus was older than God but he also had a locked and loaded gun and therefore, very much the advantage. She blew out a shaky breath. So this was how it would end for her — a bang, not a whimper, same as her father. Of course, she was close to shitting-her-pants afraid, but she would never, ever show him that fear. Instead, she summoned her most defiant expression and stared at him, straight into his dead black eyes, letting him see nothing except the granite-hard resolution to die with her dignity intact.

"Looks like you lose, Sheriff," Titus said. He spat out a wad of tobacco juice and chuckled again. "Just like your daddy."

"Who paid you to do that, Titus?" Annalee asked quietly. "Cutshall?"

The old man looked like a malevolent ghost in the indigo-gray dusk. "It was Cutshall's money what paid for it," he admitted, shrugging. "Your daddy...well, I ain't shamed to tell you he died like a man."

She bared her teeth at him. "You can kill me but you're done. You hear me? You're done, old man. I'll be gone, but there'll be others comin' along behind me, comin' after you and yours, and Hell will follow with them."

"Got a new sheriff all lined up," Titus gloated, pressing the gun muzzle harder against her head, as if he longed to punch it through her skull. There was genuine hatred in his voice. "One of my grandsons, Josiah. Pretty smart boy, Josiah, and he's got Cutshall behind him one hundred percent. Yes, ma'am, we're gonna be shittin' in high cotton from now on. Ain't nobody gonna look down on the Gunns no more. We're gonna own this county."

Flashlight beams cut through the gloom, diffuse blue with a diamond-bright center. Behind the lights clipped to rifle and shot-

gun barrels, she recognized Titus' sons and grandsons, two generations poisoned at the well. She had no doubt that if, by some
miracle, she managed to escape Titus, his boys would kill her without mercy.

"Damned straight," one of them called. The rest made sounds
of approval. "We're gonna be the kings of Daredevil County!"

Annalee did not respond to the taunts but inwardly, she was
terrified for Lunella and her kin. A corrupt sheriff would give
Dempsey and the Cutshalls carte blanche to do whatever they
wanted to the Skinners, including wholesale slaughter, mass expe-
rimentation, other horrors beyond imagining. A whole industry of
suffering and death, and there was not a damned thing she could
do to stop it. The thought of her mate locked up in a small cage,
powerless to defend herself or escape, made Annalee want to
scream.

Titus leaned forward, speaking hoarsely into her ear. The
words rang like a death knell. "Got any last words, Sheriff Crow?
Any prayers?"

"Yea, though I walk through the valley of the shadow of death,
I will fear no evil," Annalee quoted, "for Thou art with me." She
closed her eyes, knowing she had accepted long ago that her life
might end in violence when she opted to follow her father and
become a police officer instead of pursuing another career. Resignation was an accustomed companion.

*I'm sorry, honey,* she said silently to the absent Lunella. That
was her biggest regret — she would not be able to say good-bye in
person. *I'm so very sorry it has to be this way.*

She bit her tongue against a flood of pleas, recriminations,
and curses, and waited for the bang that would signal the end of
her life.

Titus' gurgling scream was a shock bursting white across her
brain. Annalee inhaled a breath and forced her eyes open, only to
squeeze them shut again when Titus' gun went off and the muzzle
flash blinded her. In the momentary explosion of light, she saw
his face contorted with fear, his mouth a round gaping hole. She
also caught a glimpse of pale fur and huge gleaming teeth before
the strobing light died so abruptly, it left her with a dazzling static
of sparks in her vision. Wetness splashed across her mouth and
jaw, warm and smelling unpleasantly metallic. Realizing it was
blood, she carefully did not lick her lips.

The night erupted into a cacophony of yelling and the boom of
gunfire. Flashlight beams crisscrossed in the chaos, jumping to
focus on men who were falling, thrashing on the ground as wolves

savaged them, pale hairy shapes that curved and darted in for the kill with deadly grace. It was not a battlefield but a slaughter. As she watched in horrified fascination, Jethro Gunn shot a wolf pointblank, then staggered backwards, his face contorting, when the wounded wolf's form shimmered into Ezra Skinner, nude and blood-streaked. Jethro screamed when a smaller wolf with darker blond fur leaped on him, bringing him down.

Titus reeled to his feet, scarlet runnels pouring down the side of his neck to soak the collar of his flannel coat. "Bitch!" he choked, spraying her with spittle. "Gonna kill you!"

He reminded her of a wounded wild boar, his little piggy eyes filled with malice, his stringy muscles rigid with fury, an enraged squeal piercing her eardrums. Titus lunged, curling his big-knuckled hands around her throat before she could fend him off. He was old and stringy but astonishingly strong. Annalee kicked his knee twice, driving the hard tip of her shoe into the vulnerable joint, but she was too close to inflict maximum damage and he was too far gone to feel it.

His exhalations stank like carrion. Annalee tried to reach his eyes with her nails but his arms were longer and she could not make contact. His horny fingers dug into her flesh, clamping down tighter, compressing her windpipe. She could not breathe. Her lungs cramped, her chest convulsed, her heart seized; it felt as if her entire torso was filled with molten lead. Annalee struggled in his grip, clawing, and thrashing, but he held her pinned to the tree trunk, his strength enhanced by rage.

Her eyes were wide open, taking in every detail of her killer's face — his bristly unshaven chin, the rotten stumps of his teeth, the scattering of moles on his cheekbones.

It was a sight she would take with her to the grave.

Sorry, sorry, sorry...

Suddenly Titus' grip loosened and he disappeared from her view. Annalee took in a whooping, agonizing breath that burned as if she had inhaled liquid fire. She coughed and spluttered and puked helplessly, drowning in air, her vision blurred by tears.

A familiar female voice asked, "Hey, are you okay?"

She tried to focus. Lunella was standing next to her, naked, her skin daubed with blood, leaf mold, and earth. "Are you okay?" Lunella repeated, taking hold of Annalee's upper arm in a grasp that was more of a caress.

Annalee tried a few more breaths, which came much easier than the first, and was surprised when a giggle erupted from her mouth. There was nothing remotely funny about the situation —

there were probably seven dead or at least injured men here, including Titus Gunn who lay unmoving at her feet — but hysteria bubbled up irrepressibly within her, and soon she was laughing, crying, and sobbing, her face mashed against Lunella's collarbone. Her professional façade was shattered, her vulnerability exposed. Tears, snot, and mucus ran freely. She clung to the other woman's firm body, laughing and laughing until she choked and began to weep in earnest. Throughout the storm of conflicting emotions that battered at her, Annalee was aware that Lunella was petting her, stroking her tangled hair.

Around her, humans were dying, killed by wolves intent on their survival. Pale-haired, blood-smeared men and women rose from the killing field, their eyes flashing gold.

Annalee fell into darkness, soothed by Lunella's touch.

# Chapter SIX

When Annalee awoke, she was in strange surroundings. Immediately stiffening in alarm, she glanced around, taking in the flowery chintz curtains at the window, the heavy quilts piled atop her on the bed, the plain pine furniture. A musky bittersweet scent permeated the room, familiar and comforting. She slowly let herself relax, only to flinch, startled, when the door opened without warning.

Lunella came into the room carrying a plate. "Hope you're hungry," she said, sitting down on the edge of the bed without hesitation. "Got an egg and sausage sandwich for you. Aunt Rachael's own sausage from our herd of pigs down in Thunderbird Valley, and the egg's from our own chickens, laid this mornin'. Better'n that fast food junk."

Annalee tried to sit up, but her injured leg protested with a twinge.

"For Heaven's sake, mule brains, let me help," Lunella said, frowning. She put the plate on the bedside table, stood and assisted Annalee in sitting up, shoving pillows between her and the headboard. "It ain't broke," she went on. "Your leg, I mean. Might hurt some, but it'll be okay. Aunt Rachael put some arnica ointment on it."

"What happened?" Annalee asked, making the unsettling discovery that while she had been unconscious, someone had stripped off her ruined uniform and underthings, washed her down, and treated her minor wounds, leaving her dressed in an oversized T-shirt and nothing else. That made her feel uneasy until she realized Lunella was the likeliest candidate, which was a whole 'nother kind of weird, but also kind of nice.

"Noah and Uncle Ezra took care of the bodies," Lunella said, looking at her sidelong as if to gauge her reaction.

Annalee grunted around a mouthful of sandwich. The Gunns had broken man's laws for sure; they were guilty of murder and worse, maybe even attempted genocide, though she would never be able to prove it. None of them had been given a proper trial...*but so be it. What's done is done and I protect my own. As Daddy used to say, "What happens in the Deep, stays in the Deep." But I'm going to make sure there are no repeats.*

"You sure about that?" Annalee asked. "Wouldn't want some tourist or weekend hunter stumbling over a mass grave next deer season."

"I'm sure."

"What happened last night can't happen again," Annalee said firmly, or as firmly as she could muster while swallowing egg and sausage and flaky buttermilk biscuit. She took a drink of coffee and gave Lunella her most serious glare. "Hear me? Never, ever again. Pass the word to the rest of your kin...they have problems with poachers or whatnot, they come to me, okay? I don't want to hear about no more hunters disappearing in the woods. I start getting reports like that, I'm going to know who did it and I'm not going to turn a blind eye. Just because I'm in on the secret don't mean I ain't going to uphold the law."

Lunella turned, looking at her directly. She licked her lips but said nothing.

"Maybe you ought to explain it to me, how your family showed up like that," Annalee said. "Not that I ain't grateful for the rescue, honey, but I'm no vigilante, either, and I can't put up with that behavior." Obeying an impulse, she put down the remainder of the sandwich and touched Lunella's hand, lacing their fingers together, willing her to understand.

"Yeah, I know." Lunella heaved a sigh, but swung herself onto the bed so that she was sitting shoulder-to-shoulder with Annalee. "After we got Bear home, me and Noah went to the church in Brightbrook," she said. "You weren't there but I smelled your blood down in the basement." She leaned harder on Annalee, who pressed back against her.

After a moment, Lunella went on, "I knew you were hurt but I couldn't tell how bad." Her eyes glinted gold for a second. "Could track you to where some men put you in a truck but after that... Anyhow, turns out the busboy who works at Twinkle's was out back sneakin' a smoke and he told Noah he seen Titus Gunn, who he knows on account of he went to school with Malachi Gunn, and the old man used to come to football practice sometimes. Soon as I heard it was the Gunns that took you away, I got Noah to bring me home.

"Uncle Ezra was all for raising the pack but Aunt Rachael...see, she ain't never going to be happy that you're my mate." Lunella's inflection was almost a growl. She cleared her throat and squeezed Annalee's fingers.

"I don't want you to be in trouble with your family," Annalee said weakly, feeling resentment on Lunella's behalf. As a patrol officer and later as sheriff, she had witnessed firsthand families torn apart because a child refused to conform to a parent's wishes. How much more difficult would such a conflict be for Lunella, who had loyalty bred in her bones? Asking Lunella to choose between her family and her mate would only lead to heartache, and she hoped Rachael had better sense than that.

"Don't care," Lunella said stubbornly. "She'll come around. She has to."

"Okay, honey, if you say so."

Lunella insisted, "She's got no choice."

Annalee was not getting into an argument at the moment. "I believe you. Go on."

"Anyhow, Aunt Rachael said you weren't one of us, not really, but I said we owed you on account of you saved Bear's life twice. I told her we was obliged, and Uncle Ezra agreed. She had to back down then and call the pack. I figured the Gunns would take you to that hunting shack of theirs over to Gumption Junction. You know the place?"

"Vaguely."

"So we went out there and didn't find no Gunns, but we found Ron Cutshall. His daddy left him behind."

Lunella sounded so grimly satisfied, Annalee covered her face with her free hand and groaned, "Jesus Christ. Tell me y'all didn't kill him."

"We didn't kill him. Pinkie swear! We just scared the snot out of that self-righteous sumbitch. Ron told us the Gunns had taken you out in the woods for a hunt."

"And what happened to Deuteronomy Cutshall?"

"Coolin' his heels in county lock-up. Noah arrested him for assaulting a police officer, hindering prosecution, and I don't know what else."

"Thank God for small favors. I'll have a talk with Ron, make him see the sense of keeping his pie-hole closed about the Skinners and Dempsey and what-not. I'll probably have to drop the charges, 'cause for sure I can't let him testify in open court."

"Anyhow," Lunella said, overriding Annalee's musings, "after Ron told us where you were, me and the family followed their trail. You were there for the rest of it."

"How come you and your kin didn't take out the Gunns before now?" Annalee asked, knowing the question might be offensive but needing to ask it anyway. "I mean, you had to have plenty of opportunities when they were poaching on your land."

"They weren't hunting *us* before," Lunella replied, "not with guns, not with intent to kill. When they took Bear the first time, we couldn't touch them 'cause we were afraid they'd hurt him. And back then, too, they weren't hunting *you*."

The protectiveness in Lunella's tone made heat prickle behind Annalee's eyes, but only briefly. She reminded herself that men were dead. "How many were killed?"

"Titus, Josiah, Dewey, Jethro..." Lunella named seven Gunn men in total. "There were a couple more at a campsite over to Devil-May-Care, but we left them be."

"Do I need to worry about a feud?"

"I don't think so." Lunella's grin could only be described as wolfish. "But hey, if they want to start something..."

Annalee thwapped Lunella on the arm. "Seriously, you goof, is there a feud in the making? Last thing we need around here is a goddamned war."

"It was mostly Titus and now he's gone. None of the other Gunns'll be inclined to make trouble without the old man stirrin' the pot."

"Well, officially, I don't know anything about disappearances unless or until somebody files a missing persons report." Annalee decided this was how she was going to handle it. If it came to her notice as sheriff, she would have to initiate an investigation, but that would not be a problem. Noah Whitlock was smart and he had the right training to ensure those bodies would not be discovered anytime this century. Of course, the surviving Gunns might decide not to file. She could think of a couple of new widows who would gratefully keep her in casseroles for life if they knew what had happened to their heavy-fisted husbands.

"We'll deal with the situation when it comes," she concluded aloud. "There's no sense borrowing trouble, as my granny used to say."

There was a brisk rapping sound. Annalee glanced over and saw Noah standing in the doorway, his expression uncertain.

"Speak of the devil," Lunella said, smiling a welcome at him. "What's up, cuz?"

"Got news about Abner Cutshall and Alexander Dempsey," Noah said, coming into the room. His uniform was clean and crisply ironed; it was clear he had taken time to go home, shower, and change his clothes. "Remember that private airfield south of Odom?"

"The one where Cutshall parks his private jet? Shit," Annalee muttered. "I'll bet he's out of the country by now."

Noah shook his head. "They filed a flight plan, but the tower lost radar contact with the plane about a half hour ago."

"What?" Galvanized, Annalee scrambled over Lunella, ignoring the woman's yelp of protest when her elbow accidentally jabbed a sensitive area. Her own leg was none too happy about it, either, but she ignored the pain. "Has the tower re-established contact? Radar or radio?" she asked, yanking down the hem of the T-shirt to cover her upper thighs and hoping she had not flashed the deputy. Behind her, she could practically feel Lunella's smirk branding her skin.

"Nope." Noah's gaze remained resolutely fixed above her neck.

"Why the hell am I hearing about this now?" Annalee glanced around and finally turned to Lunella, who was looking at her with fond exasperation. "Honey, where are my clothes?" she asked, frustrated. "I can't go out there with my ass hanging out."

"I swung by your house on the way here," Noah said to her, offering a duffel bag, "and brought you a fresh uniform. I also fed your butterball cat."

"Thank you, thank you, bless you a thousand times. I'm sure Mongo appreciates it and so do I. Leave that cat without food and he's likely to eat the sofa." Annalee snatched the duffel bag out of Noah's hands. "Give me some privacy, please."

Noah turned his back but stayed put in the doorway. "There was a call from out on Skybridge Mountain. Old Lady Murphy's got a house up there. You know, she's Jeeter's great-grandmother on his father's side. He gave her a satellite phone last Christmas, in case she needed help. You remember; she broke her hip last winter."

"That house is more like a shotgun shack," Annalee commented, yanking up her tan uniform pants and fastening the button at the waist. No underwear but it would not be the first time she had gone commando. "Mrs. Murphy's been up there a good fifty years."

"Yeah, her and her telescope. She saw the plane go down and reckons it crashed about five miles east of her place. The fire department's been dispatched, and the state police helicopter is doing a fly-over to confirm. We ought to be hearing from them any minute."

Lunella shrugged. "Ain't nobody gonna mourn Cutshall much."

"Except maybe his spoiled grandchildren, and whoever else inherits his money. Then again, maybe Cutshall isn't dead. There might be survivors." Annalee finished dressing, tucking her shirt into the waistband of her pants. She rummaged in the duffel for socks and shoes, stopping when Lunella got out of bed and leaned close to her.

"I won't come with," she said, "but when you're done, I'll see you at home."

"Yours or mine?" Annalee asked, her heart giving a sudden strong thump.

"Wherever you are is home to me," Lunella replied, dropping a kiss on her cheek.

That simple sweet kiss continued to warm Annalee through and through while the officers' SUV sped along the serpent-winding road that went up Skybridge Mountain. Noah was behind the wheel, his eyes hidden behind sunglasses. She did not ask him what he thought about her relationship with Lunella, feeling slightly awkward. He was her subordinate, after all, and a good deputy. If he disapproved, she did not want to hear about it. There was no point creating problems at work.

The radio squawked. "Dispatch to Charlie One-Oh-One," came Minnie Hawkins's voice, made tinny by the cheap speakers.

Annalee answered. "Charlie One-Oh-One. Go ahead, Dispatch."

"State police have confirmed a crash site two miles east off mile marker eighteen. Fire and Rescue are underway. NTSB has been notified."

"Acknowledged."

Noah pressed harder on the accelerator. Annalee did not admonish him, not even when he took a hairpin turn at a speed that could have ended in complete disaster. They had to reach the crash site first. If there were survivors, or if the Feds got their hands on Dempsey's research... Without her asking, as if he had read her mind, Noah sped the SUV up a little more. What she would do if there *were* survivors, she did not know, but Annalee was determined to protect the Skinners. Would she do that to the point of committing murder? The notion of killing an unarmed, possibly injured man made her sweat. She hoped she would not have to make such a choice.

Black smoke contaminated the otherwise clear blue sky, spiraling above the crowns of trees thickly clustered on the mountain's side. Noah found a spot and pulled over, parking on the narrow shoulder near the guardrail. Annalee got out of the SUV, her relief at being the first on the scene quickly obliterated by a news van she could make out in the distance, chugging along the road. *Damned journalists and their police scanners*, she thought.

"We've got company," Noah remarked, stating the obvious.

Annalee left Noah behind to organize a perimeter and keep the press out while she went over the crash site. Of course, she was supposed to wait, too, and let the professionals have first crack, but she could always claim she thought she had heard a survivor calling for help. A passing breeze blew acrid, stinging smoke into her eyes and down her throat, which already felt raw. Coughing, Annalee pulled a bandana out of her rear pocket, tying it over her face to help filter out some of the smoke. Forging down the slope, she found debris scattered around an area of roughly a hundred yards, much of it twisted metal. Several trees were on fire, the flames heating the air until it scalded her lungs.

It looked as if the plane's wings had been torn off on impact, and the nose and tail had sheared off as well, leaving a cracked metal tube that had been the main body of the fuselage. The side was open in a jagged tear, leaving the interior exposed. Annalee made her way over to the plane, trying to be careful not to disturb the scene any more than necessary. The NTSB investigators would skin her alive if they thought she'd trampled thoughtlessly over their site.

She found Dr. Alexander Dempsey next to the fuselage, his body still strapped into a seat that had torn loose. There was a length of rubber tied around his upper arm and a hypodermic needle stuck in the crook of his elbow. Dempsey was unmistakably dead. The front of his throat was mangled badly, irregular strings of crimson flesh trailing out of a wet red hole that encompassed the space from carotid artery to jugular vein. The man's windpipe was gone, ripped away with unimaginable force.

Shrapnel? Or something else...

A cold trickle of dread ran shivering through her veins.

Annalee removed the rubber tubing from Dempsey's arm and took the hypodermic, wrapping it in her bandana and sticking both items into her back pocket, being careful not to prick herself. Who knew what kind of crap might be on the needle? It could be the doctor's serum, or it might be some other drug. She was not going to leave the hypodermic at the scene, though. That would be taking too much of a chance. Patting Dempsey's body down, she did not find the flash card that contained his research, then there was no more time. A fireman hallooed at her from the top of the slope and she had to at least pretend to do her duty.

Rescue personnel found the pilot's body in the cockpit; he had been apparently killed in the impact. The cause of the crash was unknown at the moment, though pilot error and mechanical failure were the two main hypotheses. An organized party of state police troopers, local policemen, and fire department volunteers searched the side of the mountain until dusk but found no trace of Abner Cutshall's body. There was plenty of blood in the fuselage but until a DNA test was done, there was no way of telling who it belonged to. A new search was planned for the morning but no one really harbored any hope of finding the Great Man. He had simply disappeared, leaving not a trace behind if the blood was not his.

What had happened inside that plane at ten thousand feet? Annalee wondered. Had Cutshall taken Dempsey's serum? Had he attacked the doctor after changing into God-knew-what? Annalee feared that Cutshall was not dead but somewhere in the woods, a monster barking at the moon, ready to attack, to rend, to act out his madness with tooth and claw.

She swallowed the bitter taste of fear.

Cutshall might be alive, but there was an equal chance that he was dead, his body ejected from the crashing plane and swallowed up by the forest. Maybe he had taken the flash card with him, which would explain its disappearance. Whatever had happened, the wolves of Malingering Deep were safe for the moment and that was what counted most.

Tomorrow, she would call Doc Vernon and explain the way of things. The medical examiner would be made to understand that the investigation into the victim and the wolf found at the Ateeska River could go no further. All autopsy reports and DNA evidence would be buried deep in as much bureaucratic obfuscation as possible, as would be the mutated bodies of Aiden Thompson and Ruth Lassiter in the city's Potter's Field. If the doctor did not cooperate, well...a woman who kept a bottle of whiskey in her desk drawer was vulnerable to pressure, especially since county coroner was an appointed position and the man who did the appointing was a militant ex-alcoholic.

Her father would have done no differently, Annalee decided. He was a lawman but he had loved the wolves, too. He had lost his life trying to protect them.

It was three o'clock in the morning before Annalee was able to leave the scene on Skybridge Mountain, catching a ride home with a state trooper. The radio's volume was turned low, just hissing static and bursts of mostly unintelligible voices speaking in a code her tired mind refused to decipher. The sound washed over and through her, soothing as white noise. She leaned her face against the cool window glass and dozed until the driver shook her awake. When she stumbled into the house, exhausted and stinking of smoke, she found Lunella curled up on the sofa with Mongo sitting on the pillow near her head.

Whatever the future held, she had this moment, and nothing could take it away.

Lunella's nostrils flared and her eyes fluttered open. They were brown ringed with gold, and filled with a love that made Annalee's chest ache sweetly.

"Come on," Lunella said, her voice soft, "take me to bed, Annie."

Annalee fell on her knees beside the sofa, rested her head on her mate's breast, closed her eyes, and finally let herself go.

Printed in the United States
210681BV00001B/94/P